Navel of the Moon

Navel of the Moon

O

A NOVEL

Mary Helen Lagasse

CURBSTONE BOOKS
NORTHWESTERN UNIVERSITY PRESS
EVANSTON, ILLINOIS

Curbstone Books
Northwestern University Press
www.nupress.northwestern.edu

Printed in the United States of America

10 9 8 7 6 5 4 3 2 1

Library of Congress Cataloging-in-Publication Data
Lagasse, Mary Helen, author.
Navel of the moon : a novel / Mary Helen Lagasse.
pages cm
Includes bibliographical references.
ISBN 978-0-8101-3104-0 (pbk. : alk. paper) — ISBN 978-0-8101-3105-7
(e-book)
1. New Orleans (La.)—Fiction. I. Title.
PS3612.A38N38 2015
813.6—dc23

2014049542

For my beloved husband, Will—
whose love and belief in me
out-shined everything

Optima dies . . . prima fugit.

—VIRGIL

Contents

Navel of the Moon

1

Author's Notes

217

Acknowledgments

219

Navel of the Moon

PROLOGUE

I stood on the brink ready to fly. My toes turned over the edges of the rough-hewn wood—the landing of that long-defunct stairway in our backyard being the favorite of all my getting-away places.

We'd sit there by the hour, Queenie hush-hush breathing at my side, me with my nose buried in a book, my bare legs dangling over the edge of the landing so that I might look into our neighbor's backyard through the dense foliage of hibiscus leaves.

I'd snuggle my toes between the sagging planks of the moldy green fence, buoyed by the feeling that it was only Queenie and me in the world and that I'd be satisfied to spend eternity afloat on that wooden carpet, where I might know the joy of having a tail like Queenie's to wag in celebration of that instant in time.

Sometimes I'd whisper my secrets into the glossy profusion of blossoms and leaves that reached well above the landing. I'd sit 'til daylight dimmed above that dappled canopy, my thoughts dispersing like puffs of smoke with the sound of my grandmother's voice calling me to supper.

The Irish Channel—New Orleans

1

IT WAS A BAPTISM OF FIRE. Not for Lonnie, who'd actually been the one baptized by the purifying waters, but for me. As for the others, the event registered with them as nothing more than youthful silliness, yet serious enough to have caused adult consternation at the time.

The popular notion holds that the more traumatic the experience the more likely you are to remember it in detail. And it's true. I can recall the most innocuous details of that baptismal day: the throaty gutter of the vigil lights in their garnet glasses; the dull sheen of the bronze-colored bobby pins that held Lonnie's blond bangs to make way for the purifying waters; the tintinnabulation of the tower bells resounding in my chest, telling me to hurry. It's an experience that was beautiful in actuality and painful in the aftermath. Invariably it sets me off to thinking of those whom I've loved and lost—Mimy and Queenie and Valentina, Norma, the kids I grew up with, and Lonnie, of course. Lonnie Cavanaugh, who became lost in the streets of the Irish Channel. Lost, then, behind the gridded gates of the Orleans Parish Detention Center for Girls when she was picked up for shoplifting; then at the Orleans Parish Prison when she was picked up by the vice squad; and lastly at the Louisiana Correctional Institute for Women at St. Gabriel, Louisiana, sixty-four miles west of New Orleans, known simply as "St. Gabriel." That's where Lonnie is today, doing time for drugs, larceny, and prostitution.

While most visits to St. Gabriel took place in the Visiting Room, monitored by security officers, the duration of non-contact visits was at the discretion of the warden. I had satisfied any last-minute doubts he might have had with regard to the nature of my visit, assuring him that, as I'd explained by telephone, I wouldn't come in the official capacity of freelance reporter to conduct a formal interview; that although Lonnie and I had been friends since childhood, there would be no excessive displays of affection between us; and that I would respectfully abide by the prison rules as would any other visitor, as I understood that security was of paramount importance at the prison.

But it was not without some trepidation that I signed the logbook provided at Front Control, thinking that it had been more than three years since I'd last seen Lonnie, and then it had not been on the best of terms that we parted. I walked through the gates of the tall chain-link fence onto the grounds, where a wide walking path separated the rows of low, cream-colored brick structures on either side, at the farther end of which were the buildings that housed the prison's medium-security offenders, which is where I found Lonnie.

We met in the forty-bed dormitory where everywhere dimple-cheeked baby dolls and button-eyed teddy bears were propped on pillows and in chairs. We had the place to ourselves, and though it was at first awkward for us both, it wasn't long before we were sitting on Lonnie's bed chatting away, so much so that it seemed we couldn't finish talking about one subject before we were launching on to another. Our two-hour heart-to-heart ended with Lonnie telling me she'd gotten her GED and would be applying for a culinary arts class that provided offenders, within thirty-six months of their release, with the skills necessary for employment in the food service industry, and with my telling her of my newly attained job as a stringer writing for the Associated Press.

We parted as friends, vowing never again to let life's vicissitudes erode the bonds of our friendship. I drove away with the feeling of something wonderful having happened that I had doubted would ever come to pass. But not a month later, when I called to schedule a return visit, to my astonishment I was told that Lonnie had filed a written request at the front office asking that all visitors be denied.

Sometimes I think I understand why Lonnie did that, and I'm okay with it, and other times it becomes unclear and very hurtful. But I honored her wishes, just the same. And I never saw Lonnie again.

Unlike the rest of us, Lonnie attended public school, but from kindergarten onward she wanted to transfer from Laurel Public Elementary to St. Mary's Parochial. It wasn't until second grade, when the rest of us were excited about making our First Communion, that she and I dared bring up the subject to her mother.

Lonnie crooked her finger and stuck it in her mouth. She was sucking it so hard she was practically gnawing it as we came under Miss Ada's brown-eyed scrutiny. Miss Ada was a big-bosomed woman, her narrow forehead defined by a widow's peak as pronounced as that of the Evil Queen's in the Snow White movie. But Lonnie's mother was not tall or slender as was the Evil Queen, nor as malevolently beautiful. Miss Ada was ordinary-looking. She kept her brown hair pulled back in a tightly knotted bun that rested at the back of her stumpy neck, and was forever dressed in one of her nondescript zippered house frocks. But that day she arose as daunting as a thunderhead from where she sat at the kitchen table, then she practically glided to the telephone to call the religion teacher and promptly pull Lonnie out of the Confraternity of Christian Doctrine classes she attended on Saturday mornings with the other public school kids.

Lonnie and I were crushed. We'd had our hearts set on wearing the same white dotted-swiss dress we'd seen in Fisher's Department Store window on Magazine Street, the same satin drawstring bag and lace-edged veil we planned to buy at the JoAnne Shoppe on Dryades Street. And when Lonnie saw the prayer book my mother got out of the layaway plan at Umbach's holy store, she squealed with delight. With its gilt-edged pages, rococo crucifix set inside the front cover, and the purple satin ribbon marker, Lonnie said it was the most beautiful prayer book she'd ever seen. Before she'd even let herself take it out of its satiny box, she wiped her hands on her skirt to keep from smudging the pearlescent covers. It would be three years, long after First Communion day had come and gone, when we learned the reason why Miss Ada wouldn't let Lonnie make her First Communion.

When my family moved to Clementine Street, Lonnie and I weren't yet three years old. Even before we knew one another's names we were sitting side by side, digging in the bald plots of dirt in front of our respective houses, making mud pies. It's said you can't remember anything before the age of three, that what you think you remember is only what you've imagined, or what somebody else has told you. But I know these are my memories because I remember *being there*, the memory of which is embedded in me like an iridescent bead implanted in the tissues of my then baby's heart: the hard dirt arguing with the old soup spoon Mimy gave me to dig with, the March wind sending the dust in eddies that swirled through the street, the brush of leaves on pavement, the powder-fine dust speckling my lashes and gritting my eyes while the stubborn mud refused to take the mold of our play-set dishes that blustery day more than seventeen years ago.

Lonnie and I would sit on my front steps to watch the domed bell tower of St. Mary's Assumption Church scraping the clouds. Nights, we'd go to bed listening to the chiming of the tower bells and the cries of the nighthawks darting from the eaves to feed on insects caught on the wing. We'd drowse to the hoots of the tugboats on the river, to the sounds of the freight trains linking heads and tails like rusting behemoths on the railroad tracks that lined the wharves a few blocks away.

Five blocks to the north of us was the Garden District—the Silk Stocking Ward, as it was then called. To the south were the riverfront Negro shanties, and all about were shotgun singles, gingerbread doubles, camelback duplexes, and the hundred-twenty-five block St. Thomas housing project, thought of as a city unto itself by those of us who didn't happen to live there.

Those two-tiered box steps on either side of my front door were the cypress thrones on which Lonnie and I sat dreaming our dreams, the hardwood planks under our rumps recalling with their satiny striations their dark-leafed past as the summer light turned itself down, leaving us to blink at the stars, and freeing us to think we might grasp the air as if it were a silver mesh entangled with stars that were ours to shake loose and gather to our flinty breasts. There, we became what we wanted to be, had what we wished for, and there wasn't anything we could have been happier over than that we were the best of friends.

2

My house on Clementine Street was a narrow two-story shotgun with peeling yellow paint and a rickety second-story balcony that leaned like a fretful aunt over Lonnie's squatty half-double. Close up, you could read the name of "Lumière" on our mailbox in little gold letters my father bought at Clark & Roescher's hardware store. The alley that separated Lonnie's house from mine was hardly wider than the reach of our arms—so narrow that standing in the middle of it you could just about touch both clapboard sides with your fingertips.

What made my house different from Lonnie's and everyone else's on the block, or in the whole Irish Channel for that matter, was what went on inside it—everyday things that were governed by my grandmother's *mexicanidad.* No sooner did you walk in the front room than you were greeted by her El Popo Cigars calendar. Even back then the calendar was out-of-date by a couple of years. But my grandmother never kept it to reckon time with; she kept it for the picture of the volcanoes superimposed by the figures with the unpronounceable names for which the volcanoes were named—Popocatépetl, which means "Smoking Mountain," and Iztaccihuatl, which means "White Lady." My grandmother could wrap her tongue around those legendary names in a way that I, in my Irish-Channelese-tainted Spanish, never could.

As I saw it the legend of the two volcanoes was the Mayan version of Sleeping Beauty: The handsome prince, clad in his regal leather-and-feathers costume, crouches alongside the sleeping princess, guarding her as she lies in repose, her gossamer gown shrouded in the mist of the torch he has lighted in anticipation of her awakening. Throughout the years the snows enfold the sleeping princess and cover the warrior prince, but neither the perpetuity of time nor that of ice can extinguish the fiery torch or discourage the handsome prince. Unlike the happily-ever-after ending of the Brothers Grimm tale, the Aztec legend has a typical Mexican ending. Their destinies remain unresolved; the princess continues in her slumber and the prince maintains his vigil, both of them benumbed, but hopeful.

The ruins of shrines found as high as twelve thousand feet showed that the mountains were important religious sites for the Aztecs. But Mimy would have been the first to tell you it was all pagan nonsense. Nonetheless, those volcanoes were, for her, sacred mountains nestled in the Valley of Mexico, turf that my grandmother, sleeping year in, year out in the second bedroom of the shotgun house in the heart of the Irish Channel, traversed in her dreams.

And then there were the aromas that filled our house—the *achiote, cilantro, comino, hierba buena, perejil*—aromatic seeds and fragrant herbs my grandmother found at the French Market, the bouquet claiming one room after the other whenever she stood at the old Roper gas range cooking her *guisos*. The scents glazed the walls of our kitchen with an invisible patina. The scents filled my nostrils and gathered in my head so that even today they return with but the blink of an eye.

Mireya Hernandez Mendoza de Arroyo was my grandmother's full name. "Hernandez" she got from her father, "Mendoza" from her mother, and "Arroyo" she got from her husband Vicente, who died long before I was born. She named her only child "Linda" because she said my mother was pretty from the day she was born. My brother Eddie was named for my father, Edward Justin Lumière, who was from Cloutierville in central Louisiana. I was named for my grandfather Vicente Arroyo and my great-grandmother, whose given name was Maria de los Angeles. My full name is Vicenta Maria de los Angeles Lumière, but for the sake of brevity I call myself "Vicky."

Mimy left Texcoco with her young husband, Vicente, whom she married against her parents' wishes. Her parents loved her and she them, but they'd strenuously objected to the union because they wanted more for their only daughter.

In marrying Vicente Arroyo, a common laborer, Mireya had married beneath her station, an act that violated their way of life, which, in those days according to Mimy, was practically like committing parricide. Later came the poignant but bitter parting, when she left Texcoco with her infant daughter Linda to join Vicente, who was by then working in the silver mines in Zacatecas. Accidents were common in the mines, caused as much by the hazardous conditions as by the twelve, fourteen, sixteen hours the exhausted miners worked hauling 200 pounds of ore on their backs. It was on coming through a dark and narrow passageway, carrying such a load, that Vicente fell dead.

As was expected for a young Mexican woman without means, Mireya never returned to the bosom of her family after her husband's death. She left Zacatecas and headed farther and farther north until she arrived at Ciudad Juárez, where she had just enough left of Vicente's earnings to go to El Paso to obtain the proper passport to continue her voyage to "the other side."

Immigration agents at the Stanton Street Bridge that linked Ciudad Juárez and El Paso looked with suspicion at Mireya, a woman *sola*, who it was thought would likely end up a public charge. Hence, even with cash in hand, she was denied, as she said, "a regular passport." Mireya had no choice but to remain in Ciudad Juárez. She found a job working as a maid in a small hotel—her infant daughter wrapped in a rebozo strapped to her back while she scrubbed floors, cleaned toilets, and boiled pails of water to wash hotel linens on a washboard. After three months of working in Juárez, she secured a local passport and continued her journey *al otro lado*, going east to find work rather than west as had so many of her compatriots.

Except for her fair coloring, Mama didn't look much like Mimy. She was tall and slender, and having been but a babe in her mother's arms when they crossed the border, she never had the slightest hint of an accent. With my dark hair, brown eyes, my freckle-sprinkled face and slender build, I was a combination of the Arroyos and the Lumières. But I was never mistaken for a Cajun, or for being of French or Irish descent, as was my blond, buzz-cut, freckle-faced brother, Eddie, whose gangly arms and legs and gargantuan feet predicted he'd be over six feet tall.

"Where'd you say your grandma came from?" a curious Lonnie asked me one day. We were still little kids.

Mimy was sitting on the side of her bed, her attention drawn from the recessed glassed-in miniature sculpture of the pietà that was the centerpiece on the *mesita* that served as her little altar. Night and day, vigil lights guttered in their garnet glasses before the icon with its scrolled candleholders that folded out from either side of the polished oak frame. The latched lower compartment served as a storage nook for the requisite articles for Mass or for the Last Rites.

I knew exactly where my grandmother was from. Even so, at times I'd catch myself staring at Mimy, powdery and pale as a ladyfinger confection from Baher's Bakery from being indoors so much, her fine pale brown hair threaded with silver, her delicate hands and feet small for someone as buxom as she, and wearing her ever-present *chal*—the washed-thin cotton Mexican shawl she wore like a mantle.

"Lonnie wants to know where you come from, Mimy," I said, as if Lonnie's question needed translating.

Mimy laughed that husky laugh that sounded as if it belonged to someone taller and bigger than she. "*Del ombligo de la luna*," she said offhandedly.

"What?" I blurted, even before Lonnie could stammer, "W-where'd y-your grandma say she was from?"

I was as baffled by Mimy's response as was Lonnie because I knew that Mimy had been born in the town of Texcoco near Mexico City, where she met my grandfather, gave birth to my mother, and from where she'd begun her migration north—first to Zacatecas with her husband, then from Zacatecas after he died of "a burst heart," to wind up in, of all places, the Irish Channel in New Orleans. I thought I knew everything there was to know about my grandmother.

Mimy, who spoke in English when it behooved her to do so, said very precisely, "I—am—from—the—navel—of—the—moon." She looked from Lonnie to me, and then tipped her head for us to look up at the window behind us, set close to the ceiling. The screen, billowed by the evening breeze, framed the black-on-blue silhouette of our neighbors' weather-worn chimney that threatened to tumble brick by brick down the steep-pitched slate roof to land on my grandmother's bedroom floor.

Lonnie drew her eyes from the window. She smiled timidly, twisting her arms to pretzels. Then she retreated behind me to conceal her disappointment of that moonless sky.

El ombligo de la luna? I was utterly enthralled. My childish mind envisaged a big navel orange of a moon that transformed to a diaphanous sphere that glowed with a soft radiance in the far side of the sky beyond the two volcanoes of my grandmother's El Popo Cigars calendar.

That evening, staring at that patch of moonless sky, I created a physical place for where my grandmother said she was from, and I retained that image, and imagined myself there, secreted within the big navel depression on the surface of the moon, a place where I didn't have to be like anyone else, where I could make up my own mind about things, a place where I would sing a song of belonging, unafraid that anyone would think of my voice as weak and wavery—a place not to be found on any map of the moon, but more, a place for the undoing of fear.

3

WHEN MY FAMILY MOVED to the Channel, Zofia Borack, the Cat Lady, was already living at the end of our block on the corner of Clementine and Laurel, and Norma Costanza was living with her mother, Miss Etheline, in a two-bedroom project apartment directly across the street from us. Being among the first residents of the St. Thomas project when it was completed not long after the war, the Costanzas lived in the neighborhood longer than anybody—longer than my family, and long before D.D. Dillenkoffer and his sister Becky, who'd in time become two of my closest friends, moved with their mother into the house around the corner, or Mrs. DeSales moved into the duplex apartment upstairs.

By the time we'd reached fifth grade Lonnie decided that no matter what, she couldn't put off being baptized any longer. Her decision to defy her mother shocked all of our friends but me, because I knew that Lonnie was more afraid of not being baptized than she was of her mother.

"Well—the catechism says any Catholic can baptize in case of emergency," I said to Lonnie confidently.

"For true?" Lonnie said, popping a shriveled forefinger from her mouth. You'd have thought that being nearly ten, she'd have broken that nasty habit!

"Don't take my word for it. Look it up in the Baltimore Catechism," I said unabashedly.

We decided on the Grotto as the perfect place for Lonnie's baptism.

The Grotto, whitewashed, bumpy, and hunched in the shadows of St.

Alphonsus Church (the "Irish" church in our neighborhood), looked like a giant turtle shell made of divinity fudge. Inside, the scent of the lighted candles, the flowers and the sooty walls, the pipe-fed spring gurgling with holy water, the mementos, medals, expressions of gratitude for favors granted and miracles performed, and the hundreds of faded photos of World War II sons, grandsons, and husbands never failed to glaze you with a patina of sanctity. The Grotto was a scaled-down version of the Lourdes cave, where the Virgin Mary was believed to have appeared to the peasant girl, Bernadette. Long past its World War II heyday, it was venerated in the 1960s by parishioners who collected its waters for the healing of everything from melanomas to ingrown toenails. The place made you feel downright holy even before you'd dipped your fingertips in the holy water.

The venture that began with Lonnie and me wound up including D.D. Dillenkoffer, his sister Becky, Stanley Cunningham, and Ollie DeSales—six in all participating in the secret baptism. We waited until three o'clock, which marked the beginning of the two-hour period during which confessions were heard in St. Alphonsus, and there'd be little chance of our getting caught by a priest, or by one of the brothers who were always flittering about.

"First, let me put Queenie in the yard," I said before we left. The last thing we needed was a dog tagging along. I led Queenie by the collar through the narrow alley that separated Lonnie's house from mine. When Queenie saw what I was up to, she put on her brakes. I had to pick her up and carry her whining and wiggling to the backyard gate. We'd be lucky if she didn't try to scale it. Small dog though she was, she'd scaled the six-foot gate countless times before to follow us to Woolworth's or to any of the stores on Magazine Street from where Lonnie and I would be promptly evicted for having ignored the NO DOGS ALLOWED sign.

At first, everything went as planned: D.D. and Stanley went inside the church to act as lookouts while the rest of us headed straight for the Grotto. Lonnie and I took our places at the front, where the pre-blessed water surged from a groove in the faux rock, flowed in a narrow gully grooved in the bumpy wall, and disappeared down a hole I imagined led to an underground pool as blue and pristine as the waters I'd seen in photos of the Blue Grotto in Capri. Becky and Ollie headed straight for the prie-dieux that squealed as if on the verge of collapse when they knelt on the wooden kneelers. Assuming the proper solemnity, they bowed their heads, but their ears were perked like terriers' listening for the slightest sound that would signal the approach of an intruder.

D.D. and Stanley drove us crazy, running in and out like a couple of nuts with whatever excuse they could muster: "Lettin' y'all know nobody ain't comin' . . . Priests are still listenin' to confessions . . . Coast still clear . . . !"

I was ready to strangle the next one—be it D.D. or Stanley—who showed his goofy face at the grotto entrance.

The church bells gonged and Lonnie urged in a trembly voice, "Forget about those ignoramuses, Vicky, and let's hurry." She promptly plunked down on the stone floor, winced from the coldness of it, and leaned back, holding her head as far back as she could manage over the bumpy lip of the trough.

It was the way Lonnie looked at that moment that I will never forget—she, sitting on that stony floor, glowing with "holiness" is the best way I can describe the soft luminescence of her face, her eyes closed, her blond bangs held by two bobby pins to make way for the sacramental waters, the gold cross and chain her grandparents had given her for her birthday glinting in the flickering candlelight. Even in the half-light, the star-shaped scar left by a huge boil that had festered on her forehead for weeks on end the whole summer long glowed with a satiny luster.

"Ready?" I croaked.

Lonnie nodded. "After this I can't be sent to Limbo if something bad happens, can I?" she murmured in the tiniest voice.

"And you can take Holy Communion," Becky chimed.

"And Original Sin will be washed away," Ollie said.

"That's right," I chortled, anxious to have it all come true for her.

Lonnie folded her hands to her chest, taking it all in.

D.D. never failed to bump the folded expansion gate, which never failed to emit a blood-curdling screech. It was nowhere near time for the priests to be finished hearing confessions and D.D. knew it.

"For goodness' sake, Vicky, don't pay him any mind!" Lonnie urged. "Somebody is gonna be coming in if we don't hurry."

"Ready then?" I grumbled.

"Yes, yes, *yes*! Lonnie said, closing her eyes again.

I scooped some water from the bubbling little spring, held my dripping hands over Lonnie's forehead, and assumed as priestly an air as I could manage. "I baptize thee in the name of the Father . . . and of the Son . . . and of the Holy Ghost—," I pronounced, parting my hands just enough to let the water trickle through my fingers. All along I prayed that the words, measly as they sounded coming from me, had the power of bestowing on Lonnie the sense of worthiness and belonging she longed for.

"Ah-men," I said, letting the remaining water splash on Lonnie's forehead.

"Ah-men," sniffed a wet-faced Lonnie.

"Ah-men," echoed Becky and Ollie from their prayer benches.

No sooner was the word uttered when Father Butterworth appeared!

I suspected that D.D. had let it happen on purpose—his revenge for not having been invited to participate in the baptism. Since he couldn't conduct the ceremony, he'd insisted on reciting the baptismal words, or on pouring the sacramental waters. After all, he'd declared, it would've been "more legit" for him to perform the ceremony because I was a girl and there was no such thing as a girl priest!

"What's going on here?" Father Butterworth sputtered.

"We're reciting our devotions to the Blessed Mother," I said, the words falling like pebbles from my mouth.

We flew out of the Grotto like bats flying out of a cave. How we got past the priest without one of us getting caught, I'll never know. Ahead I could see D.D. running up Constance Street, taking a left turn onto Clementine, and Stanley hobbling after him like all get-out on the wooden peg of his shorter leg. In less than the five minutes it took for us to get home, Father Butterworth had telephoned our parents and had them waiting for us on the doorsteps.

My parents and Miss Ada argued head-on; D.D.'s spitfire mother, Miss Ruth, put in her two cents' worth, as did Ollie's parents, who came from Gretna to collect Ollie from his old grandaunt, Mrs. DeSales, who lived upstairs from us.

It was decided that Lonnie was a victim of my bullying and that the others were innocent bystanders. Despite all the apologies and concessions that followed, in the end my parents agreed with Father Butterworth and with Lonnie's mom that I'd acted with utter disregard to the Catholic faith and without respect for Ada Guggenheimer Cavanaugh's religious beliefs, the charge of which took me totally by surprise, because I had no idea what Miss Ada's religious beliefs were!

"*¡Qué hipócrita!*" Mimy huffed. "Carrying on as if she were such a devout Jew! I'll bet the last time Ada Cavanaugh was inside a temple was when she was a fetus floating in her mother's belly!"

"Mamá, how can you say such a thing!" my mother said, properly indignant for my sake.

"*Lo digo porque no soy hipócrita,*" Mimy retorted. "I say it because I am honest, and because it is the truth. That Ada Cavanaugh! Acting so righteous!"

"There's such a thing as being *too* honest, Mamá" my mother chided.

"One can never be too honest," Mimy protested. "The woman is behaving like a born-again Christian who's recovered her Jewish faith!"

"I agree with you, Mimy," I said, butting in. "If being Jewish was such a big deal, why'd Miss Ada keep it a secret from you, from Mama and me, from everybody—even from Lonnie?"

Mimy's eyes flew at me, her eyebrows weaving in the task of searching for right answers.

"Lonnie's mother has her own reasons, *niña,*" she admonished. Still and all, she kept telling me I'd done the right thing in baptizing Lonnie, no matter what anyone else said, including the "*padre sanguíneo,*" which is what she called Father Butterworth because of his ruddy complexion. But Mimy always kept her bases covered—whenever mentioning the clergy in anything but a good light, Mimy would make the sign of the cross for insurance.

The next day I was summoned to the rectory. No sooner had I walked in than Father Butterworth started lecturing me on the dangers of losing my immortal soul. In baptizing a Jewish girl, I'd made a mockery not only of the sacrament of baptism, but of Mother Church herself.

"I wasn't mocking baptism, or Mother Church, Father Butterworth," I protested. "I was doing what I thought was right."

"Ri-*ight*? Ri-*ight*? Who are you to decide what's right, girl?" the priest said, looking around as if he expected somebody to corroborate his indignation when there was nobody in the rectory office but him and me. "*Hwhat*, in your opinion, was right about what you did?" he wanted to know.

"I did what I did because when a person is in danger of dying without being baptized, anyone can, and should, baptize. That's what it says in the Baltimore Catechism in the chapter 'Who May Baptize.'"

"That's a church doctrine that does not apply to Jews," the priest said, rearranging his rump in the wooden clasp of the captain's chair.

"But the Catechism doesn't tell us that Jewish people are excluded if they want to join the Catholic Church," I countered.

"Enough!" he boomed.

But I wouldn't shut up: "—and what about the *Irish* half of Lonnie, the half of her that isn't Jewish?"

"You're talking about the girl as if she were a side of beef!"

"What happens to that half of her?" I persisted, undeterred.

"You are one bold girl!" he snapped, making "bold" sound like a punch in the eye. At that instant, one eye squinting, the other one searching my face, he reminded me of the walleyed actor who played the brutish Bill Sikes in the *Oliver Twist* movie.

"I didn't know at the time that Lonnie was half Jewish," I murmured, cowering like Sikes's dog, Bull's-Eye.

"Even so, there still has to be good and sufficient reason for doing what you did. Your friend isn't in danger of dying—. She isn't suffering from a terminal disease—." He lifted a rusty-colored eyebrow, waiting.

"No, she isn't suffering from a terminal disease," I said, having regained some of my former bravado, "but there's a chance she might have been hit by a car, or her heart could've stopped. It's true, isn't it? I mean, 'Who of us can predict?'"

I said it exactly the way I remembered my teacher in second grade saying it.

"Sister Felicia said dying could happen at any time. She said you can't let your guard down, that you have to be in God's good graces at all times 'cause 'death comes like a thief in the night.'" The quotation sounded deliciously ominous.

I wanted to let the priest know that *that* was exactly what Lonnie was afraid of—of death coming in the night, sneaking into her room while she was sleeping, and pulling her from under the bedcovers by her toes. It was the reason Lonnie was afraid of the dark, why she always slept with her knees touching her chin, why she often kicked hard in her sleep. But I couldn't and wouldn't have said any of that to Father Butterworth, or to anyone else for that matter. That was nobody's business but Lonnie's. Besides, I didn't want to be alone with Ol' Butterfingers any longer than I had to. I kept one eye on the shadow of the old secretary, Miss Vollenweider, wavering behind the frosted glass–paneled door of the outer office, another on the priest. "May I be excused now?" I asked, tucking the hem of my skirt under my knees and scrooching further back in the chair.

It was no easy task going against the grain of everything you'd been taught. Challenging a priest's authority was tantamount to challenging the authority of Jesus Christ, and from the look on Father Butterworth's red-and-ready face, I was thinking that he was thinking the same thing. I was shaking so badly I had to wrap my legs around the chair legs to keep from bolting out of the room.

"You're half Spanish, aren't you?" he asked, pressing his tented fingers to his lips.

"Yes—I mean, no," I retorted.

"Well—your mother's Spanish, but your father . . . 'Lumière,' that's French, isn't it? You're half Spanish, half—"

"Half Mexican, half French," I interjected.

"It's all the same," he said with a wave of the hand.

"Not the same, Father Butterworth," I mumbled.

"The two new girls in Sister Philomena's class, they're—"

"Nicaraguan," I said, waylaying him before he presumed to guess. Had Mimy been there, she'd have promptly enlightened "*el padre sanguíneo*" as to the distinctions between Spanish and Mexican and Nicaraguan. But "Spanish" was the umbrella under which I stood with Mimy and my mother (the only persons of Mexican heritage I knew of then living in the Channel), and the Nicaraguan girls, Carla and Carmen, and the scissors man, Mr. Rodriguez (who *was* Spanish straight out of Valencia). Mr. Rodriguez trekked the streets of the neighborhood playing his pan flute to announce himself and the big wagon wheel knife and scissors sharpening station he pushed for blocks on end and pedaled vigorously to run the wide leather band on which, for ten cents apiece, he sharpened the knives and scissors of everybody in the neighborhood.

When all the squabbling was done, I had to write the Baltimore Catechism lesson on baptism fifty times and was grounded for a whole month. But worse than anything else that could have happened, Miss Ada forbade Lonnie to talk to me, effectively ending our friendship and plunging me into a state of depression. Throughout the following weeks, Mama and Mimy took turns trying to cheer me up.

Mama: "Vicky, why don't you invite some of your classmates over?"

Mimy: "Bee-Kee, why don't I bake some of those *roscas* you love so much?"

Mama: "It isn't Miss Ada doesn't like you; it's your interfering she doesn't like. Hadn't you wondered why she never allowed Lonnie to make her First Communion? Why she made Lonnie quit religion classes and never let her go to Catholic school? Guggenheimer is a Jewish name. Didn't you ever think of that? And if Lonnie's Grandpa Eli is Jewish, that makes Miss Ada, his daughter, Jewish—and Lonnie and Rudy . . ."

"Yeah, right! I've thought of all that, Mama. But what I still want to know is if Lonnie's being part Jewish is so all-important, why did Miss Ada's own father, Grandpa Eli, and his wife, Aunt Lizzie, give Lonnie a gold cross and chain? And why'd they bother to have it blessed in church, no less?"

"Because that's what Lonnie wanted for her birthday, which they thought was more important than—," Mama caught herself.

"See! That's exactly what I think they thought! And more than anything in the world, Lonnie wanted to be baptized. If Lonnie ever knew she was part Jewish, which I don't think she did, it wasn't important to her, s-so why should it be important to me?" I squeaked, the muscles in my throat tightening.

"How the Guggenheimers choose to express their love for Lonnie, whether with a crucifix or a Star of David, is none of your business!" my mother snapped. "This is the end of it, understand? The end!"

I loved the old Guggenheimers almost as much as I loved my own grandmother: Grandpa Eli with his thatch of gray hair, his skin the color of autumn leaves, and his button-down suspenders that reminded me of inverted wishbones; Aunt Lizzie and her plump, downy cheeks, her

Irish button nose, her hairnets flimsy as spiderwebs, and her voice which always sounded as if it were on the verge of singing.

I think of the sign that swung from the wrought iron arm in front of their laundry shop on Magazine Street:

LIZZIE THE LAUNDERER

—SHIRTS EXPERTLY DONE—

—HATS BLOCKED—

and I can still see the old couple steaming and pressing linens with those big metal pressers and handing customers their laundry packages over the chest-high counter.

The Guggenheimers lived in the two back rooms separated from the laundry shop by a stiffly starched curtain that failed to hold in the aromas of Aunt Lizzie's cooking, so that invariably, the shop smelled as much of veal chops smothered in onions as it did starches and soaps and cleaning fluids.

Since the time we were old enough to cross the street holding hands to walk the few blocks from our house to the laundry, Lonnie and I were in and out of the shop—scooting under the drop-leaf panel of the counter, where Aunt Lizzie would be gossiping with one of her customers.

Lizzie Guggenheimer, whom Lonnie called "Aunt Lizzie," was Grandpa Eli's second wife and not Miss Ada's real mother. She was a big woman, taller and all around bigger than my grandmother. But where Mimy shuffled along, looking as if she were barely going to make it on her tree-stump legs, Aunt Lizzie pranced about in slippered feet, toe-first, like a dancer.

Grandpa Eli, an unlit pipe clenched between his teeth, would sit in his chair behind the counter, his good ear pressed to the Emerson radio that *whee-ohhed* every time he turned the dials in search of transatlantic news.

"You'd think," Aunt Lizzie would say, shifting on her nimble feet, "that after all these years World War II was still going on, the way Eli searches that dial, trying to summon ghosts, or what all—I don't know."

Since the day I walked into the laundry shop for the first time, when Lonnie and I were still too young to walk the four and a half blocks there on our own, I'd been fascinated by the giant WAR BONDS wall poster that sighed with the slightest shift of air and cast the shop with a sadness that tinged the bright yellow walls and the shiny linoleum-covered counters. It pictured a dark-haired girl sitting in the grass, clutching her doll in the shadow of a giant swastika.

More than once, Lonnie gave that ancient poster a sideways glance and said she thought the poster girl looked like me. Grandpa Eli and Aunt Lizzie would look at me, then at the poster girl, and nod their heads yes, they thought so, too. Except for the dark hair and the eyes whose color you really couldn't distinguish, I didn't think so.

Yellow and tattered, the poster was still on the wall of the shop when Grandpa Eli died of a stroke and Aunt Lizzie died of congestive heart failure two years after him; and the LIZZIE THE LAUNDERER sign out front stayed swinging on its rusty hooks until the place was reopened as the electronics repair shop it is today.

"No matter what—Lonnie and her brother *are* Jewish," my mother said, intent on discussing the issue again, which she said would be the end of it.

I lifted one shoulder as if to say none of it mattered to me no how! But behind my smart-ass attitude I was fighting back tears that kept threatening to spill every time I heard mention of Lonnie's name. I'd secreted my disappointment in Lonnie under layers of insouciance and would have chosen death by suffocation before admitting that I'd been hurt by her compliant renunciation of our friendship.

Grandma Mimy and Mama urged me to make new friends. Even my dad got into the act. "That new girl down the block? The little redhead? What's her name? I bet she'd be a nice friend for you," he said, as if you could pick new friends the way you did cantaloupes, pressing their centers and rapping their roundedness to see if they were ripe enough to satisfy you.

I could have told him I'd already been to Gloria Callahan's and didn't much cotton to the idea of her telling me about all the fun things she and Becky Dillenkoffer and Lonnie Cavanaugh were doing, and the places they'd been to, one being Kingsley House, that I'd self-imposed "off-limits" for me because I wasn't about to chance bumping into the Lonnie Cavanaugh Fan Club.

In the 1800s, when the Planters' Press property with its four acres of open ground was donated by a local benefactor, the plans were to create an ambiance unlike that of the dreary, sometimes threatening atmosphere of the tenement dwellings and the mayhem of the Shot Tower Gang and the Ripsaw Gang, and other teams of Irish boys that roamed the streets.

One of the gracious ladies of the time made the pithy observation when Kingsley House was founded:

If you are a Jew and belong to Kingsley House you are a better Jew.
If you are a Protestant and belong to Kingsley House you are a better Protestant.
If you are a Catholic and belong to Kingsley House you are a better Catholic.

For us, Kingsley House, on the other side of the projects from where we lived, was an island of green amidst the sometimes grim, sometimes turbulent milieu of our working-class neighborhood.

The wrought iron grills set in the twenty-foot brick wall left standing from the old cotton press days lent an old-world look to the place, as did a flagstone courtyard where the fragrance of sweet olive, Cape jasmine, and clianthus colored the air. Dark green pittosporum climbed the walls of the three-storied colonial-style communal buildings with their arched windows, galleries, stairways, and fluted columns. Standing at the wide carriage entrance that opened onto the sweep of a grassy quadrangle. Any which way you looked, you could choose the site of your day's activity, whether it would be in the new brick gymnasium to shoot baskets, the crafts building to make your own creations from gushy clay, the wading pool where mostly little kids and mothers hung out, the big open spaces where field games were played, or the beautiful, big-windowed library.

While Lonnie and the others crowded the workshops to finger-paint or to fashion clay figurines that would later be glazed and fired in the kiln by Miss Mancuso, I headed for the library, where early on I discovered the big-pictured books whose satiny pages ever after carried the exotic air of the beautiful librarian, Miss Gouri Mehta of the silk saris, the sleek black hair, rose-gold bangles, and cinnamon hands.

To satisfy my dad, my mother, and Mimy as well, I sought Gloria Callahan's company and did my best to tolerate her simpering ways. But I avoided my other friends as best I could—especially D.D. I wasn't about to give him the satisfaction of ragging me about the falling-out with Lonnie, my so-called best friend. But more and more I retreated to the peace and safety of the moon's navel, where nobody could find me.

Lonnie and I were about nine when the Dillenkoffers moved into the house around the corner. I thought of the Dillenkoffers' house as a Noah's Ark of a house because it was long and narrow and had wavy clapboard siding that ran the length of the house so that it looked like a seagoing vessel listing on open waters.

Skating around the block on the new Union skates I'd gotten for my birthday, I slapped at what I first thought was a bug sting on my neck. The second time I skated past the chinaberry tree in front of the Noah's Ark of a house something pinged the top of my head. The third time I skated by, the sting was so keen, so clearly defined, I actually defined the ovoid imprint of the chinaberry through my tee shirt. I went straight for the tree and would have climbed up it, skates still on, had Norma Costanza not materialized—a thirtyish, wild-haired, barefooted hellion who took hold of the lowest tree branch and shook it until the tree shed half its leaves, and out fell the culprit.

"Somufabitch!" he shrieked, scrambling to his feet. He was a scruffy-looking kid, shirtless and shoeless, with sun-bleached brown hair and ears that stuck out like the loops of a sugar bowl.

Norma and I were friendly but not yet real friends. Until that day we'd hardly exchanged more than two words: "hello" and "goodbye." I'd see her sitting at her window across the street watching the cars and passersby; or I'd see her crossing the street on her way to and from Matthews' Corner Grocery, and I'd wave and say hello and she'd wave and mouth a soundless hello.

The kid's stunned-deer eyes focused on Norma. "Ma'am. I'm sorry, I wasn't cursin' you, I was just tryin' to get your girl's attention. Didn't mean to hurt nobody," he said, obviously thinking Norma was my mother.

"What've you got there?" I demanded, pointing at the Y-shaped contraption that was an amalgamation of twisted wires, gobs of electrical tape, rubber bands, and a sling pouch cut from an inner tube.

"It's my Super Triple-D," the kid said, adding before I could ask, "Triple-D stands for D.D. Dillenkoffer, and it's super 'cuz it don't miss."

"Doesn't look so super to me," I sniffed.

"Looks got nothin' to do with it," he said. "Wanna take a shot?"

"No, she don't wanna take no shot," Norma said, snatching the contraption from the boy and flinging it back at him.

D.D. grabbed the contraption in midair, sucked in his belly until his rib cage defined itself, and tucked the slingshot inside the waistband of his cutoffs.

"What'd you say your name was?" I asked him, tipping forward to show how deftly I could balance on skates.

"Name's D.D. We moved here last week. Used to live on Fourth Street, six blocks up. What's your name, if it's okay to ask?" he said, shifting his eyes from me to Norma for a split second.

"Vicky."

"Vicky what?"

"Vicky Lumière."

"Vicky. That's short for Victoria, ain't it?"

"If you must know, it stands for Vicenta," I said.

"That don't match, Vicky and Vincent-tah," he hedged.

"It's Vicenta, not Vincen-TAH."

"Anyway you say it, it still don't match. 'Vinny' woulda been better—if you don't mind my sayin' so."

"I'm named for my grandfather Vicente Arroyo and for his mother, whose name was Maria de los Angeles. My full name is Vicenta Maria de los Angeles Lumière," I said right up against his face, "but I call myself Vicky, if it's any of your business."

"I was only askin'," he murmured, scratching a bare foot against the other.

"Forget it," I said. "This is Norma. She lives across the street." I pointed toward the window that served as Norma's watchtower to the world.

"I thought she was—"

"—just a friend," I snapped.

"Pleased to meet ya, Miss Norma," the boy said, eyeing Norma warily.

"It's Norma!" Norma said, clutching her ever-present canvas tote bag.

"Whew. I thought she was your mother," the boy said, whistling through his teeth as we watched Norma cross the street in a huff, going home.

"My mother's at work," I told him.

"Mine too," D.D. said. "She works at Earl's Restaurant."

"We go there a lot," I said it as if I were a frequent customer. I'd been there a few times with my parents, who were steady customers when crabs and crawfish were in season.

"She got 'ny kids—Norma, I mean?"

"She's an old maid," I blurted. "What I mean is, she isn't married," I said, correcting myself. "And I'm telling you for your own good, don't ever call her an old maid."

"You don't need to worry about that—"

"I'm not worried about it," I snorted.

"What's she got in that old bag she's carrying? Gold or somethin'?"

"It's for me to know and for you to find out," I huffed. I'd always been as curious as anyone about what Norma carried in the canvas tote she always wore slung on her arm. I figured it was a bunch of odds and ends Norma fancied in her own oddball way. I'd once seen her pick up a camellia blossom when it fell from the bush, too heavy for its stem, and saw her inspect the husk of a cicada before dropping it into the bag, but I didn't know what all she carried in the bag any more than did the new kid.

You could say that my first meeting with D.D. was amiably contentious. Our relationship would stay that way—one day on the offensive, the next on the defensive. We were always challenging one another, until we got older and things started to change.

After three interminable months, Mama cornered Miss Ada in Matthews' Grocery around the corner at the far end of the block, and managed to convince her that when I'd baptized Lonnie, I hadn't meant to be disrespectful, that in my misguided way of thinking I thought I was helping Lonnie.

Miss Ada finally relented, I suspect more because she got tired of seeing Lonnie moping around the house than anything else.

So, Lonnie and I became friends again, putting an end to the first of the two serious falling-outs we'd ever have. She slept over and we spent the night giggling and whispering until we heard the chirping of the first sparrow when it nudged the fledgling morning, and finally we drifted off to sleep.

We became as close as we'd been before. But something was different. The picture I had in my mind was of a metal rod broken and soldered together again. It was the same, but different. I just know that there were things I kept to myself. Like the day my father caught my brother Eddie playing cards for money; my father and Mimy quarreling over Eddie's "gallivanting"; nights of my mother crying into her pillow, thinking no one could hear her; and my need more and more to be by myself.

I became too restless for the solitude once offered by the backyard stairway landing where I had idled with Queenie in timeless reverie what seemed a hundred years ago. I clamped on my skates and headed toward the Lee Circle monument, then passed it and skated all the way to Julia Street, the forbidden zone where winos and junkies hung out. Or I'd jump on my bike, ride and ride until I found myself riding through the paths of bearded oaks in Audubon Park. I walked my bike through the mist rising from the meadow of cooling grass, and found myself standing atop Monkey Hill—the thirty-foot slope sitting on the western edge of the park, rutted with two deep paths we'd ride down at breakneck speeds. At dusk I stood on the summit of that man-made hill and gazed at the sky where, in place of the orange-navel of a moon, there was a gauzy see-through lemon-slice of a moon.

I'd often wondered about my best friend: wondered if she had ever had a chance encounter, a discovery that altered her way of seeing things. Like coming upon a chunk of granite half buried and shimmering through the clay-sludge of the riverbank, or coming upon a box turtle there, cozied in its shell, waiting to emerge to explore a world not of its making. Or, had she seen the swirl-beauty of oil on water in a rain puddle, those same colors riding the rainbow-skin of a bubble, or refracted to prismatic brilliance by the beveled edge of an old mirror, so that deep down she *felt* what iridescence was? And had she ever had the feeling of leaving her skin, like a cicada that works its way out of the soil from where it lay buried, to emerge a winged creature that abandons its husk whole and intact as its real self flies away?

No matter. I knew more about Lonnie Marie Cavanaugh than anyone. I knew to hold her left hand when we'd walk down the street because the index finger of her right hand was always damp from having been stuck in her mouth. I knew how self-conscious she was of the scar left by a boil big as Stromboli at the center of her forehead, and how much better she felt about it whenever I told her it looked as if she'd been star-kissed. I knew how self-conscious she was about smiling because of her two overlapping front teeth, knew she made teensy farts if she laughed—the harder she'd laugh, the louder her farts!—and how that caused her all kinds of embarrassment, knew she lived in fear that one of her farts would escape in front of boys.

I knew she was sensitive about her brother Rudy's bedwetting, knew she was scared of the dark and afraid of her mother. And yet there'd been that something about Lonnie that I hadn't known that nearly ended our friendship. For, however much Lonnie and I laughed and talked and traded secrets the night of our reunion, the sense of loss and bewilderment I'd felt when Miss Ada forbade Lonnie and me to be friends stayed with me, entrenched beneath the pulsing depression at the base of my throat.

4

WE TOOK NORMA COSTANZA'S oddballness for granted. But the grown-ups' consensus of opinion was that she was a wild woman, too old to be hanging with us kids. It wouldn't have taken much for any, or for the pack of them, to find Norma guilty of the slightest infraction to have her sent to "the home of the fruits and nuts," as my brother Eddie called the state mental asylum in Mandeville.

"Your daughter should be ashamed of herself, playing with children," one or another of our mothers complained to Norma's mother whenever they'd chance to meet the old lady on the street. "It borders on the obscene, watching a grown woman jump rope with children, all loose, without the proper undergarment."

Etheline Costanza, a sallow-faced bag-of-bones woman older than any two of our mothers put together would retort that it was the other way around. "'Li'l chil'ren,' my skinny Scottish ass!" she'd snivel. "They the ones always eggin' Norma Mae on. Always comin' over and draggin' my girl out the house when she's inside mindin' her own damn bidness."

"It wouldn't be so bad if Norma wore proper underclothes—like a brassiere, to begin with," my mother interposed.

"My daughter don't mean no harm, missy. If Norma Mae gits a little excited and outta hand, those dumb-ass chil'ren of yorn have only theyself to blame!" she'd spit back in a voice angry as a wasp caught in a bottle.

Although the grown-ups thought of Norma as being "a little loose in the skull," the fact that she was thirty-four going on ten suited us fine. We called her "Crazy Norma" because winter and summer she went around barefooted, always carrying around that mysterious hands-off canvas bag she hugged like a security blanket, and because whenever she got overexcited she was as liable as not to heist up her big gypsy skirt, and wiggle her butt at you. Chances were that you'd find yourself staring at her bare ass as you would at the seat of the bloomers her mama made from the surplus swaths of unbleached cotton my mother brought to them from the Whitney Cotton Mills where she did piecework.

The old lady always remembered to thank my mother profusely and reiterated each time how much she was saving by not having to "spend good money on them expensive silk drawers they sell at Woolworth's." My mother said she always wondered why Missus Costanza didn't explain to Norma that wearing drawers was the decent thing to do.

There was one time when the situation did get hairy—the time Norma caught D.D. trying to peek inside her "baggy," as she called it. Norma took hold of D.D. by the shoulders and shook him so hard I thought his melon-size head would pop off his scrawny neck.

"Are you nuts?" I said to him after I got Norma to calm down and go home.

"Jeezus-Gawd," D.D. croaked, rubbing his neck. "I thought she'd never stop."

"I've told you a hundred times how Norma hates anybody touching that tote bag, haven't I? More so, anybody trying to dig in it! What if it were you and it was your treasure Norma was trying to get to?"

"You think she's got treasure, I mean like money hidden in that bag?" D.D. asked, unrepentant.

"That's nobody's business but Norma's!"

"She didn't havta get her nose so bent outta joint. Gawd almighty. She acted like I was tryin' to rob her, or somethin'."

D.D. pooh-poohed the whole incident, but I caught the look in his eyes that said having Norma Costanza mad at you was no laughing matter.

The other adult in the neighborhood we all took a liking to was Louis Champagne.

Our upstairs neighbor, Mrs. DeSales, couldn't have been happier when Louis asked to rent her extra bedroom. He was a Redemptorist brother and the sacristan at St. Alphonsus Church when he decided to leave the order to live what Mrs. DeSales called "the bachelor's life."

The arrangement worked out perfectly for both of them: Mrs. DeSales's meager widow's pension was nicely supplemented by Louis's monthly rental payments, and Louis was able to live in close proximity to the church and rectory where he worked as a salaried employee, performing all of his former duties without the official title of "Brother," and not having to wear the ankle-length cassocks he so detested.

"Such a good, good boy, that Lou-ee," Mrs. DeSales would say, looking like a kindly old horse with her long narrow face and big yellow teeth. Five years out of Mamou, her frenchified accent was as thick as a Cajun roux. She frenchified English the way my grandmother latinized it, including the way she pronounced Louis's name "Lou-ee," in the French manner, which got us in the habit of doing the same.

Louis always looked as if "he just stepped out of a bandbox," as the old women would say whenever he passed by. He wore crisp white shirts, ties, sharply creased trousers, and smelled of Lifebuoy soap. His dark hair covered his small round head with the velvety texture of a tennis ball, and his rimless bifocals, which sat high on his bumpy nose, gave him the look of a laboratory technician.

At four o'clock twice a week we'd be on lookout for Louis coming from Ellzey's on Magazine, hugging his big bag of groceries. We'd race to see who of us could reach him first. It wasn't candied goodies we were after; it was the plain gray box that contained the broken pieces of the flour pressed into the rectangular form out of which the wafers for communion were produced.

Sometimes we'd go to the workroom behind the sacristy where Louis spent much of his time arranging the vestments for Mass, cleaning and polishing the vessels and artifacts, or standing at the press where he etched and cut the paper-thin hosts. Louis got as much of a kick as we did when we'd take the boxful of broken "host" pieces and gathered in his apartment to play "Communion."

Mealy-mouthed Gloria Callahan, who claimed that she liked *host* flavor even more than she liked her all-time favorite, chocolate, said that the pretend game we played was sacrilegious.

"God's gonna punish you-all. And you, Vicky, He's gonna paralyze for putting on that old Mexican poncho, playing like it's a church vestment, and making like you're a priest, having everybody stick out their tongues and swallow those phony hosts. If I were you, Miss Vicky Lumière, I'd be afraid of being struck by lightning."

"Ka-*boom*!" Stanley Cunningham cried and collapsed on the floor clutching his chest.

We howled with laughter. I crossed my eyes and D.D. pulled down his eyelids, pushed up his nose, and hunched his back Quasimodo-like.

"Wait 'n see. God's going to punish you and make you all stay like that," Gloria warned, wagging a finger in D.D.'s face. "And don't start that ix-naying, wix-naying pig Latin, thinking I can't understand, 'cuz I do."

"Ouyay eanmay like alkingtay in igpay atinlay?" I lisped.

Gloria's nostrils whitened with righteous indignation. "One of these days, you're gonna be sorry, Vicky Lumière. You're gonna get your comeuppance and I hope I'm not around to see it."

"Yeah—right. You'd buy tickets!" Stanley said, yanking Gloria's pin-straight hair.

Next day, Mimy gave me more needlework to do than the Mothers' Sewing Club did at their annual quilting bee. Lucky for that mealy-mouthed Gloria I was hanging around when Ol' Butterfingers came moseying around.

Bored to the point of apoplexy with unraveling embroidery knots and sucking my needle-stuck fingers, I told Mimy I needed a break. "I'll be just across the street. You can watch me from the front door if you want to, Mimy," I hollered, bolting before she could object.

I was sitting on one of the stone benches in the project courtyard thinking about nothing in particular when I heard a noise like a stifled sneeze coming from the direction of Norma's apartment building. I'd developed a keen sense of hearing to compensate for my myopia so that from that one nonsensical sound I recognized Gloria Callahan's sniveling cry of alarm. I ran up the concrete steps, wondering what the little Goody Two-shoes snitch was doing in the dark project hallway. The pneumatic hissing of the screen door hadn't died when I saw her, pale as a ghost in the half-light, the priest holding her against him with one hand, the other hand fumbling under her skirt.

Had it been any one of us other than Gloria that Butterfingers cornered in the project hallway, it wouldn't have happened. Over the years we'd grown wise to the wily old priest. We'd even made a game of snatching the holy pictures he held out as bait to lure us within fondling range. He'd laugh and wink an eye as if to say he wasn't angry we'd gotten the better of him. But Gloria Callahan deferred to all priests as if they were flesh-and-blood representatives of Christ on earth—-not surprising for a girl who'd enter the Dominican order novitiate at fourteen, just two years down the line.

Gloria was clutching the half dozen or so holy pictures and the priest was holding her so tightly against him, her toes barely touched the floor. His eyes were dead on me while he kept trying to get his hand inside Gloria's panties. I couldn't think fast enough to do anything other than to run up and yank the holy pictures from Gloria. I threw them hard. They scattered all over the place.

"Those pictures have been blessed!" the priest growled, and promptly dropped Gloria, who slumped to the ground a helpless pup. Then she started scrambling around on all fours, gathering the holy pictures and bawling so hard she started hiccupping loud as a hyena. I thought she'd faint for lack of air.

"Gloria, stop that!" I commanded, and slapped her hard enough between the shoulder blades as to have dislodged a couple of molars. Ever the drama queen, Gloria clasped her throat, held it, and drew in a series of long, whooping breaths.

"We'll forget this happened," the priest muttered, snatching the holy pictures from Gloria, who was on her knees offering them to him one by one.

The three of us turned to the click-and-swoosh of the door opening at the end of the hallway. Who was it but Norma Costanza trying to make sense of the scene unfolding before her: of Gloria bawling, of Gloria and me huddled together on the floor, of the priest hovering over us, his red face and Roman collar fluorescent as Day-Glo colors in the half-light of the hallway.

"This is none of your business, woman!" he bellowed over our heads, his voice rebounding from the cement floor, the ceiling, the ceramic tile walls.

Norma bellowed something undecipherable and then turned around and around, swiveling as fast as the groaning bear target caught in the crosshairs of the air rifle in the shooting gallery at the penny arcade.

"Whatever is happening to you, woman?" the priest cried. He was looking at Norma as if she were possessed.

Norma froze. With all of us gawking, waiting for her next move, she charged toward us, came to a standstill in front of the priest, and spun around one more time.

I prayed, crossing my fingers so tightly, they hurt.

"No, Norma, please! Don't!" I screamed. But Norma was already flipping up her skirt and shaking her bare ass at the priest.

"Harlot!" the priest screamed. He shoved the rumpled holy pictures inside the bosom of his cassock, turned, stomped back through the hallway and out of the door.

I clamped my hand over Gloria's mouth to staunch her bawling, but the more I shushed her, the louder she bawled. She was still sniveling when we crossed the street and got to my house.

I couldn't take the chance that Butterfingers would beat me to it, accusing Gloria and me of being disrespectful and Norma of being an immoral woman, so I told my parents what had happened. Our chances of surviving unscathed were akin to the proverbial snowball's chances of surviving a fall down a fiery shaft. Worse than anything would have been the wrath rained on Norma, who would surely have wound up in jail, or been sent packing to Mandeville. But the next day came and went, and the next. Then a week went by and not a peep did we hear coming from the rectory.

I saw the incredulous look on our parents' faces when we described the history of abuse we'd suffered at the hands of Father Benedict Butterworth: how he'd brushed his consecrated hands across our budding breasts, how he tried to get us to sit on his lap, how he rubbed his crotch, groaning all the while, and his double entendres, half of which we didn't understand. Our parents couldn't understand why we'd waited so long to tell them.

They were more skeptical than disbelieving, as if in our youthful naïveté we had to have gotten something wrong. They tried not to believe that the consecrated hands that raised the Body of Christ at the Offertory at Mass could have raised Gloria Callahan's skirt to fondle her privates. Or, perhaps they just had our best interests at heart, because when it came down to the nitty-gritty, it would have been us—and this included "Crazy Norma"—against the unimpeachable Father Butterworth.

5

EVERYONE HAD THEIR VERSION of how the Channel got its name. The popular notion was that when ships came into port on fogbound nights, Flanagan's, Bailey's, Murphy's—one Irish pub after the other—would keep their lights burning to guide the ships safely along the sinuous course of the river. And, as a result, the grateful seamen called that section of the riverfront "the Irish Channel."

The poor Irish immigrants that came to America in the 1800s, the period of the Great Famine, having no means of moving on, were forced to settle in their port of arrival.

In New Orleans they settled in the section of the city where Howard Avenue became Howard Street, and the path from Howard Street met Magazine, then Constance, Annunciation, Tchoupitoulas, Front Street, and the river.

In the brightly lit saloons along the river front, brawls occurred between roistering sailors and the hot-tempered Irishmen whose brogue led the visitors to call the area "the Irish Channel." It was then a thriving section of the city. The remnants of fine residences belonging to more affluent families who had lived there could be seen in the brick walls, iron grillwork, wide balconies, and verandas of apartment houses scattered here and there among the storefronts and more modest houses of the Channel.

The story I'm more inclined to believe is the one about McMullen's Riverfront Bar on Adele Street. McMullen's was a popular watering hole and a great vantage point where the patrons could sit at the bar and watch the ships maneuver through the river. It's said that when the ships made their turns at the extra sharp bend fronting Adele Street, the tide rose so high it flooded the whole area, and the patrons sitting on McMullen's bar stools would have to hoist their feet up to keep their shoes from getting soaked. Hence, there never was a real channel, but "Irish Channel" stuck, and in time came to include the area between the river and Magazine Street, and from St. Joseph Street to Louisiana Avenue.

Lonnie would get all dewy-eyed about being Irish when St. Patrick's Day rolled around, and D.D. got on his high horse about how much more the old-time Germans had done for the Irish Channel than the Irish ever had.

"Rightfully, it shoulda been named the German Channel—hear them bells?" he said, cupping an ear to vex Lonnie even more. "My great-great-great-grandmother donated a buncha silver heirlooms and bracelets and earrings, and all kindsa silver stuff that was melted down and put into them bells to give 'em that tone. Y'all have my great-great-*great*-grandma Julia Dillenkoffer to thank for the silvery tones of them bells, y'know. Her and her German friends."

"What was your great-great-great-grandmother, a gypsy that she had so many bangles and baubles?" I tittered.

"And if y'all ever get a chance to go up in the bell tower," D.D. continued without skipping a beat, "y'all would see the Dillenkoffer name on one of them bells alongside the names of all the other German people who built St. Mary's."

"As if you went up there and looked," Lonnie said, popping a glistening question mark of a finger from her mouth.

"Y'all are so damn jealous," D.D. snorted.

"Jealous of you?" I said, hoping my voice didn't sound as tinny and unconvincing to him as it did to me.

"Jealous is exactly what I said. 'Specially you, Vicky. At least Lonnie can say her people, the Irish side, that is, staked a claim in the Channel. But you, bein' half Spanish—"

"Vicky's not half Spanish. She's half Mexican, huh Vicky? From her grandmother's side of the family, that is," Lonnie informed him.

"Whatever. It's all the same to me," D.D. shrugged.

"That just goes to show how ignorant you are," Lonnie said.

"Don't call me ignorant," D.D. said, glaring. "Or stupid!"

"And don't call me Spanish," I said.

"Mexican then—," he chortled. "Big deal."

"And don't forget French. Lumière is French, in case you don't even know that," Lonnie said.

"Mexican, French, who gives a flyin' fart? What I'm sayin' is, your ancestors never had no claim in the Irish Channel," D.D. said to me.

What D.D. knew about the Irish Channel he owed to me. In my endless nosing around I'd researched the Louisiana section of the school library and discovered the old lithograph prints of what the Channel looked like in the 1850s when the Irish immigrants filtered in from Canal and St. Peters Streets, crossed Federal Road, passed the cotton presses and foundries that bordered the river, and settled in what came to be known as the Irish Channel. According to the record books, the area was already predominantly German—a fact I'd related to D.D., much to my regret.

D.D. started to do some digging on his own, then his mother took an interest and together they'd go to the main library to research the Dillenkoffer name. From then on you couldn't shut D.D. up about his Teutonic ancestors—"the ancients" as he and Miss Ruth called them.

Leonhard and Julia Dillenkoffer, D.D.'s great uncle and aunt, came from Düsseldorf and helped build St. Mary's Assumption Church, D.D.'s uncle hauling tarred cotton bales in a mule-drawn caisson for its foundation, his aunt carrying bricks for the walls and bell tower in her apron, both of them donating whatever silver pieces they had for the casting of the bells. St. Mary's was a Gothic church built by Germans for Germans. "Not until years later," D.D. was quick to remind us, "was St. Alphonsus, around the corner, built by the Irish for the Irish parishioners because they couldn't understand when the German priests talked to them because they said their English sounded more like German than it did English!"

"You only know what you know because I told you," I said, aiming to knock him down a peg or two.

"Just 'cuz you're always readin' a buncha silly ol' books you think you know everything," he said. "There are lotsa things that aren't in them books, y'know," D.D. snickered.

"All things worth knowing are written."

"Yeah—right," D.D. said, hesitantly. "And what stupid egghead said that?"

"That's an oxymoron." I snapped.

"A oxy-what?"

"A contradiction in terms, you moron."

"I don't know what the heck you're talkin' about and don't give a good shit. But you still never told me who said that about all things worth knowin' being written down, or whatever it was you said."

"*I* said it, that's who!" It sounded good to the ear, but actually, I hadn't thought out what it meant when I said it.

"You think you know everything . . ."

"You're repeating yourself."

"—And you think you can *do* anything."

"Anything and everything you can do," I said, that being a proven fact.

His brown button eyes started ricocheting. "Betcha can't," he sniffed.

"Can't what?" I said.

"Jump," he said, wearing a self-satisfied smirk that told me I was being had. "Like, I double-dog dare you to jump from the landing onto the old mattress."

He was talking about us jumping from the broken second-story stair landing in my backyard onto the old mattress my brother Eddie and his friends had dragged in from the street and wedged in the space left by five missing bottom steps. The landlord hadn't bothered to have the back stairway fixed because old lady DeSales never used them, preferring to use the side alley entrance between Lonnie's house and mine. Eddie and his friends had jumped from the landing onto the mattress until they got bored.

"Anything you can do, I can do," I repeated, thinking that attempting to clear those steps without a running start was suicidal.

"You jump first. I'll follow," D.D. said, having second thoughts of his own.

"How about now?" I said, daring him.

"Now's too soon," he said, letting rip one of his famous belches. "We gotta wait until we get back from the movie at the Happy Hour."

We were still in the clothes we'd worn to Sunday Mass that morning, slipped out of for dinner, and slipped back into for the matinee movie.

On our way home from the movie matinee we stopped by The Best Ice Cream Parlor for the chocolate cones wrapped in paper, frozen so hard biting into them made your teeth ache. Not twenty minutes later I was standing in my sock feet at the edge of the second-story landing, my arms outstretched as if I were preparing to dive from the hell-diver of a springboard at the Audubon Park pool. I stood without twitching a muscle, letting my eyes drift from their myopic stare to Queenie, who was running around the yard with one of my good patent-leather shoes clenched between her teeth. Lonnie, Becky, and Gloria were standing on either side of the mattress, and D.D. and Stanley were standing behind them.

Even as I looked down—a cocky, nothing-to-it smile plastered to my face—the mattress shrank to postage-stamp size. I took hold of myself, set my sights on the center of the postage-stamp mattress, and made a wide arc with my hands. If I was going to die, I was going to look good doing it. I held my breath and jumped. I hit with a muffled thud that flattened the center of the mattress, chattered my teeth, and sent me crashing against the weatherboard wall ahead. I threw out my hands to keep from being splattered against it. Then I looked back, half expecting to see the vestiges of my dry-mouthed fear hovering above the landing like the Cheshire cat's grin. Lonnie and the others were hooting and jumping and Queenie was howling like a wolf.

"It's your turn!" Lonnie nagged at D.D., but he was already climbing the frame of the broken stairs. He hopped onto the landing and looked down, still wearing that smirky grin of his. The tips of his shirt collar fluttered in the breeze. I had to admit that he reminded me of Errol Flynn in the old black-and-white swashbuckler movies you saw on television.

"Eat y'all's hearts out!" he screeched, all vestiges of an in-like-Flynn image having evaporated. His lips were moving, no doubt in silent recitation of a final Act of Contrition, then he made a rapid-fire sign of the cross and jumped. He hit the mattress with a *whoosh* and rolled off it like a balled-up chimp onto the pebbly dirt.

Stanley Cunningham scrambled over to help, but D.D. pushed him away. He sat in the mud, rocking and hugging his injured leg. He whistled, blowing the dirt off the brush burn where his bare knee poked out of the torn trouser leg. "Aw, pissin' ant! These are my good pants," he said, pinching the ragged edges of the fabric as if they were supposed to stick together.

"Pissant," I muttered from the side of my mouth.

"What'd you say?" he blustered.

"The word is 'pissant.' There's no such thing as a pissing ant."

"How do you know ants don't pee?" he sniggered.

"Because if ants peed, I'd have seen them." My short-range vision past ten feet was like looking through Vaseline-coated lenses, but close up I could count the eyes of a spider.

"Jeez! Don't you ever stop teachin', preachin', and braggin'?"

D.D.'s cackling spurred Stanley Cunningham into a hysterical fit of his own. He flopped onto my back step and rat-tat-tat-tatted us with his wooden peg leg.

"Your mama's gonna have a total hissy fit when she sees that," D.D. said, pointing at my ravaged dress. I hated when D.D. took other people's expressions and made as if they were his. "Hissy fit" coming from him didn't sound the same as it did when Gloria Callahan said it, tossing her straight copper-colored hair and giving you that tight-lipped grin that made the rims of her nostrils whiten.

Until then, I hadn't noticed the torn hem and the ruffle of the tattered underskirt: two big loops dragging in the dirt. My mother would surely throw a conniption fit when she saw how I'd wrecked the dress she'd made from the McCall's preteen pattern we'd chosen together. It was a polished cotton print of tiny white flowers on a field of burgundy, with a fitted bodice and a circular skirt with an attached frilled-hem underskirt. Mimy had said it looked "store-bought," which delighted my mother no end.

Committed as Mimy was to making a "señorita" of me, she was sure to initiate a transformational knitting and embroidering marathon.

My knitting efforts had never gotten beyond the knit-one, purl-one stage. As for embroidery, I'd attacked the stretched fabrics with a vengeance, but after a week of Mimy's coaching I hadn't advanced one iota. I stuck my fingers so often that the edges of the pillowcases were decorated with the tiny red dots left by the stigmata of my wounds.

Mimy accused me of threading the needle with yarn lengthy enough to circle the block so that I could have more time to go "golly-benting." She'd heard my father use the term whenever he complained about my brother spending too much time running the streets. "Too much gallivanting" was the reason for why my father said Eddie never got his chores done, why Eddie did poorly in school, why Eddie had lost his part-time job bagging groceries at Ellzey's, and why my father and Eddie never got along.

There were knots in my handiwork Mimy would help me untangle and knots she missed seeing. Those knots, big as raisins on the underside of the hoop, I'd snip before displaying my handiwork for my mother's inspection when she came home from work.

I lifted my torn hems daintily and sashayed over to where Lonnie was standing. "What's your mama gonna say when she sees *that*?" Lonnie whispered, gaping at my tattered hem.

"What can she say? What's done is done," I snapped.

"Well, you'd better not break these or you'll really be in trouble," Lonnie huffed, drawing my cat-eye glasses from her blouse pocket and plunking them into my outstretched hand. She hadn't gotten the words out of her mouth when from the corner of my eye I saw D.D. standing at the back gate waving his arms to get my attention.

I threw my hand up instinctively and *plink-a-plink!* the rock he'd thrown so forcefully shattered my glasses.

Later I caught up with D.D. in the stairway vestibule of his house and lit into him. The racket brought Miss Ruth running downstairs taking the steps by twos, the end result being that she paid for the repair of my shattered eyeglasses with the tips from how many nights of waitressing at Earl's. And it was for this that D.D. nursed a long-standing grudge, the payback of which would come months later, would involve the dead Cat Lady, would satisfy the grudge D.D. bore me, and would have calamitous consequences for me.

6

I CAN PICTURE IT as clearly as if I'd been the one who'd found the Cat Lady dead; as if I'd been the one peeking through Zofia Borack's kitchen window, my breath steaming the glass as I stared, unable to take my eyes off her sitting at her kitchen table rigid as a pharaoh, the big tomcat Bubby a black yellow-eyed boa lying across her shoulders big as you please.

It was the Cloverland Dairy deliveryman coming to collect an overdue milk bill who found her, dead three days without anybody having noticed.

The bunch of us stood around gaping when Mr. Moneypenny, the undertaker, took the Cat Lady away in a body bag big enough to accommodate a longshoreman or any two flimsy old ladies the size of Zofia Borack. It took two men from the SPCA another four or five days to round up all of Zofia Borack's twenty-two cats—except for Bubby, who, biding his time, had sprung from the Cat Lady's shoulders and split the second they opened the door.

"They would sooner capture *una fantasma* than capture that black devil!" Mimy scowled. Being from Mexico, my grandmother had always been more preoccupied with shadows and spirits than with things you could see and touch.

"Mimy, the Cat Lady died and she was all alone," I said in defense of Zofia Borack.

"And may God rest her soul," Mimy said, crossing herself, "but that creature, Bub or Bubby, however he is called, you can't tell me that that old woman didn't have 'Beelzebub' in mind when she named it."

Mimy and her old-country superstitions! She knew less than I did about Zofia Borack. I myself was in for an education where the Cat Lady was concerned, learning things about her I would never have imagined. Yet, with two brushstrokes, *zip, zip,* my grandmother had painted Zofia Borack red and black. She'd never had the chance to see the Cat Lady's nice side, as I had: her concern for the mama cat Puss, how she tenderly cared for the street cats she took in, and how concerned she was for Queenie the day the SPCA wagon came sniffing around.

Mimy had sent me to the corner grocery for a box of Silverleaf pure lard. When it came to Silverleaf, there was no substitute good enough for Mimy to grease her *plancha* for the crisping of tortillas for whatever dish she had in mind. As well, it was the indispensable ingredient for the flaky biscuits she baked on Saturday mornings, as it was for the buttery-gold *roscas* she baked on special occasions.

I was standing at the curbside ready to scoot across the street to the grocery when I heard somebody calling my name. That I was totally dumbstruck when I turned and saw it was the Cat Lady calling from her door goes without saying. As good as I was at recognizing anybody's voice with but the mere utterance of two syllables, I hadn't recognized that it was the Cat Lady calling because I'd never heard her speak in a voice other than the one she used to call in her cats, which was more like a series of hisses and tongue clicks, or the low growling voice she used to make us go away whenever we played too close and the ball would bang against the old weatherboard siding of her house.

"Vicky," she called, "how is it—?"

I looked at her, perplexed.

"'How are you?' is what I mean to say."

"I'm fine, Miz Borack. And you?"

"I'm fine, too. The mama *kot* Puss is ready to have her kot-ties, and she will not come from under the house. I fear she—I think she knows that . . ."

"She knows what?" I said, and turned to see if Mimy was standing at our front door waiting for her box of Silverleaf lard. I'd never hear the end of it had she seen me chatting with the woman she said was at best a pagan, at worst a *bruja.*

"The gas wagon is to be on our street today. It was on the radio. It can come at any time now. Do not let Queenie out of the door that she might be taken. Puss got afraid. She ran out and hid under the house," she said, all in a breath.

I remembered having heard a TV announcement earlier in the week about the SPCA planning to launch a citywide campaign to pick up stray animals and I'd been mindful to make certain Queenie was wearing her tags even when she was indoors minding her own business.

"Can you fetch the kot?" she asked gently.

"Yes, ma'am," I said, "I can fetch the kot."

I took the big towel she offered for me to catch Puss and I crawled under the house on elbows and knees. All the while I was trying to numb my senses to the low warning growl that emanated from one of the central supports in the crawl space under the Cat Lady's house where Puss's silhouette, round as a melon, crouched. I managed to catch her in time to evade the gas chamber on wheels that cruised by not ten minutes later.

Flashing a gap-toothed smile that I hadn't seen before that day and haven't seen since, the Cat Lady took Puss from me, held the round-bodied cat in the clasp of her sunken bosom, and invited me inside. "Please, will you come inside?" she said, holding the shuttered door open for me.

Not wanting to hurt her feelings, but at the same time not wanting to have Lonnie or D.D. or any of the others see me stepping into the Cat Lady's house, I glanced around to make sure none of them would see me before I scooted inside.

I watched as Puss poked and kneaded, making her nest in the large rag-filled box under the Cat Lady's kitchen table before she settled, purring and grooming herself nonstop, getting ready to birth her kittens.

"*Dziękuję*, Vicky," the Cat Lady said, satisfied that Puss was comfortably settled.

"Djin-co-ya," I echoed phonetically.

"*Dziękuję, tak*," the Cat Lady nodded. "You've a fine ear for the language."

I thanked her for the compliment and sounded the word in my head, as I did other Polish words she came up with, but she must have seen the look of puzzlement on my face. "It means 'thank you' in Polish," she said.

"Polish? I thought you were speaking in German," I blurted.

The old lady's face darkened. "Why is dot?"

"I kind of thought you had a German accent," I mumbled apologetically.

The old lady shook her head, and kept on shaking it as if she were having a fit of palsy.

"No, no. I am no German. *Polska!* I am *Polska*!" she said vehemently.

She smoothed her long skirt, went to the fridge, and drew out a quart bottle of milk. Then she took a glass from the cupboard, poured the milk, and set the glass on the table in front of me. "For you," she said, and then she dug in her pocket, took out a coin purse, and pressed a quarter in my hand.

"Jen-qui-la," I said as I placed the coin on the table next to the glass of milk, "but I can't take this, Miz Borack. I was glad to be of help to you and Puss."

"But you must accept the *mleko*—the milk," she urged. "It is good for you."

I looked at the frothy glass of "mleko"—too frothy for my taste—and all of the speculations I'd made of witchery and the Cat Lady and Mimy's denunciations of black cats whirled in my brain. I stared at the bright, enamel rings on the glass, multicolored and stark against the whiteness of the milk. My choices were to offend the old lady or to gulp down the milk and possibly drop dead from poisoning. My face grew hot. I was ashamed for having thought such a thing, but at the same time I was wary.

I swallowed my spit, lifted the glass, and drank as delicately as I could manage. The cold milk burbled going down, and rumbled, making room for itself in my stomach. I set the empty glass on the table and wiped my mouth with the back of my hand.

"It is good for you," the Cat Lady assured again.

I made my excuses and started to take my leave. If I'd swallowed poisoned milk I wanted to die in my own house, in my own bed.

The notions we had of Zofia Borack's witchery were based on the descriptions of witches I'd found in books on witchcraft. Witches were malicious and spiteful crones that kept satanic-looking cats and operated in secret at night. At that moment, seeing her standing there watching me and with the big tomcat black as midnight slinking by, my speculations about Zofia Borack didn't appear to be too far off the mark. My imagination had been fueled as well by the way the Cat Lady went around wearing those black long-sleeved dresses with ankle-length hemlines summer and winter, and by the way she purred and hissed, communicating with her cats better than she'd ever communicated with any of us, and by her foreign accent that I'd suspected was from the region of the Black Forest, or Transylvania, which I'd read had been overrun by Germanic tribes in the ninth century.

As I walked through the shotgun rooms, I took mental notes so that I could tell Lonnie, D.D., and the others what the inside of the Cat Lady's house looked like. But I knew they'd be as surprised and as disappointed as I when I told them I'd seen nothing out of the ordinary. No bat-wing lampshades. No beeswax candles or crystal balls. Nothing but an ordinary house that smelled faintly of overripe fruit, had overstuffed furniture with lace doilies like my grandmother's, a clock radio, a big Metropolitan Insurance calendar, and bored, squinty-eyed cats snuggled on cushions and purring in boxes all over the place.

"*Dziękuję*," she said in her language.

"Djin-co-ya," I sounded in mine.

"No, it is not for you to say 'thank you'; it is for me to say it," she said. "You will come back and visit Puss? She will have her kot-ties soon, very soon," Miz Borack said.

"I'll come back," I promised. But I never did go back.

"You mean to say you saw absolutely nothin' different in her house?" D.D. said, lifted to a toe stand by his disappointment.

"Did I say, 'absolutely nothing'? I don't think so!" I retorted. I didn't want to lie, but neither did I want D.D. or the others to think I'd been misleading them. I'd almost single-handedly created the witch mystique about Zofia Borack. "What I said was that the house was totally bald."

D.D.'s smirk dissolved like a broken egg yolk. "Bald? What does that mean, 'the house was bald'? Can't you ever talk normal, like everybody else?"

"I meant that there wasn't a single picture anywhere. No photographs. None on the walls, none on the mantelpiece, or on the end tables. Nothing that would connect the old lady to a family. Got me?" My mind was churning with images of photographs in pressed metal frames like the ones my mother positioned in special places throughout our house, and the sepia-toned photographs of Mimy's that hung alongside the panoply of saints' pictures on the walls in her room.

"No, I don't get ya," D.D. sulked. "Why don't you stop tryin' to sound so darned mysterious and put things in plain ol' English?"

"When people don't have pictures in their houses, nobody can know where they came from, or who or *what* they are. Now do you get it?"

D.D. cocked his head, waiting for enlightenment.

"I don't get it myself, kiddy," Lonnie murmured.

"Neither me," Becky said in her froggy little voice.

"Don't you all think it's kinda odd the Cat Lady has *no* pictures of *any* kind anywhere in her house?" I returned, rapping my own skull with my knuckles.

"If you wanna know the truth of it," D.D. said, "I don't see nothin' particularly odd about it, period. Some people just don't like to have a buncha pictures hangin' around. It's your imagination working overtime, as usual. I think you're trying to make something up where it don't exist."

"You're hopeless—all of you," I said, and let it go at that. But fantastical beliefs die hard. That's why after the Cat Lady died, and Milton Moneypenny, Jr., told us about a secret something his undertaker father had discovered about her, I jumped on it, ready to prove that that secret something would substantiate all the mysterious things I'd conjectured about the Cat Lady. Even so, the image of that orange-colored melon of a mother kot, Puss, kept coming into my head, and the Cat Lady offering me that ice-cold milk in the tall glass with the bright colored rings of blue, red, yellow, orange, and green. I had to forget about all that. *Had to*, I told myself. Truth was truth, no matter what.

Milton Moneypenny, Jr., said that after his father collected the Cat Lady's body in his black Cadillac hearse, he'd overheard his father say he'd have to break the Cat Lady's legs to straighten them to fit her body inside the coffin, she'd been sitting dead at her kitchen table for so long.

"It isn't that my father hasn't got a coffin in the showroom that wouldn't be satisfactory," Junior explained, "it's that there are none to accommodate Miz Borack's S-shaped body. Rigor mortis had set in," Milton Junior pronounced in his best mortician's son's voice.

Just as I was about to inform Junior that by the time the Cat Lady's body was discovered a few days after her death, the rigor, well past its thirty-six-hour duration, would already have eased, starting from the Cat Lady's paper-thin eyelids down to the tips of her horny old toes. But before I could open my mouth, Milton Junior added, "And there's something else . . ."

Milton Junior paused for dramatic effect, readjusting the medicated cotton stuffed in his ear. "But it's a secret I'm sworn not to reveal no matter what," he said, crossing his heart.

"A secret from who?" D.D. demanded.

"From whom," I snapped.

"I can't tell you, D.D.," Milton Junior said.

"What—kind—of—a—secret—was—it, Junior?" I muttered through clenched teeth.

"All I can tell you is I overheard my father telling my mother about this secret, but I'm not allowed to talk about it. My father forbids me to tell anyone, un-under p-pain of d-death."

"Give us a friggin' break!" D.D. cried.

Behind the bottle-butt thickness of his eyeglasses, Milton Junior's eyes shrank to the size of BBs. "The m-most I can tell you all is that it's—er-ah—it's about something that's on the—er-ah—the Cat Lady's body."

"That's it? That's the big secret?" I shrieked, incredulous. But some skeeter of a thought kept buzzing around in my head.

Determined to get Junior to tell us what that secret something was, we fell on him, tickling him in the gut until the tears of laughter dried on his cheeks.

"I can't tell you all anything! I just can't!" he screamed, laughing and crying. He scrambled to his feet and started backing away like a crawfish. We circled him and pounced once again, D.D. and Stanley holding Milton Junior's arms and legs while Lonnie, Becky, and I tickled him until his stomach muscles turned to stone under the blanket of baby fat.

"You're out of the club," I said, disgusted when the laughing tears turned to genuine crying ones.

"We have a club?" Lonnie asked, popping her glistening finger from her mouth.

"Yeah, we got a club?" D.D. echoed in his inimitable way.

"Well—no. We don't have a name for it, but we are a club, aren't we?" I said. Except for Milton Junior, they all nodded in agreement.

"Don't put me out of the club, Vicky," Milton Junior pleaded. "It isn't that I don't want to tell you. It's that I can't. A mortician's duty to his client is as sacred as a, a priest's vow of . . . of confi-den-chi-ality!" he sniffled.

"Whatever are you talking about? You're not a mortician," I said, putting my face so close to Milton Junior's I could smell the ear ointment fumes that exuded from his nostrils whenever he stood close—or so it seemed.

"No, but my father is. He's a certified mortician, and besides that, he's a cosmetologist and a grief counselor with an M.B.A."

"What's a M.B.A.?" D.D. snickered.

"A master of business administration," Junior sniffed.

"Which makes you a M.M.B.A., a master of *monkey* business administration," D.D. snorted.

"Get away from here, Junior," I said.

"But I'm sworn to secrecy!" he pleaded.

"If you say that one more time I swear I'm going to wring your neck," D.D. warned.

"But I gave my father my word," Junior sniveled.

"I think you're lyin'," D.D. said, squinting an eye.

"It's true. I swear it's not a word of a lie," Milton Junior said, his voice wavering. "But the real honest-to-God's truth of it is I didn't just overhear my father tell my mother, like I told you all. The real honest-to-God truth of it is that my father was discussing it with my mother right in front of me while I was still sitting at the dinner table. He didn't tell me to go to my room, or to go look after Christopher, like he usually does whenever he doesn't want me to hear something. This time he included me in the conversation. He looked straight at me and told me not to breathe a word of it to anybody. 'Nobody. You understand son?' he said. And I gave him my solemn word I wouldn't."

"If you gave your word, you gave your word," I shrugged. But Milton Junior wasn't about to get off the hook that easily.

After Milton Junior left, the rest of us talked amongst ourselves, considering that because he'd lied about the rigor mortis business, he might also have made up the whole business of something secret on the Cat Lady's body because he wasn't able to come up with anything original or more fanciful to satisfy our hunger for the macabre. As a mortician's son, Milton Junior was privy to lots of things none of us would ever have known about the art of embalming. He knew about embalming fluid, how it was pumped in the vein of your right arm while your blood was being drained from your left arm. How, when pickled in formaldehyde, your skin turned bottle green (something we found hard to believe because we'd all sneaked a peek at the pale gray corpses awaiting Mr. Moneypenny's attention) and how sometimes the dead moaned and farted and sounded as if they were whispering. I can still hear him and still get goose-pimply thinking about it.

We decided to let the matter rest for a while. If there was any truth to Milton Junior's story about the Cat Lady, we had a couple of days to break his mortician's son's code of honor. We figured it would take at least that long for Mr. Moneypenny to get in touch with Zofia Borack's only living relative, somebody who Milton Junior said would be coming from out of town for the funeral.

"I didn't want to say anything in front of Junior, but did y'all ever stop to think that what Junior's dad discovered could have been one of them third titties witches are supposed to have?" D.D. said, squinting both eyes for maximum effect.

"You're disgusting!" Lonnie said.

"Absolutely disgusting," I emphasized. But sure as I was that a third boob was not the case, D.D.'s speculations made me more determined than ever to uncover the truth, so to speak.

Three days after he'd pounced from the Cat Lady's dead shoulders and vanished, Bubby the cat came straggling into our yard. Mimy found him sitting atop the ridge of Queenie's doghouse, licking his paws. He licked and polished his dull coat with his raspy tongue, indifferent to Mimy's threats, or to Queenie's incessant barking.

Queenie kept circling the doghouse and leaping straight up as if she were bouncing on springs. She hurled herself against the doghouse, and fortunately for her, was unable to catch hold on the slanted tar paper roof.

"It's that Beelzebub creature come back!" Mimy said, letting the screen door clatter against her wide-ass butt as she turned to come back inside. She went directly to the broom closet behind the back door.

"Be-*el*-ze-bub? Good God, Mimy. His name's Bubby," I chortled. "He's a plain ol' cat, and the poor thing looks like he's starving."

"Here, *mocosa*, swat that *demonio* before he attacks la Queenie!" Mimy ordered, thrusting the broom at me.

I'd never known Mimy to talk with the Cat Lady; I never knew if they'd ever seen one another other than from the distance of three houses down, through the dusty blinds and screens of their respective front doors.

The differences between the two women were as wide as the ocean that separated the countries of their birth. Where my grandmother was short and plump as a pillow, with an unlined face, quite smooth for being as old as she was, Zofia Borack was as slight as a birch branch, with a face as creased as a pecan half. Moreover, Zofia Borack was considered a heathen because no one ever saw her in either of the two big churches that were the hubs of activity in the Irish Channel, whereas my grandmother was devoutly religious, and everyone on the block knew it. Not that Mimy ever attended church regularly. Instead, the mountain came to Mohammed, so to speak, in the person of Father Seamus Murphy, C.S.s.R., who brought the Eucharist to Mimy every Friday morning. But I knew the reasons for why Mimy harbored that hostility for the deceased Zofia Borack—it was as much for her own ingrained superstitions as it was for my suspected willingness to have subscribed to them.

I pushed away from the table, glad to be relieved of the tepid Ovaltine and buttered cinnamon toast floating in milk that was Mimy's idea of a nutritious afternoon snack. At the same time, I wasn't looking forward to confronting a tomcat as big as Bubby, particularly one grown mean for not having eaten for a number of days.

When I squeezed out of the screen door, broom in hand, I pushed the thought of Puss and her kittens having fallen victim to the gas chamber on wheels from my mind and the memory of the Cat Lady's voice when she asked for Queenie and thanked me in Polish and in English for saving Puss's life.

Bubby stopped his grooming and peered at me with squinty eyes. Worse for wear, he could still stop you dead in your tracks with those yellow-green 3-D eyes. He stood up and stretched, effortlessly balancing himself on the ridge of the doghouse roof.

"Git!" I said not too convincingly.

The cat arched his back and hissed soundlessly. The ridge of his spine under the tatty fur looked like a bent coat hanger. His formerly glossy black coat had an orangey cast to it, like the fading tinted hair of bottle-dyed brunettes.

"You'd better get!" I said, raising the broom, more a promise than a threat. I swung the broom in Queenie's direction, trying to make her stop barking.

Queenie sat, her furiously wagging tail unsettling her enforced composure.

"Go on, Bubby!" I said swatting the side of the doghouse.

The cat flicked a ragged ear.

Closer, I noted the lines fine as paper cuts across his nose, and the triangular gauntness of his face, and I recalled the Bubby of old—a wisp in the shadows, eyes that gathered invisible light, the deathwatch mini panther—not identifiable with this poor disheveled creature who sat there, nonetheless defiant.

"Ha! I wouldn't have believed it if I hadn't seen it with my own two eyes," D.D. said, coming into the yard. "You, feeding that mangy ol' cat."

I was standing there, watching Bubby lap up the watery oatmeal I'd embellished with the meatball I'd swiped from the platter Mimy was preparing to dump into a simmering pot of marinara sauce—the supper she was preparing for when my parents returned from work—when I heard a *pang!*

The reddish, watery oatmeal splashed from the tumbling pie pan, and the cat sprang back, electrified. In an instant, Queenie abandoned her enforced watch, yelped as if she'd been mortally wounded, and bounded after the lightning-fast hunk of fur that flew across the yard.

Bubby was over the fence in the time it took me to realize D.D. had bull's-eyed the pie pan with a projectile from his rubber gun. I was at him even before the self-congratulatory smile could settle on his face.

We hit the dirt together, D.D. not knowing what had hit him and me getting in what punches I could before he'd come back swinging. I tasted the salt of my own fury and of his sweaty fist, smashed against my teeth, and I saw a white-light flash from the ground that was neither up nor down, but everywhere—dirt and sky and D.D. all whirling together.

"You crazy or somethin'?" he shrieked, wrenching away from me.

I went at him again, hitting him in the chest full force with the heels of my hands. He crashed to the ground, dug in with heels and elbows trying to gain a foothold, and I fell on top of him, pummeling him with my bony arms and knees.

"What the hell's going on here?" Eddie yelled. In one fell swoop, he grabbed me by the waist and yanked me off of D.D.

"What do you think you're doing, hitting my little sister?" he screamed, hoisting D.D. up by the arm.

D.D.'s face was a splotched canvas of fear and fury. He was rubbing his neck and smoothing his tee shirt that was outrageously stretched from my having used it to gain leverage.

"Hitting her? She's the one who started it!" he whimpered. "I didn't mean to hit her. I'd never hit no girl. I was just kiddin' around with that friggin' cat when all of a sudden she came at me like a tigress. What was I supposed to do?"

"*Ha!* You wouldn't hit a girl," I sneered, shaking my fist at him, "but guess what? This girl damn well wouldn't hesitate to beat the crap out of you!"

"Jesus!" Eddie yelled, taking me by the arm. "When are you gonna start actin' like a girl?"

"D.D. shot the cat with a band from his rubber gun!" a voice said from behind. It was Milton Junior. I hadn't realized he was anywhere around, less so that he had tagged after D.D.

D.D. shot Milton Junior a look that could have split a telephone pole down the middle.

Milton Junior blanched. It took guts for a cream-puff kid like Milton Junior to take a stand against the likes of a D.D. Dillenkoffer.

I tore from my brother's grip and, with Queenie hot on my heels, ran out the back gate and through the rear alleyway that cut between our backyard fences—mine, Lonnie's, the Callahans', and the Cat Lady's—

and the side of the Dillenkoffers' Noah's ark of a house. I ran to the end of the alley, to the last gate, and peeked through the wooden planks into Zofia Borack's weed-choked backyard.

I squeezed my arm through the gate slats, flinched from the splintered edges that bit into the tender flesh of my underarm, and felt around for the bolted lock. I worked the bolt from its rusted fasteners and I thought of the Cat Lady, gone; of Puss and her kittens and all the other cats wasted in a gas chamber on wheels; of Bubby, lost and fearful, and tears sprang to my eyes.

I entered the yard and looked for Bubby inside the yawning screen door, under the cement steps, around the grassy patches where the coiled mottled garden hose and jam jars of dry sprigs lay forgotten in the sun. I looked under the house, trying to decipher a shape in the dark spaces between the runty brick pillars that supported Zofia Borack's old house where Puss had once taken refuge.

Queenie was sniffing the darkness. She crouched down, her black-and-white plume of a tail sweeping the dirt as she crept on her belly under the house. Then she broke into a zigzag all-out effort to flush out whatever lay in hiding. But there was no sign of Bubby. He'd vanished—this time never to be seen again.

Milton Junior was still hanging around when Ruth Dillenkoffer came downstairs. She headed through the back alley and burst through the backyard gate, D.D. in tow. She banged on our kitchen door, demanding to know how the new tee shirt she'd bought for her son at Kress's had gotten stretched and torn, and who—she was looking straight at me—was responsible for the huge knot on her son's head.

For the second time in one day Milton Junior rose to the occasion; and because he was so shy and never stood up to anybody about anything, everyone believed him when he lisped that it was D.D.'s meanness to Miz Borack's cat that had instigated the whole thing.

"It wasn't Vicky's fault, Miss Ruth. D.D. started the whole thing, and that's the honest-to-God's truth," he said, avoiding D.D.'s eyes.

Ruth Dillenkoffer gave Milton Junior the once-over.

A stiff lace-trimmed hankie bloomed big as a cabbage from the tiny pocket of her pink-and-white waitress uniform. A tiny waitress cap sat atop her magenta, tightly permed hair, looking much like a bird that had just landed there. She squinched her eyes, much as D.D. himself was doing, took D.D. by the nape of the neck, and rapped the top of his head with her knuckles. She was a stocky woman, used to lifting seafood platters and slinging trays weighted with frozen beer mugs, and a knuckle rap from her was nothing to sneeze at.

"Ouch!" D.D. cried, his eyes brimming. He jerked his face away to hide the unshed tears.

"That's for lying!" Miss Ruth said, "And this is for hitting a girl," she added, grabbing him by the chin and slapping his face with a report that made me cringe. "That ain't the way you were brought up young man!"

I was fuming. I didn't need her protecting me from the likes of D.D. any more than I needed my brother coming to my rescue. I suspected Miss Ruth was angrier for D.D.'s having gotten the worst of it from a girl. But I felt sorry for him because in my heart I knew he hadn't meant to hurt the cat; he'd acted without thinking, which was often the case with D.D.

D.D. pushed his hair back, once more displaying the lump grown to gumball proportions on his forehead. We traded glances. It was a foregone conclusion that he'd get his revenge—for this, for the jump from the stair ledge, and for a host of things too numerous to mention.

7

IT HAD BEEN FIVE DAYS since Zofia Borack was found dead and Mr. Moneypenny had put her in cold storage to await the arrival of her relative. Having gotten the information of the relative's whereabouts from a stack of letters he and the grocer's wife, Miz Matthews, had found buried in a trunk in Zofia Borack's house, they'd traced the Cat Lady's relative to Oxford, Mississippi.

We were surprised the Cat Lady had family of any sort, because in all the years she and her cats lived in the corner house she never once had a visitor that we knew of, and never talked to anyone socially, unless you counted talking to her cats and delivery people and hollering at us from her window as dialogue!

Moneypenny's Funeral Home on Jackson and Laurel sat at the opposite end of the block from Matthews' Grocery. In the still of morning, the Leidenheimer Bakery man would be setting warm loaves of French bread in the big wooden bin outside the grocery when, at the opposite end of the block, Mr. Moneypenny's black limo would be delivering the body of somebody who only a day before had been dipping a nub of Leidenheimer's French bread into a mug of café au lait.

The pale blue neon sign above the front entrance of Moneypenny's Funeral Home drew us like gnats. We'd squeeze past the bank of pointy-leafed oleander bushes that grew under the windows on the Laurel Street side of the main parlor and take turns making baskets to hoist one another up to look into the parlor windows and gawk at the dead people lying snug in satin as fancily tufted as the trimmings on birthday cakes, their faces set in waxen passivity, their hands clasping their lifeless bosoms as if they'd meant to hold onto their last dying breath.

Mr. Moneypenny thought of the neighborhood kids the way Grandma Mimy thought of cats—we were devilish creatures not to be trusted. His dislike of us intensified every time he had to come chasing us away from the funeral home when services were being held. Invariably, he'd run outside and take us by surprise.

"I'm calling your parents and then I'm informing the juvenile authorities," he'd threaten, keeping his voice low enough so as not to disturb the patrons inside. "I'm forbidding Milton to associate with you young hooligans."

It was a threat he couldn't enforce because when it came to friends, his kid, Milton Junior, couldn't be choosy. You couldn't be around him five minutes that he wasn't snuffling or whining or sticking a Vicks inhaler in his nose. But Junior had one ace up his sleeve—his father was the local undertaker.

Milton Junior milked that ace for all it was worth. He loved to hold court telling gross stories about the bodies his father brought home for embalming. We'd sit there mouths agape waiting for him to throw us a gruesome morsel. Half the time we didn't know what to believe of his fantastical tales.

Once he told us his father had to saw Shea the Reed Man's shinbones shorter to get his long skinny legs to fit inside the undersized coffin bought with funds collected in the neighborhood because the only money Shea ever had was what he managed to earn selling his custom-weaved crafts.

The only thing that had separated Shea from trampdom was the soft basket he carried slung on his back stocked with long wavy leaves of latanier, the strong silky reeds with which he fashioned whatever you could imagine: rings, bracelets, baskets, mini-size animals, and the world's best Chinese finger locks, for the couple of coins you could pay him. On those rare occasions when we'd have a dollar bill, he'd fashion it free of charge into a ring we'd wear until we surrendered to the lure of the five-and-dime on Magazine Street.

Whether from malnourishment or from something he'd caught from living on the streets, Shea turned the same pale green color of the leafstalks he carried. It wasn't surprising when one November night he was found dead, curled in a corner of the Jackson Avenue ferryboat terminal building, lying with his head propped on the big basket of latanier, as if he were sleeping.

There were scary stories Milton Junior recounted of dead bodies that wheezed and snorted, that twitched and popped like corks from shook seltzer bottles as they awaited embalmment on his father's stainless steel table.

The most horrific of all the stories he told was what we came to call "the beating heart story." It stuck in my mind so that never again did I look at Mr. Moneypenny the same way.

Junior said his father was preparing to embalm the body of a one-month-old baby boy who'd smothered in his sleep—a "crib death," as SIDS was then known. He said that when his father reached into the infant's chest cavity and drew out the tiny heart, it was still beating.

Milton Junior swore on his baby brother Christopher's head that the story was true, that his father vowed he'd never again handle baby cadavers. From then on, his father referred the grief-stricken families of deceased babies to Wightman-Burns Undertakers on Washington Avenue, six blocks up; and it was from then that his father began to drink.

Nevertheless, we were shameless in our lust for funereal tidbits—the grosser the story, the better we liked it. But I agreed with D.D. you had to take everything Milton Junior told you with a grain of salt because you didn't know when he was stretching the truth and when he was plain manufacturing it.

"Guess what, Vicky? He, or she, or whoever, finally got here."

"What in the dickens are you talking about?" I asked, tightening my hold of the telephone receiver as if it were D.D.'s neck.

"The Cat Lady's relative," D.D. said. "The wake's gonna be tonight. I bumped into Lonnie comin' outta the grocery."

"She never told *me* anything about that," I huffed.

"I guess 'cuz she never got the chance to. She said Milton Junior just told her. You goin'?"

"I think we should all pay our respects, don't you?" I sniffed.

"Does that mean you're goin'?" D.D. groaned. "What I mean to say is, do you think they'll let you go?"

"And what I mean to say is that you're an idiot of the first magnitude," I snapped.

"What's that supposed to mean?"

"'Idiot' in capital letters."

"You can call me whatever you wanna, but I'm bein' dead serious: do—you—think—they—will—let—you—go—to—the—wake?"

"Stop trying to be so *effing* cute! To whom are you referring when you say 'they'?"

"I'm referrin' to your grandmaw, that's whom*mm*."

"Grow up, will you? I thought I knocked some sense into that pea-size brain of yours!"

There was a long pause. I practically felt his steamy breath flushing my face through the earpiece. "Well, I'm askin' 'cuz you know what your grandma thought of the Cat Lady—she never liked her. You said so yourself."

"Mimy couldn't have liked or disliked the Cat Lady because she never knew her."

"That's not what you said. I remember it distinctly. You said your grandmother never liked the Cat Lady 'cuz she had all them cats, in particular that 'black devil of a cat.' That's exactly what you said she said."

"What's that got to do with it?"

Like the others, I'd be going to the wake more out of curiosity than anything else; but there was something more. I felt an obligation. I was plagued by a sense of guilt, more so since Bubby had appeared to remind me of the ugly images I'd conjured about the Cat Lady and how in all the years she was our neighbor, I'd never once taken the time to get to know her better, or even to talk to her, not until the day I went after Puss. After I'd forgotten to keep my promise to her of a return visit, Miz Borack went back to being her cranky self, and I went back to my old indifferent ways, just as if the Puss episode had never happened.

Still, I couldn't stop thinking of the Cat Lady lying in a freezer drawer in Mr. Moneypenny's embalming room, waiting for a relative from Oxford, Mississippi, to show up, and worrying and wondering what had happened to her cats. I was glad she'd been spared seeing them—Puss and her kittens and all the rest of them rounded up and put in the SPCA gas wagon, dead before they'd reached the next block; all of them but

Bub, whose flight to freedom I'd cheered, and whose total disappearance left me feeling guiltier than ever.

"Even if your grandma lets you, I don't think you'll go," D.D. kept on yapping. I pictured him, standing at the threshold between the dining room and kitchen with the telephone receiver sandwiched between head and shoulder, his hands tucked under his armpits the way he did whenever he was trying to think of something smart to say.

"Come again?" I said.

"I said that even if your grandma lets ya, ya won't go because of . . ."

"Because of what?" I squawked.

"Because of the way you used to get spooked about the Cat Lady and her cats . . ." He was no doubt holding the receiver with both hands by then.

"Me? You're the one that flipped out every time you saw Bubby creeping around, 'like a panther in the night like in the *Cat People* movie.' Those were your exact words," I hackled.

"I was only teasin', tryin' to scare y'all, and you know it, Vicky. 'Sides, I'm not the one whose grandma thinks that all black cats bring bad luck and have the Devil in 'em."

"Mimy's old-timey; that's how those old people think—"

"And I'm not the one whose grandma said Bub stands for Beelzebub!"

"You sound like a broken record," I yawned.

"And, too, I'm not the one who said the Cat Lady looked like a witch 'cuz she always wore them long dresses with long sleeves, and if I remember correctly, Miss Know-it-all, ain't it you who said witches and vampires can't be photographed and that's why she had no pictures of herself or her family hanging on the walls. You said 'her house was bald.' Them were your exact words!"

"I can't believe you could be so gullible," I spat. "I was teasing."

"How come when you're teasin', you're teasin', and when I'm teasin', I'm lyin'?"

"Because lying's what you do better than anybody I know."

"All right, then, I'll bet you that *if* you do go to the wake—and I don't think you will—you won't go anywheres near her."

"What are you talking about?"

"I'm sayin' you won't go anywheres near the Cat Lady's coffin."

"You wish!"

"I'll betcha!"

"You'll bet me what?" I could've kicked myself.

"That I'll touch the Cat Lady and you won't." There it was.

"Ha! I've got a picture of that!" I retorted, having taken the bait with my big, wide grouper-like mouth. "I'll do you one better. I'll even hold her hand," I said, thinking of nothing but satisfying my own ego.

"And I'll do the same," D.D. said.

I had a mental picture of D.D., the way he always managed to scrooch right in the middle of everyone on the crowded steps of my house whenever we sat out nights telling scary stories, and how his voice got shaky when he spotted Bubby coming out of the pitch-black alley between Lonnie's and my house, and stealing into the bushes across the street, stalking something only he could see. I started laughing so hard I dropped the receiver.

"Why're you laughin'?" D.D. was saying when I recovered the telephone. "You sound like a stupid hyena!"

"I'm laughing at the picture of you touching Miz Borack's corpse!"

"Wait and see, Miss Smart-ass. Just wait and see!"

I hung up and got Milton Junior on the telephone.

"I called you first before I did anybody, Vicky, honest, but nobody answered. My father said you all can pay your respects at five thirty, before the adult visitors come."

"Okay then, I'll call the others," I said.

"My father said to remind everybody to act respectfully. I know that you and Lonnie will, Vicky. It's D.D. and Stanley I'm—"

"Junior, don't worry. I'll see to it they act decently. I want to ask you about something else. What was that secret you couldn't tell us about the Cat Lady's body? I know you said you'd never tell in front of the others because of your promise to your dad, but it's just you and me now. Can you at least give me a hint?"

"I've been thinking about it since the other day," Milton Junior said, "and I figure I wouldn't be breaking the code if I told you from a sideward angle. It wouldn't be like I was telling you exactly . . ."

"Right," I said, not knowing what he meant, but nudging him onward.

"It has to do with something that's on her arm, a—a kind of a mark."

The hair on my arms rose like metal filings to a magnet. "Like a sign of sorts?"

"That's all I can say," Milton Junior said, "that's all."

I pictured the Cat Lady in her coffin, her skinny arms like tree roots grafted to her body, and under her long black sleeves a witch's pentagram, or three 6's, or another satanic sign even more mysterious and more powerful than the others. My imagination knew no bounds.

"It took my father and the grocery lady Miz Matthews two whole days of being on the telephone, calling up different postmasters and such asking about forwarding addresses on some of the letters they found. Some were in a desk drawer, but most were in a trunk. Some of the letters were very old, from foreign countries, and some were from different places in the U.S., all of them written in a foreign language—Polish is what I think my father said."

"That was good of your father and Miz Matthews to go through all that trouble," I said.

"It's all part of a mortician's job," Milton Junior countered.

I drew in a deep breath. "I know, Junior," I said.

Later, I went to sit on one of the park benches in the project courtyard across the street, ready to intercept my parents on their return from Whitney Bag.

"You're saying Mimy won't let you go?" my father asked.

"Why not?" my mother said.

"You know Mimy isn't keen on kids going to wakes and funerals, and you know what she thought of Miz Borack," I sulked.

"You've been fighting!" my father cried, inspecting the brush burns and bruises that were becoming all too apparent on my face and arms.

"Not exactly. It was D.D. and me, wrestling, sort of."

"You were wrestling with a boy?"

He drew back. All of a sudden and for whatever reason, my thirty-nine-year-old father seemed older to me. It was as if at that moment the little pouches under his eyes and the heavy traces of veins in his arms and in his hands chose to make themselves visible, the black rims of his cuticles from the oils and lubricants he used to tool and repair the factory machines reminding me as well of how hard he worked, and shaming me for being the way I was: smart-alecky and stubborn—the all-encompassing *necia*, as Mimy would've said of me had she been standing there.

"I couldn't help it, Dad. He was teasing that old cat of Miz Borack's; the one that was lying across her shoulders when they found her dead. He showed up in the yard today, scraggly-looking, hungry and begging for something to eat. D.D. starting teasing him and shot at him with a rubber gun—"

"You're a girl and much too old to be wrestling with boys!" my father boomed.

"Dad, I had to stop him. He'd have hurt the cat!"

"Linda, you'd better handle this," he said, trudging up the front steps. "You'd better talk to her!"

"That's true, Miz Lumière," Lonnie said, coming out of her house at the perfect moment. She hadn't been there, but talked as if she had. "D.D. shot the cat with a rubber band while it was eating," she said, rubbing her arm as if she'd been stung by the same projectile.

Lonnie was already dressed for the wake. Her blond chin-length hair sparkled. She wore a pink cotton blouse and the navy-blue wool pleated skirt Miss Ada had just gotten out of the layaway at the JoAnne Shoppe.

"You look very pretty, Lonnie," Mama said. I nodded in agreement, grateful for the change of subject.

"Thank you," Lonnie said. As usual when she smiled, she shielded her crooked front teeth with the tip of her tongue. "Can Vicky come with us to the wake, Miz Linda? We're all going."

Mama urged me to hurry and get dressed, and said that I had forty-five minutes in which to pay my respects. "That's time enough. No need to let Mimy know." She glanced over our heads at my dad, who nodded in acquiescence, a little reluctantly. "And we'll have to talk, Vicky—soon, very soon."

When we arrived, Mr. Moneypenny was already standing tall and haughty at the gallery entrance of the funeral home, dressed in his black suit, his hair slicked back to match the spit and polish of his patent leather shoes. Milton Junior stood beside him, looking every inch his father's son and heir. Mr. Moneypenny lifted an eyebrow at D.D. and me, looking beyond our smiles to our bumps and bruises, probably wondering why he had ever let Milton Junior talk him into granting us the privilege of a visit.

"Yes—well—Junior tells me you all did little chores for Mrs. Borack?" he said.

Milton Junior was nodding to us from the background. Lonnie, Gloria, D.D., Becky, Stanley, and I nodded in unison.

"That you were all her little helpers?" Mr. Moneypenny added.

We stood there nodding like a bunch of bobble-head dolls yessing on a dashboard.

"I'm allowing you to pay your respects to Mrs. Borack, but one show of disrespect and out you go," he warned. He took in a wheezy breath and coughed into the handkerchief he whipped from his coat pocket.

Unswerving in our willingness to please, we dutifully followed Mr. Moneypenny through the hallway that smelled of flowers and floor wax. When he stopped, I stopped just short of ramming my nose into his coattails, and D.D. bumped into me, dislodging the heel of my shoe. "Oops. Sorry 'bout that," he said, stifling a giggle with his hand.

Mr. Moneypenny shot us a warning look. "Half an hour," he said, glancing at his Bulova. "I'm leaving you in charge, son," he said to Milton Junior. "I'll be in the office if you need me."

"Yes, father," Milton Junior said as Mr. Moneypenny strode away.

"So cute, son," D.D. teased, reaching over to pinch Junior's cheek.

"Better stop it, D.D.!" Milton Junior hissed, pulling back.

We stood under the archway that opened to the funeral parlor, its filigree woodwork hanging above us like frozen lace. Lonnie popped her finger out of her mouth and reached for my hand. The brocade-covered casket floated in the rosy glow of the uplight floor lamps that stood like sentinels on either side of the bier. A spray of calla lilies and peonies lay on the bottom half of the coffin, and from where we stood we could see the toast-colored nub that was Zofia Borack's nose poking from the whipped-cream interior of the open casket.

"You still wanna go first?" D.D. whispered, so close I felt the rush of his peanut-butter breath against my cheek. He was wearing his usual smirk, but his eyes were fidgeting, searching for a way out of the predicament he himself had initiated.

"Ya wanna, or ya want me to?" he said from behind his hand.

I let go of Lonnie's hand, which was getting uncomfortably sweaty. "I'll go first," I blustered, "then you!"

I ambled forward, but my heart was pounding. I walked toward the bier, listening to my footsteps muted by the Oriental rug, whose designs were a blur of colors to my short-range eyeballs.

I'd never seen a dead person close-up, only through the funeral parlor window, in movies, or in dreams when dead people were will-o'-the-wisp phantoms trading places with the shadows. Closer, I wondered if it was my blurry vision or Mr. Moneypenny's cosmetic expertise that had erased the convolutions of Zofia Borack's wrinkled face, leaving it smooth as parchment. Nor did I remember the Cat Lady's face ever having been as small as it appeared, snuggled in a nest of gray polyester curls. And I'd been unprepared for seeing her dressed in anything other than the dark clothes she'd always worn.

I breathed in a sickeningly sweet breath of air, and concentrating on the task at hand, I forced myself to think of the Cat Lady's hands not as human dead ones, but as lifeless ones, like the stone hands of the Bernadette and Virgin Mary statues in the Grotto. Meanwhile, I looked for marks that I might decipher through the pink chiffon sleeves of her shroud. I shifted my head just enough to see if the others were watching, and then I pinched the lace-trimmed cuff of one of the sleeves and drew it back.

"Forgive me, Miz Borack," I whispered, and at that very moment I felt the force of a cupped hand at the back of my head, pushing it downward.

I resisted the downward thrust as best I could, but my neck muscles capitulated to the unrelenting force of D.D. pushing with all his strength. Down went my head, my shoulders, my face thudding against the wooden torso sheathed by the pink chiffon shroud.

The lampblack imprint of the words "Now we're even" sooted the air and everything appeared as if in slow motion—gnarled hands, pink chiffon, rose-tinted lights, D.D. slack-mouthed, Lonnie talking without sound, and the Cat Lady herself hovering over me, her face as deeply furrowed with worry as on the day of Puss's dilemma.

Then everything whited out.

8

D.D. SWORE IT WAS a spur-of-the-moment thing.

"I didn't mean to do it. Honestly. I was gonna do just like we'd said. We were both gonna touch her hand; first you, then me. All of a sudden I saw myself pushing your head down. It was like someone forced me to do it. Jeez! When I saw you slump on her coffin, then slide to the floor like a wet noodle, at first I thought you were kiddin' around. Then I thought you might be having a heart attack, or a stroke or somethin', and that maybe you were dead," he said. "I was never so scared . . ."

"Listen to me, bonehead, if you think my fainting had anything to do with what you did, forget it! My stomach was growling from not having eaten and from the sickeningly sweet smell of flowers, and then the candles and everything else got to me."

To have admitted that he'd gotten the best of me would have given him satisfaction no end. So I kept that to myself, as I did the apparition of the Cat Lady before I conked out. I saw her! Still, my common sense told me I'd been hallucinating, but yet I shivered when I thought of the Cat Lady's face hovering in the dusky pink light, smiling, or, more than likely, glowering down at me. I know I saw the Cat Lady herself hovering over, as if she were floating.

It wasn't until the following day when Mr. Moneypenny called to ask my mother how I was feeling that things started to fall into place.

"It's Mr. Moneypenny for you, Vicky," Mama said, handing me the phone.

"Hello, Mr. Moneypenny. How are you? And Mrs. Moneypenny? And Milton Junior and little Christopher?" I said, cheerily as I could.

"Fine, we're all fine, Vicky. Thank you for asking. I'm calling to see how you are. Junior said you were still a bit under the weather. Your mother just told me you hadn't had supper before you came to pay your respects yesterday. My wife and I can't stress enough to Milton Junior how important it is for young people to have their proper meals—"

"I'm much better, Mr. Moneypenny, thank you."

"I also called to tell you I have a message for you—from Mrs. Dreyfus."

"Mrs. Dreyfus? I don't believe I know a Mrs. Dreyfus . . ."

"Valentina Dreyfus—the late Mrs. Borack's sister," he elucidated.

"I didn't know the Cat Lady had a sister."

"The what? I mean, the who?"

"I meant to say, *Mrs.* Borack, sir," I sputtered, sidestepping the issue. "I hadn't known she was married."

"Mrs. Borack was a widow. You don't remember seeing her sister Mrs. Dreyfus in Parlor A? She was sitting on the divan across the room."

It dawned on me then that the face I'd seen hovering over me in my delusional state had not been a figment of my overwrought imagination after all; the spectral image was a flesh-and-blood person. I breathed a sigh of relief, but at the same time I became worried. I wondered what the lady could have been thinking when she saw D.D. and me acting like a couple of jackasses at her sister's coffin. Especially me. Had that been my loved one laid out for viewing, I'd have been pissed no end.

"Mrs. Dreyfus wants to talk with you."

"D-did she say what about, Mr. Moneypenny?"

"No, Vicky. She didn't," Mr. Moneypenny said with finality.

"So—what do you think the ol' Miz Dreyfus is going to say?" I asked Lonnie. We were sitting on Lonnie's back steps, our backs pressed against the sagging screen.

The Cavanaugh house remained in shuttered darkness whenever Lonnie's father, Rudy, Sr., a Toye Brothers Yellow Cab Company taxi driver, was on the 4 P.M. 'til midnight shift. The five front rooms were verboten to anyone but to Lonnie's mother, who glided about in terrycloth mules with nary a creak of the floorboards. The only room accessible to us during the day when Mr. Cavanaugh was sleeping was the kitchen, where we were allowed to speak only in whispers.

"Vicky, you mean to say you actually were trying to peek under the Cat Lady's sleeves to see what Milton Junior said his daddy saw?" Lonnie asked.

"I already told you once what I was doing," I bristled.

"Did D.D. see you?" she asked, the shriveled index finger of her right hand held in suspension.

"If he did he never mentioned it," I remarked.

"I don't see how he could have missed it," she said.

"You wouldn't have been able to shut him up if he had. You're the only one I've said anything about it to, and you have to swear you won't tell anybody."

"As if I'd breathe a word," she scoffed.

"It isn't as if I'd exactly planned it, y'know. It just happened."

"You're beginning to sound like D.D.," she said.

"Lonnie, get off your high horse, will you? Didn't *you* want to know as much as me what kind of a secret the Cat Lady had up her sleeve?"

"Not enough to want to do *that*," she said.

"What do you mean by 'that'?"

"'That' meaning to fool around with her dead body."

"Do you mean to say you thought that I was desecrating her remains? Is that what you're trying to say?" I asked.

"You know what I mean, kiddy. And if you want to know the truth of it, after you told me about some kind of a mark Milton Junior said was on the Cat Lady's body, I, for one, forgot about it. It just didn't make the same impression on me as it did you, that's all."

Unable to make a worthy comeback, I sat there smirking.

"What are you going to tell Miz Dreyfus if she comes right out and says she saw what you were doing?" she asked.

"I don't know what I'm going to say. I just keep hoping she didn't notice."

"I was right there and I know I didn't see you doing anything but looking at Miz Borack when that stupid D.D. pushed your head down. There was no one else around but us when you fainted; at least that's what I thought. Then all of a sudden this lady comes out of nowhere and kneels on the floor beside you and starts fanning you with one of those cardboard funeral home fans, and then Mr. Moneypenny came running in, all embarrassed and mad until he saw you there, passed out on the floor." Lonnie paused. Her eyes were studying my face, reliving the whole incident.

"You had me so scared, kiddy—falling to the floor the way you did, with your eyes rolling back and all that. You scared me half to death. I never have seen anybody faint like that before, or be unconscious. Nobody except your grandma, that is."

"Neither me—and Mimy, well, she's a whole 'nother story."

We laughed, thinking of the many times Father Murphy had come to administer the Sacrament for the Sick and Dying in response to Mimy's weak spells and *vértigos*, reciting the litany of prayers half in Spanish half in English and anointing Mimy with undiminished solemnity however many times he was called to her bedside after not having died previously.

"I hate to have to face that lady," I confessed. I'd glimpsed the old lady's face and form briefly, but the picture I had in my mind was of a vengeful Teutonic muscle-woman in spite of the deceased Cat Lady's having informed me that she was Polish.

Lonnie pressed her finger against her lips for us to quiet down before her mother would come to the door mad as all get-out to tell us to shut up and remind us that Mr. Cavanaugh was on the night shift and sleeping.

"Maybe you can wait a couple of days and by the time you call Miz Dreyfus, she'll already have left. It wouldn't be your fault if she did."

"Mr. Moneypenny said she's staying at the big brown-and-yellow rooming house on Jackson off Annunciation Street. You know the one."

"If you want, I'll go with you," Lonnie offered. She turned and looked at the sagging screen and the forbidding wooden door behind it.

"You would, Lonnie?"

"Shh! Like I told you, kiddy," Lonnie whispered, "I don't think she saw you messing with the Cat Lady's shroud, but just in case she did, you've got to get your story straight."

"You don't have to put it that way!"

"Keep your voice down!" she muttered.

"I don't like the way you said I was messing with her shroud," I whispered hoarsely, my throat aching with dryness. "And you can say whatever you like, but you know and I know that you were as curious to know about that so-called secret mark as I, or any of us, were."

True or not, this time Lonnie didn't bother to deny it.

After all the equivocating, I drummed up the courage to call Miz Dreyfus. The lady was very pleasant on the telephone, without any hint of the hostility or sarcasm I'd expected, and with a voice that reminded me so much of the Cat Lady's, it gave me chills. When I agreed to pay her a visit the following Saturday, I still didn't have a clue as to whether she'd seen me poking around, nor what excuse I'd give her if she had. By then, the secret of what lay hidden under the Cat Lady's sleeve seemed insignificant. I had just about accepted that it was a secret the Cat Lady had taken to the grave.

The next day, Norma Costanza's life as the neighborhood eccentric came to an abrupt and sorrowful end.

The neighborhood was still snoring when a drowsy Norma wandered out of her front door to sit with her baggy on the cement steps in front of her apartment building, when soft-stepping angelic Father Murphy appeared. No doubt, he approached as soundless as a ghost, guarding the Eucharist he carried in a little gold compact buried in the folds of his tunic and totally absorbed in his mission of bringing the Body of Christ to one of the elderly project residents. Reluctant to disturb the drowsing woman, he lifted the tote bag and set it aside to pass.

Norma awoke with a start. She grabbed the startled priest by the wrist, forcing him to release the baggy.

The baggy safely grounded, Norma grabbed the priest by the shoulders. Ever mindful of the sacred charge ensconced within the folds of his tunic, likewise, the priest took his attacker by the shoulders. They grappled momentarily, then fell from the steps to the ground, Norma on top, buffeting the anguished priest, who even in his torment lay with his eyes closed and arms folded across his chest like Tutankhamen lying in his sarcophagus, protecting the little gold compact that held the host from all harm.

From under the relentless rain of blows, the priest, whose voice ordinarily never rose above a whisper, screamed loud enough to awaken the whole Irish Channel.

That afternoon, Lonnie, Becky, and I sat on my front steps, three brass monkeys watching people running in and out of the Costanzas' back door—Lonnie seriously at work on her finger, Becky wide-eyed, her eyelashes flicking her too-long bangs, and me, cracking my knuckles until my fingers ached.

When we saw Norma emerge from the door, subdued and handcuffed, a policeman and policewoman escorting her and her mother to the squad car parked outside the gate, we choked back the tears.

We hung on the edge of the sidewalk when the squad car drove out of the driveway and turned onto Clementine Street on its way to the Second District Police Station. We waved and waved, trying to catch Norma's attention, but all we could see through the side back window was Norma's downcast profile, her blunt-cut loose-hanging hair shielding her face like a fringe.

No sooner had the police car sped away than the three of us ran across the street, through the chain-link gate, and up the rear yard steps. It was the first time any of us had actually been in the Costanza apartment. What we found was a pyramid of dishes drying on the drain board, an old card table that had served as their dining table, two folding chairs, a shiny-bald sofa, an old-timey round-screen television set, stacks of old movie books, and enough dust bunnies in the corners to restuff the two sagging mattresses of the twin wagon-wheel beds in the bedroom.

"I wonder what happened to that bag of Norma's, the one she always carried around," Lonnie said, whispering as if she were inside a church.

"I think her mother had it with her," I said, realizing that it was more wishful thinking on my part than recollection.

"It's gonna feel real funny not seeing Norma sitting in her window and coming over to see what we're doing. I wonder what's ever gonna happen to her," Becky said in that froggy little voice that expressed the sense of desolation we were all feeling.

"I don't see why they had to take Norma away like a common criminal," I said later across the supper table.

Mimy looked from me to my mother with eyes that were absurdly round through the magnifying moons of her bifocals. My mother's eyes shifted from Mimy to my father, who was shifting peas around with his fork.

"Because she is that," Mimy said. "Now finish your supper, *niña*."

"She's what?" I demanded of Mimy.

Mimy's lips worked with thoughts she wouldn't express. "Your food's getting cold," she said at last.

"She's a criminal because she frightened that creepin' Jesus of a priest?" I persisted.

"Insolent *muchacha*! You dare speak of Father Murphy with such vulgarity?" Mimy gasped.

My father's fork screeched across his plate. "It's that gutter language she's learning from her brother—him and those hoodlums he hangs with."

"Why are you bringing Eddie into this, Dad? This has nothing to do with him," I said, pushing away from the table.

"Sit down and finish your supper," my father commanded.

"Norma didn't hurt Father Murphy. He's got a couple of bruises, but so has she, and besides, he's okay," I said, caught between sitting and standing. "Norma thought—. Oh, what's the use," I said, seeing how devoid their faces were of any semblance of understanding.

"Vicky, honey—," my mother said, reaching for my hand.

"I know you never liked her, Mama," I said, pulling my hand away. "None of you did. And I also know she didn't mean to attack Father Murphy in the way everyone's saying. She got over-excited, no doubt thinking he was trying to take her baggy—that's what she calls her tote bag. She was utterly surprised by the priest, and, too, she could have gotten excited thinking of what had happened to Gloria in the hallway. She just didn't know *how* to react—she just reacted!"

"*¡Oígame tú!*" Mimy commanded. "What happened to Norma has nothing to do with who likes Norma or who doesn't like Norma. She has created her own bed, as the saying goes, so let her lie on it. It's enough to tell you that she is responsible for the mess she's in. Her *historia* speaks for itself."

"What 'historia' are you talking about, Mimy?"

"Not now, Mimy," my mother cautioned.

"There's nothing you can tell me about Norma I won't understand. What do you all think, that I'm too young, too naive?"

"Calm yourself, *niña*. Norma Costanza is not the *salvaje noble* you think she is," Mimy said, weaving those infamous eyebrows of hers.

"She is an innocent, you could say, and if you're accusing her of something bad, Mimy, I think I have a right to know. She's my friend and she's got nobody else to speak up for her."

"What we mean is that Norma had a reputation when she was younger—before we moved here—," my mother said, measuring her words.

"Mama, how do you know that?" I demanded.

"She'd disappear for days on end, leaving her poor old mother in a panic."

"One can only surmise where she was, or what she was up to," Mimy interposed.

"Anyone could have taken advantage of her," Mama added disconsolately. "What could Norma have known of the consequences of—"

"I can't believe my ears! You're saying that she was a tramp because of what people *told* you?"

"That's enough!" my father exclaimed, slamming his hand on the table.

I excused myself and left the supper table in disgust. I had to keep thinking that things would work out, that Miz Etheline, Norma's hornet of a mother, wouldn't rest until the matter of her tussle with Father Murphy was investigated and the people at Mandeville had had a chance to observe for themselves that Norma was a danger to no one, and release her.

A couple of days later I saw Mr. Micelli, the project manager, going into the yard where the Costanzas' few pieces of furniture sat silent as tombstones in the weedy grass.

I ran over and hung out at the Costanzas' door, watching as he went through the apartment taking notes on what needed retouching and repainting, what doors and hinges needed repairing, and the door locks that needed changing. I watched when the Salvation Army truck backed into the driveway and carted the rickety pieces of furniture away, and watched when the painters came with ladders and drop cloths to ready the apartment for the next tenant, all traces of Norma Costanza and her mother having already been erased.

9

THE SLIP OF PAPER with Valentina Dreyfus's address was tucked in my jeans pocket.

Lonnie and I both knew the house where she was staying—a dusty, mustard-colored house in the row of houses whose tall withering facades, full-width galleries, and floor-to-ceiling windows that in times past served to draw in the river breezes that fluttered the French lace curtains and flowed through the once-gracious high-ceilinged rooms. Now the grand old mansions were rooming houses divided into apartments rented by the week, or by the month.

For all my shilly-shallying to stave off the inevitable, it took us twice the time to make the ten-minute walk from my house to the house on Jackson Avenue. We climbed the wide front steps and stood on the porch waiting as if we expected that someone would come out and tell us to step inside.

The massive front door was ajar, flattened against the wall by an ancient shoe scraper that served as a doorstop. We stood in the foyer waiting for our eyes to adjust from the glare of the streets to the gloom of the vestibule before we approached the lengthy stairway.

"Guess we'd better go up," I said, clicking a convenient light switch. In the vaulted ceiling above us a naked bulb blinked ineffectually.

We dragged ourselves up the ancient staircase and when our eyes leveled on the second floor, we saw three doors through the baluster spindles: one nearest the window that overlooked the street, one at the opposite end of the hallway, and the middle one with the raised numbers barely distinguishable under layers of cream-colored paint.

"That's it, number 22," I said, giving substance to the musty silence.

"What are we going to say to her?" I whispered.

"You mean what're *you* going to say to her," Lonnie muttered, drawing her finger from her mouth. She rubbed her finger on her blouse and tapped the door lightly.

"Dammit, Lonnie," I said, pushing her hand away. "I wasn't ready to knock yet."

"You don't have to bite my head off," Lonnie huffed.

I ignored her and tapped the door gently.

"Miz Dreyfus?" I said, wishing to God she was on a Greyhound bus heading back to Oxford, Mississippi. But I could hear small noises of life on the other side of the door—the tinkly sound of glass, the patter of footsteps gaining strength as they approached.

"Yes," came the voice, even as the dead bolt rasped and the door opened.

I smiled at the visage whose features I couldn't distinguish for the brightness of daylight that flooded the room from behind her.

"The Cat Lady!" gasped Lonnie.

"W-what my friend meant by that is that you and Miz Borack look so much alike—I mean that you 'looked' alike—," I stammered, having gotten a good look at the lady. "What I mean to say is that we called Miz Borack the 'Cat Lady' because she had so many cats—b-but we meant no disrespect." While there was a very close resemblance, close enough for her and the Cat Lady to have been twins, Valentina Dreyfus was, if not taller, more erect and not as stoop-shouldered as the Cat Lady had been. Her voice, unwavering, had a bit of a foreign accent, though it was not as pronounced as her sister's had been.

"My dear, there is no need to apologize. I know that my sister was very fond of cats, and I have no doubt that the name would have pleased her."

"She loved her *kots*, as she called them," I said, sighing with relief.

"Come in, come in. You are both most welcome."

The apartment was a large high-ceilinged room with tall windows overlooking the avenue, and another set of double windows that afforded a generous view of the dark, steep-pitched slate roof next door and the wispy pink-and-blue sky above it. An oaken pedestal dining table set between the bedroom and kitchen areas dominated the apartment: the front area with its quilt-covered bed, rocker, and cedar chest, and the kitchen area with its efficiency stove and refrigerator, windowed wall cabinet, various articles sitting on the drain board, and boxes on the floor waiting to be shorn of their brown paper wrappings.

"I beg you to excuse the condition of my apartment. I don't have yet all the things put away," the old lady said. "This beautiful dining table and the rocking chair and cedar chest I purchased only yesterday from a very nice young man who calls himself 'Peacock' at a furniture store on Magazine Street. He has so many nice things there. Yes, and he was kind enough to deliver these this morning."

I smiled to myself thinking of Peacock, who, with his feathery white-blond hair, his bleached-blue eyes, and his pointy Adam's apple looked more like a turkey buzzard than he did a peacock. Ever the salesman, he'd given the old lady a grand tour of Young's Collectibles & Furniture Store, no doubt calling her attention to bric-a-brac and odds and ends as old as the dust that had settled on them.

Even in its disarray, with the curtain panels billowing in the breezes that glanced off the slate roof of the house next door and the late afternoon sun casting the room in sepia tones, the apartment was warmly inviting.

"My chiffonnier is yet to come from my house. —And my desk," she added.

Lonnie and I glanced at one another, no doubt both of us wondering simultaneously why the old lady would have wanted to move from Oxford to New Orleans once her sister had died.

"Mr. Moneypenny said you're from Oxford, Mississippi," I said.

"Do you know Oxford?" she asked.

"I've never been, but I know something about it. It's where William Faulkner lives—Rowan Oak," I answered promptly.

The old lady drew back. "You know his work?" she asked, unabashedly impressed.

"He writes about Yuk-na—Yok-na—Yoke-na-potta-pa," I brazened.

"Yok-na-pa-taw-pha County," Mrs. Dreyfus articulated with a smile.

"Yoknapatawpha," I repeated. "Yok-na-pa-taw-pha,"

"*Tak*. It's a tongue twister, indeed, but I suspect Mister Faulkner had his reasons," the old lady laughed.

"You've read his books?" I asked her, surprised, because she was a foreigner.

"*Tak*, I have read them," she nodded.

"I didn't know his books were read all over," I blurted. "—in foreign countries, I mean."

"Mr. Faulkner's works are indeed read all over, as you say, and translated into several languages. But I am myself surprised that one as young as you has read his works."

"Oh, no, Miz Dreyfus, I didn't mean for it to sound as if I've read all his books. I've read some short stories, and read *about* him, but I haven't read his books, his novels that is—not yet, anyway," I said, my lie of omission being that I'd tried but dismally failed to understand what I was reading when I'd decided to tackle *The Sound and the Fury*. It would be some time before I'd understand the primacy of point of view in Faulkner's work—when *who* becomes *you*, one might say—and stumble onto the realization that there was something of value to be gained in seeing the world through the eyes of someone such as the mentally retarded Benjy Compson.

"My impression is that you are well read for one so young."

"I like to read," I said, befuddled by the compliment.

Valentina Dreyfus ushered us to the round claw-footed dining table, then went to the drain board beside the sink. Our eyes followed her as she unwound the newspaper wrappings from a cup and saucer, rinsed them, drew a teaspoon from this drawer, a linen napkin from that one, and set the articles on the table, where two settings were already in place. "For you," she said, smiling at Lonnie.

Lonnie smiled, drawing her lip over her two overlapping front teeth. She was probably thinking the same as I—that despite having been identical twins, Miz Dreyfus seemed years younger than her sister. Her hair, which she wore in a loose chignon held by two large tortoiseshell hairpins, was the color of tarnished silver, and she possessed a dignity and grace of movement the poor old Cat Lady had lacked.

We munched sesame cakes and drank tea from cups thin as parchment, and talked an hour or more, both of us telling the old lady the things we thought she needed to know about the neighborhood.

I pressed the sesame seeds to the roof of my mouth—flat little seeds that bloomed to roundedness on my tongue, and I crunched them between my teeth; and the taste, at once bitter and sweet, colored my perceptions of that orange-gold afternoon and the memory of my first meeting with Valentina Dreyfus.

"Miz Dreyfus," I said when Lonnie and I got up to leave.

"Yes, Vicky?"

"I have something I need to talk to you about; something I need to tell you." I glanced at Lonnie who was busily studying the wooden floorboards when we heard a frantic scratching at the door.

"Vicky, you in there? It's me," D.D. said through the door. "Queenie led me and Stanley straight here. 'Sides that, we thought you'd wanna know your grandma's been yellin' her head off lookin' for you."

No sooner did Miz Dreyfus crack the door than Queenie poked in her muzzle and squeezed through, bumping everyone like a ricocheting pinball and dusting everything with her tail.

"Excuse us, Miz Dreyfus, I have to go," I said, pissed as a lizard at D.D. for having used Queenie to track us down. Secretly, though, I couldn't have been more relieved.

"I'd like to come back and talk, if it's okay, Miz Dreyfus," I murmured, standing in the doorway, half in, half out. "I have something I want to say to you."

"I will expect you tomorrow then?" she said and gently closed the door before I could ask her what time.

"Why are you so mad at me? It isn't like I made Queenie come look for you, y'know," D.D. said as we trundled homeward.

"I didn't want Queenie to follow us here!" I shot back. "I don't like her crossing Jackson Avenue. It's too busy!"

"I toldya, didn't I? She shot out the door like a bullet before we even knew it. I hadn't gotten the words outta my mouth askin' your mama for you when she was already in the street headin' in this direction. And for your information, I caught up with her and managed to get hold of her collar before she could run across Jackson. If you wanna know, I carried her across both sides of the street. I coulda let her run across and get herself kilt, y'know." D.D. huffed, looking for backup from Stanley.

"Yeah," Stanley said on cue. "A person's got about as much a chance of gettin' Queenie to do somethin' she don't wanna do as they got of gettin' you-know-who to do somethin' she don't wanna do once she's made up her mind not to, huh, D.D.?"

The next afternoon I was sitting at Valentina Dreyfus's round table. I made a ceremony of sweetening my chamomile tea, of stirring it to tepid blandness, of sipping the tea as if it were in a bottomless go cup as I summoned the courage to bring up the subject of the funeral home fiasco.

Valentina Dreyfus listened intently. She clasped her hands and pressed them to her lips; her gray eyes held steady above the peaks of her knuckles. She unclasped her hands, waiting, set them on the table, and began to smooth the tablecloth in ever-widening circles. "You have something more you need to tell me?" she asked.

I couldn't do more than purse my lips, moving them side to side.

"Is it about your gesture at the funeral home?" she asked.

My gesture? I hesitated, the remark having bothered me for its delicacy. "Yes, ma'am, that's what I want to talk to you about," I said at last. Clear as day, I envisaged the pink lace-edged frills of Zofia Borack's sleeves, the daintiness of it contrasting with the speckled near-fleshless hands. I smelled the sweetness of the flowers and candle wax and a wave of nausea washed over me.

"My dear, are you feeling unwell?" Valentina Dreyfus asked.

"I'm fine," I said, not too convincingly.

"I was very much touched by your gesture," she said.

"You were?" I gasped.

"It has brought me great comfort to know that in you Zofia had a friend."

Her gray eyes, more expectant than accusing, studied mine.

"Miz Dreyfus, what you saw, it wasn't what you think. That's what I've wanted to tell you. It's been on my mind ever since . . . I shouldn't have ever touched Miz Borack. It was disrespectful and wrong and had it been someone in my family, someone like my grandmother, I don't know what I'd have done. I needed to tell you how sorry I am, and how ashamed." Would that the floor had opened and swallowed me, chair and all!

"The truth of it is Miz Borack and I never got a chance to become real friends. I think we might have been very good friends, if—" The words, utterly disingenuous, failed me.

"What was it you were looking for, Vicky?"

I knew then that somehow she knew the truth of it; and that I was obligated to own up to it then and there.

"You were expecting to find something on her arm?"

"Yes, ma'am." I said, swallowing hard. I could see the pentagram and the triple 6's as if they were emblazoned one on each of my eyeballs.

"What exactly was it you sought, Vicky?" she persisted.

"It was stupid. 'Stupid's' the only word I can think of for what I did. No, it was worse than stupid. It was wrong, and terribly insensitive," I uttered lamely.

There were no words that could have mitigated my stupidity, my dimwittedness, my gross insensitivity—self-deprecations that were flying at me like frenzied crows.

The old lady was pushing back her dress sleeve. The implication of the gesture didn't register in my mind even when I saw her extending her arm, resting it on the table before me, her palm up and open.

Realizing what was happening, I was afraid to breathe, and yet I was arrogant enough to believe she was about to reveal a configuration that would be the mirror image of the one borne by her sister.

What I saw were bluish markings, sloping downward as if they'd slipped from their original place halfway between her wrist and the crook of her elbow.

"Was it a mark like this that you thought you would find on Zofia's arm?" she asked, holding her arm closer for me to inspect.

I saw the letter *A* followed by a set of numbers.

I was dumbstruck.

"Do you know what this is, Vicky?" she asked.

I shook my head yes and no at the same time. "It must have hurt when they did it," I said, stupid as ever.

Something that passed for a smile crossed the old lady's face.

"The first prisoners who arrived at Auschwitz-Birkenau had no letter. The Germans put the letter before the numbers later," she said, tracing the slanted *A* with her finger. "Zofia and Magda and I arrived at

Auschwitz-Birkenau at the end of 1942. The *B* designation was given to Jews and Poles arriving later, say, in the years of 1943 or 1944."

I'd seen pictures of the horrible things that had happened in those places. I'd read about the Nazi death camps in the World War II history section of the school library; had gone through pages and pages of photographs in old issues of *Life* magazine at the public library; had watched the grainy newsreels in television documentaries where American soldiers saw what their minds couldn't have registered. I wanted to tell Valentina Dreyfus about all these things, but I kept my mouth shut.

The old lady touched the tattooed numbers again. Her hands, faintly veined, the fingers somewhat knobby, were nonetheless long and graceful.

I drew my eyes from the blurred tattoo and concentrated on the lace window panels, on how gracefully they caught and rounded the March wind, and saw through their fluttering the slate-shingled roof and the pink wisps of clouds that drifted like torn veils in that rectangular patch of darkening sky. The tears welled hot in my eyes. I could see through the watery veil the old lady's eyes on me, and I dared not blink for fear of burdening her with tears that had come too late.

"It is all right, *Dziewczynka*," she said just above a whisper.

I looked at her. "Div-chun-ka?" I said.

"*Dziewczynka*. Yes. D-z-i-e-w-c-z-y-n-k-a is how it is spelled. It means 'little girl' in Polish—and I say 'little' with affection, *Dziewczynka*."

"Divchunka," I faltered, enunciating again what I'd heard.

The old lady nodded. Although she never put her forgiveness in words that day, or anytime thereafter, I knew she forgave me for the desecration I had committed.

The image of Valentina Dreyfus that I carry from that afternoon in March of 1960 until this very day is that of a face translucent as a moonstone, with eyes that are blue-gray, and eyelashes that are sparse and moist and clustered like the tiny triangles of a six-pointed star.

10

WE WERE WALKING BACK from shooting baskets in the school yard when Lonnie yelped as if she'd been stung.

"What?" I said, jumping out of my skin.

"Your red flag—it's showing."

"Red flag? What in heck are you talking about Lonnie?" I said, instinctively drawing the basketball that was tucked under my arm to the front of my shorts.

I shifted the basketball aside, looked down, utterly flabbergasted by the hugeness of the stain that was nearly purple in the dusky evening light. I was angered by the sight of it; felt as if my body had gone off and done this thing on its own. I'd thought of menstruation as happening in the distant future, when I'd be ready for it to happen—certainly not before my twelfth birthday.

"What're you gonna do?" Lonnie asked.

"Just stay close to me," I urged.

We walked into the house in tandem, without anybody taking notice of us, and went directly to my room, where I whisked out a fresh pair of panties from my dresser drawer and headed straight for the bathroom.

"Don't say a word of this to anybody," I told Lonnie as I wedged a football-size wad of toilet paper in my crotch. "I don't want anybody to know about it just yet." Mimy and Mama would make a big fuss, my father would have to be told, and eventually my brother would start looking at me as if I'd grown a third eye.

I used up an entire roll of toilet paper that day. I half expected that Mimy and Mama would ask me why all of a sudden I looked taller than usual sitting across from them at the breakfast table the next morning. I didn't know how long it would last so I had no choice but to tell them that I'd gotten my period.

Just as I'd feared, right off Mimy instructed me on how I was to conduct myself now that I was a "señorita," and Mama enumerated the things to be expected now that I'd received the official badge of womanhood.

Unlike all the other girls, who couldn't wait to get their periods, which was the demarcation line between girlhood and womanhood, or the attainment of "true femininity," as they liked to say, I was in despair. For me, menstruation marked the end of the world as I knew it. I'd have to mark the days of the calendar, have to take a backseat to boys. I'd have to sit on the sidelines and watch them do all the fun things I'd been better at doing than them. But in the weeks and months that followed my rite of passage, I discovered that I wasn't crippled for life, that I could still compete and still outdo the boys in most things.

My spirit of competition had been encouraged by my brother since I was a "pint-sized punkin," as he called me. He'd showed me how to scale the school yard's tall picket fence—to run straight for it, to grip the iron bars with both hands, shimmy and hoist myself 'til I topped the crossbar, then to plant my feet between the spear-tipped pickets for the split-second it took to stand and balance before jumping; all of it in one uninterrupted flow because to hesitate was to freeze; and to freeze was to hunch and hold on for dear life until somebody came to the rescue—or worse!

It tickled my brother to see how fast I learned, how well I executed the skills of the root-the-peg game my father had taught him from when he himself was a kid in the hinterlands of central Louisiana. I'd center the gleaming point of the ice pick in the tender flesh of my open palm just as he showed me and flip it in a perfect arc before it plunged into the lush black dirt where fat earthworms abided, under the corrugated tin roof of the shed in our backyard.

As much as I tried and for the most part succeeded in not being bothered by "that time of the month," I'd have been happy enough to put the whole biological mess on hold indefinitely!

"Wanna know what I heard?" Lonnie said after she'd gotten her own period. "I heard that boys can tell by the dampness of your hands and your skin temperature when you're having a period."

"The boys we know are so lamebrained and thick-skinned they wouldn't react to a hundred ten volts of electricity shot up their butts," I snickered. "Anyway, who'd ever want to be holding hands with any of those boneheads? Not me, that's for sure!"

"Neither me!" Lonnie huffed, wiping her hands against her shirtfront.

In spite of my outwardly contemptuous opinion of boys, more and more I found myself liking the deliciously forbidden feeling I got from being around them—cute boys that smelled of blustery weather and clothes rumpled and forgotten in dresser drawers. More incredible than anything, I found myself attracted to that goofy-looking D.D., with his brown-button eyes, the silly cowlicks that sprouted like twin fountains from the back of his head, his muscled legs, and the way he stood with his toes pointed inward, agile and ready to grip the ground to head in whatever direction whimsy took him.

And I delighted in the boys' awkwardness. While they leaned forward on their skates, looking like Frankenstein monsters flailing the air with stiff, surgically attached limbs, my Union skates became a part of me soon after I buckled the straps.

I'd run my sawed-off broomstick along picket fences, leap over tree roots and broken sidewalks like a ballerina pirouetting, would leave the boys trailing behind like the clumsy oafs they were. I'd plunge full-speed down the low rounded steps of the Lee Circle monument, and cross the streetcar tracks racing to beat the oncoming trolleys that sparked blue when their poles met the cross-wires; and one auspicious day I found myself standing in front of the main library.

I'd take off my skates, take the rounded stone steps by twos, my eyes glued to the entrance portico where on a high podium, four Corinthian columns loomed above me, and where countless times before I'd entered the hushed majesty of the library where hundreds of thousands of books awaited me.

It wasn't until the magical day I skated across the street from the Lee Circle monument to the main library that I found books of weight I pulled from the shelves by their spines; musty books, too, that I found in the stacks after climbing the winding staircase to aisles where sunlight squeezed in from windows set high against the vaulted ceiling and fell in mote-filled shafts of light. The floor on which I stood glowed with the soft luminescence of fluorescent lights that shone through thick translucent glass floor insets that reminded me of the camphor squares my grandmother crumbled and dropped into her bottles of rubbing alcohol.

"Mimy, they're showing a *Tarzan of the Apes* movie in honor of Edgar Rice Burroughs," I argued one day when my grandmother insisted that I put my skates back inside the broom closet.

"Apes, rice, burros! *Pu-fa-lé!*" she said wrinkling her nose and dismissing me with a wave of the hand. "I don't care about such things. What I care about is you getting your proper rest." She stood like a gendarme, arms folded and watching as I flopped onto my bed. What my grandmother wanted more than anything was the peace of mind derived from seeing me tucked safely in my bed rather than "golly-benting the streets" so that she herself could nap undisturbed.

My brother had escaped Mimy's clutches long ago. School days and summer vacations, he went off with his friends while I became the focus of my grandmother's vigilance, which was all the more keen whenever my parents weren't home.

Determined to skate to the main library and return before my parents got home from work, I lay in bed feigning sleep, patiently biding my time until Mimy, fresh from her bath, would emerge in a haze of Cashmere Bouquet, to doze in her bed.

I arose from my bed and tiptoed to Mimy's room to find her sleeping the sleep of the innocents.

I hushed my skates as I retrieved them from the broom closet, tiptoed back through Mimy's room, drew the skate key from the drawer of my night table, careful to open and close the tricky little drawer as quietly as I could. Then I fashioned my pillow and blanket to look like I was asleep under the chenille bedspread, and tiptoed through the shotgun rooms, my skates hanging by their straps over my shoulder, the ball-bearing wheels tinkling like little bells against my back.

I opened the front door to the invitation of fresh air, sunlight, and the open street, and that's when I heard Mimy.

"*Por Dios*. Who goes there?" she quavered as if from a distance greater than the two shotgun rooms that separated us.

I turned to see my grandmother standing at her bedroom door, open-mouthed and doing her best to see through her talcum-frosted eyeglasses. She was clutching her chest with one hand, and holding onto the door-jamb with the other. Frightened, she was—but not too frightened to ask the apparition for its ID.

"*¿Quién eres?* Who are you?" she asked in both languages, in case the apparition wasn't bilingual.

To be caught in the act of sneaking out of the house would mean I'd be grounded until the Second Coming. I had to act fast, had to appease my grandmother, giving her what she most wanted, namely, the opportunity to confer with one of the mysterious presences from the past she was always talking about. Mind you, it wouldn't be a puny American ghost wafting thinly in the background, but a solid bulk of unknown origin more frightening because of its undeniable presence. A *bulto*!

Banking on Mimy's respect for the supernatural, on the bright sun-light behind me, and on Mimy's talcum-challenged eyeglasses to make her recognition of me difficult, if not impossible, I lifted my arm slowly, investing what I thought was a ghostly, dreamlike quality to my move-ments: lifting and lowering, lifting and lowering. I let my hand drift, my shoulders and torso sway ever so slowly. To my surprise, my grandmother waved and swayed in harmony.

"*¡Váyate!* Leave. Be gone. There is nothing for you here," she said, real-izing she was being held in sway by the *bulto*.

Being an accommodating specter of substance, I nodded my head in a leisurely fashion as I stepped back to let myself out of the door. Holding my skates by their straps with one hand, I closed the door behind me, my mo-tions designed to emulate what I imagined to be that of a bona fide *bulto*.

That Mimy didn't attempt to approach the *bulto* and didn't appear at the door to see in which direction the mischievous mass had gone was proof that she'd swallowed my act hook, line, and sinker. I hid in the alley, listening for her retreating footfalls, waiting just long enough to see that she hadn't discovered that the bulk under the bedspread wasn't her peacefully sleeping "Bee-Kee" and come to the door yelling for me.

I crouched in the alley, the backs of my knees tingling from lack of circulation. I pictured my grandmother sitting on her bed, plumping her pillows, utterly enthralled by the *bulto* visitation. I sat on the cool velvety bricks to put on my skates and started laughing so hard I could barely see to buckle the straps.

That evening I overheard my grandmother recounting the experience to my parents, "—and it waved at me like so," she was saying. She planted her hands on the kitchen table, lifted herself from the chair, and raised her arm to demonstrate the entity's movements. "It bid me farewell, letting me know that it was not yet my time, that my days on earth, like the numbered beats of my heart, are resolved in the mind of *Dios poderoso*, who will take me to his bosom at the appointed time."

My parents never discussed Mimy's story with me, so I never knew what they thought of it, but I imagined, by the way they sat in rapt attention as she spoke, that either they believed her story or, at any rate, believed that she believed in the *bulto* visitation.

Still, my grandmother was nobody's fool. She was just a willing slave to her beliefs, and many times she'd sweep you right along with her. When lightning forked through roiling clouds and thunder made the dishes chatter on the cupboard shelves, Mimy, her face glowing like Moses's descending from Mount Sinai with the Ten Commandments, would stand at the back door, strike a match on the doorpost, and light one of the wilting Palm Sunday palms she kept behind the Sacred Heart's picture that hung over her bed for just such an occasion.

She'd brandish the sparking palm like a fiery sword, lifting it to the sky while Lonnie and I crouched behind her wind-whipped skirts, hoping that before Mimy's palm burned halfway, the thunder would back down, the lightning would fizzle out, and the skies would open and smile once again. More than once Lonnie and I were witnesses to it.

Yet, Mimy was nothing if not reverential in her religion. Three times a day, at the tolling of the Angelus, she recited her devotions in Spanish. She carried a rosary with her the way other women carried their hankies, stuffed in the bosom of their dresses; and she received the Eucharist brought special delivery by Father Seamus Murphy.

"Here comes creepin' Jesus," Eddie and friends would jeer, catcalling when they saw Father Murphy rounding the corner of Constance and Clementine.

From the minute he entered our front door, Father Murphy began his recitations. In dulcet tones, he'd mix Latin verses with Spanish phrases. He'd unfold the narrow purple stole he carried inside his tunic, kiss it with something akin to ecstasy, and hang it around his neck, assuring Mimy in a voice as intimate as a lover's of *Jesusito*'s boundless love.

Ego te absolvo ab omnibus censuris, et peccatis in nomine Patris et Filii et Spiritus Sancti . . . he'd pray in Latin over the anointed Mimy, who could be found on death's door after there'd been a bad argument in the house. "*Ay, Jesusito mio*," he'd whisper in Spanish as he fed Mimy the minuscule pieces of the consecrated host with teaspoons of holy water.

After the priest left, Mimy would follow his ministrations with two healthy doses of Hart's Elixir.

I'd tried a number of times to get Mimy to understand that Hart's Elixir wasn't an elixir for the heart as she supposed it to be, that it was a solution of herbs and minerals with a 5 percent alcoholic content, as the ingredient label plainly read. But Mimy popped her lips and refused to hear that it was anything other than a heart-strengthening potion.

Although Eddie had been much spoiled by Mimy because he was the firstborn, he'd always remained detached when it came to her death's-door dilemmas. Either he arrived in the midst of one of her attacks of disorienting weakness, too late to be affected by the unfolding drama as were Lonnie and me, or he'd take off the instant it was determined Mimy would live to pray another day.

My father accused Mimy of having spoiled Eddie rotten—something that angered my father, who'd never forgotten how tough life had been growing up poor and having to work hard for everything he got in the town of Cloutierville on the banks of the Cane River in Natchitoches Parish.

"Your mother refuses to understand that by spoiling that boy, she's making a bum of him," he'd say, lambasting my mother as if she were to blame for Mimy's mollycoddling. "Me—I had to quit school to help out, or else *ma mère* and me, we would damn well have wound up in the poorhouse after my papa died. Me, I've been working since I'm sixteen, and even before then doing odd jobs, helping out whenever and which-ever way I could. That kid—he's got no sense of responsibility, never has had—never will have."

My grandmother Lumière, whom we called Mémère, was a sweet but detached old lady who gummed the little cut-up pieces of meat from her plate until she'd extracted all nuances of flavor before she discreetly deposited the cuds in the large handkerchief she kept in her lap for that very purpose. Being only ten when she died at the age of eighty-four, doing her own chores to the very last, I never really knew my Grandmother Lumière.

It was only natural, then, that Eddie and I didn't identify with our Cajun grandmother from northern Louisiana, but rather with Mimy who'd lived in the Channel with us all our lives.

It was my compulsion to take risks, fostered and encouraged by my brother, that caused a serious rift between us.

I was skating around the cement apron that encircled the Robert E. Lee monument across from the library when I came across these two boys. I'd seen them before, smoking their cigarettes and lounging on the wrought iron benches around the monument, or slouching forward on the handlebars of their bikes as if they were masters of all they surveyed.

They were about fifteen, older than me but not as old as my brother.

"Wanna go up?" one of them called as I flew by.

"Go up where?" I asked, stopping spur-of-the-moment.

"Up there," the boy with spiky blond hair said, thumbing upward. "Ever been?" he asked, taking a long drag from his cigarette. He wore a man's suit vest and no shirt, and had on a pair of leg-hugging jeans and wore pointy-toed boots that appeared too big for him, far as I could tell. The sum total effect of it was that he looked cool and self-assured, which was, I suppose, his intention.

I shaded my eyes and looked up at the statue of General Robert E. Lee keeping its coppery green vigil of St. Charles Avenue from atop the giant fluted column.

"See them little slots like up there?" the dark-haired boy said. "Them's actual windows." He stopped to aggravate a zit on his chin. "They ain't fake."

"You can see clear down to Canal Street from up there. All you gotta do is shine a flashlight through that big iron grate and you c'n see the steps leading down towards the tunnel, which takes you to the winding stairs that go all the way up," he said, pointing to the segmented grating over which I'd leapt countless times. "We saw you skating around yesterday—you and your dog there. Fact is, we been seein' you a lot around here."

"I come to the library just about every other day," I said.

"We were gettin' ready to go up and wondered if you'd want to come along," the darker boy said. He dismounted his bike, rolled it behind the iron bench, and tucked it between the ligustrum bushes. "You can put your skates here, too, if you wanna. Nobody'll steal 'em."

"Definitely, I'd like to go if it doesn't take too much time . . . ," I said, my heart thumping.

"We loosened the grate yesterday. Man, you wouldn't have believed the muck we dug outta there! Must of built up since Christ knows when, huh Joe-Boy?" the spiky-haired guy said. "By the way, I'm Mickey and this here is Joe-Boy. What's your name?"

"M-Maddie," I blurted, not knowing where that came from.

I wagged my finger at Queenie, who was sitting a little distance away, questioning with her brown liquid eyes. "Stay, girl," I told her. She was such a good companion, patiently waiting on the sloping lawns of the library until I reappeared, and sticking as close to me on my skates as if she were on a leash.

We dug our fingers into the square holes of the iron panel, so thick and heavy you'd have sworn it was medieval. We grunted and pulled it hard as we could, dragging it aside by the hardest, just enough to leave a shoulders-wide wedge of space for us to climb into. Once below, we stood in the semidarkness, our arms above our heads, all thirty fingers thrust into the grid holes to drag the grating, heavy as a dungeon door, and set it back into place.

The tart odor that emanated from the boys, one in front and one in back of me, coalesced with a darkness so complete that I was in a state of near panic when we stumbled onto the corkscrew staircase that led to the very top of the monument. I took hold of myself and clanked onward, holding onto the central pole around which the stairs wound as tightly as the chambers of a nautilus.

When we reached the uppermost landing, twelve feet or so in diameter, I went directly to one of the two window openings, anxious to catch a breath of fresh air, anxious to please the boys with an awestruck reaction and to make the obligatory comments so as to be out of there as fast as my feet could take me. But I calmed down, made it my business to peer through the narrow openings at leisure, took the time to look at the cars filing up and down the avenue, the occasional glitter of chromium and glass winking in the late afternoon sun.

"It's a view nobody's seen for a long time, that's for sure—except maybe for General Lee," Mickey said, drawing away from the window opposite. He came to where I was standing. In the narrow bar of sunlight the stubble on his chin glinted like thistles on a prickly pear.

"What you say your name was again?" he asked me, winking. I didn't know if he was winking at me or at his friend who was standing next to me, practically breathing down my neck.

"Maddie—why?" I said, unnecessarily loud in the turret-like enclosure.

"Just askin'," he shrugged.

"How old are you?" Joe-Boy asked, running his finger down the back of my neck.

"How old are *you*?" I asked flippantly, hoping they hadn't detected the shakiness in my voice.

All along I was fighting the feeling of being smothered by their closeness. It wasn't the smell of the moldy walls that was getting to me, it was that sour wheaty odor oozing from their pores that left me feeling dizzy—that damnable predisposition toward dizziness I'd inherited from Mimy!

I groped for the central support of the spiral staircase, and I toed the floor searching for the first step.

"Where ya going?" they called after me. I wrapped my arm around the support post as I descended, praying to God I wouldn't miss one of the wedge-shaped steps and break my neck as I tumbled round and round 'til I'd hit bottom.

I couldn't tell if they were still at the top of the stairs, or right behind me, for all the clanking racket I was making, practically stumbling all the way down.

The ground met me with the jolt of an elevator that hit the bottom floor, and without stopping I ran blindly through the dark passageway toward the waffled light that filtered through the grating. A shadow kept cutting back and forth, back and forth, and I could hear Queenie's snuffling and whimpering whenever she stopped her pacing to scratch and dig at the steel grating.

"You going to wait up for us, or what?" one of the boys said behind me.

"I'm supposed to meet somebody at the library and I'm late," I shouted back at him.

Hearing me, Queenie started barking.

"Be right out, girl," I called, mentally urging her to bark all the louder.

Depleted, I willed the muscles in my legs to climb the granite steps where I might sit and huddle in the dappled shadows, thrust my fingers through the eyelet openings, and push the grating with my shoulders, my arms and hands, my entire body!

"Tell that mutt of yours to shut her yappin' or some cop'll be over here findin' us!" Joe-Boy snarled.

The two of them squeezed in and flanked me on either side. Their doughy odor filled my nostrils as they pressed against me.

"Why are you all of a sudden in such a big hurry?" Mickey said against my ear.

Joe-Boy yanked me by the collar of my tee shirt and he thrust his hand inside it, his hard, groping fingers kneading my breast mercilessly, and in a cleft in time I heard myself explaining to my mother, to Mimy, to Lonnie how I'd gotten the bruises and scratches.

"We just wanna fool around some. That's all. We ain't gonna hurt ya none," he rasped against my ear.

"Damn right you *ain't*," I blustered, pulling away. But my words rang hollow. They knew how scared I was. They kept grabbing and poking, and laughing at me slapping at them and cursing them out to keep from crying.

At that instant Queenie's barking ceased, chopped off by the eardrum-splitting screech of the grating when it shifted, letting in a rush of air and light and my brother's face looking down at me, his hands reaching for me and yanking me out with one tremendous jolt.

"Lucky for you I had a few things to look up at the library and came along when I did, or you'd have been up the creek. Do you understand what I'm sayin' to you, you little fool? I coulda killed those fuckin' little punks!" he screeched, doubling his fists.

"Pooh!" I said, incapable of uttering anything substantial.

Eddie looked as if he could have strangled me.

"You stupid little twerp! You're no little kid anymore, y'know that, don'cha? You ought to be realizing what could've happened to you, what those bastards would've done to you if I hadn't heard Queenie barking her head off. To put it bluntly, it would have been your ass, you know that—?"

"So? Nothing happened! Satisfied?" I yelled back. I clapped my hands over my ears and starting singing something, "*The Old Gray Mare She Ain't What She Used to Be*," I think.

He grabbed my wrists, held them tightly, and released them before he stomped out of the room.

I threatened and cajoled, swore never to speak to him again if he told my parents, but I couldn't talk him out of telling them any more than I could talk my parents out of grounding me for the next three weeks until school closed, and forbidding me to go anywhere they hadn't approved of beforehand.

My parents talked about sending me to boarding school if I didn't straighten out, and Mimy chimed in that she knew just the school—an out-of-state institution run by the Sacred Heart nuns where I'd be kept *interna* until I graduated from high school—all within earshot and for the shock value, because my parents could never have afforded sending me to a private boarding school of any kind; and short of my having assassinated the Pope, I *knew* they would never have sent me away.

"Eddie told them for your own good," Lonnie said when I told her what had happened. Best friend or not, I was sorry I'd told her anything! I could read her mind. She was thinking that her brother Rudy would have done the same thing.

"I mean—do you think it was even worth it, kiddy, taking a chance like that with two strange boys just to be able to tell everybody you got to go all the way to the top of Lee Circle?"

"You wouldn't understand, kid-*dee*," I retorted derisively. "For your information, it makes not a fly's fart of a difference to me what you or anybody thinks!"

The truth of it was that when it came to derring-do, Lonnie had always been as much of an egger-on as Becky and Gloria—content to cheer from the sidelines while I took the flying bust-your-ass leaps. She'd never been one to weave her way through the coco-grass that grew on the levee, to slosh in the riverbank mud; she'd never cared to coax box turtles from the coziness of their shells, and watch them poke out their heads with those yellow beaks and imperious nostrils. She had never been one to catch frogs for fear of getting warts, or to go after lizards for fear they'd pee in her hand. She'd never been one to tolerate smudged dresses and barrettes dangling from her hair if there were boys anywhere around.

"Eddie should've minded his own business," I snapped, bringing our disagreement to an irrefutable end.

Not in a million years would I have admitted to Lonnie or to Eddie that things had gotten so scary in that subterranean tunnel that I was petrified, not knowing what to do when those guys had me pinned between them, their fumbling hands all over me; and that when the grating lifted and I saw Eddie's face staring down at me, I was so relieved I threw up.

It wasn't until I locked myself in the bathroom that night and sat in bathwater as hot as I could stand it, the smell of rotting oats emanating from my skin, that I thought of how close a call it had been; and it was then that the all-knowing, scared-of-nothing Vicky Lumière blubbered like a baby.

11

It was the middle of summer vacation. We'd retreated from the midday heat to sit in the relative coolness of my kitchen, where the big-paddled window fan whirred tirelessly, pulling in the street air that layered everything with dust as fine as talcum powder.

"We could boil some of your grandmother's chili peppers, dip the candied apple in the pepper water, rewrap it in its cellophane, and give it to D.D. He'll grab it like a baby taking his ninny-bottle—until his tongue catches fire," Milton Junior sniggered.

Under the table, Queenie opened an eye, stretched out full-length on the cool linoleum floor, and dozed off again.

"I think it would be fun, don't you, Vicky?" Milton Junior continued.

I shrugged and rubbed Queenie's belly with my foot.

"Sounds kinda fun to me," Lonnie said, stifling a yawn.

Making D.D. miserable didn't hold the appeal for me that it once had. Besides, I was too comfortable to move from where I was sitting at the receiving end of the flush of air that ran through the corridor of the six consecutive doorways of our shotgun house. Nevertheless, I contemplated the candied apple that sat on the table glistening as if it were glazed with glass.

"D.D.'s not one to be tricked easily," I offered.

"We can make a flip for it maybe, and let him think he won," Lonnie suggested.

"The only way you could trick him into taking the apple would be to argue about who'd get the first bite. Something like that," I suggested halfheartedly.

"That would work!" Milton Junior said.

"Whatever," I followed.

"If you don't want to get involved, Lonnie and I can do it," Junior said petulantly.

"I'm really not that interested either," Lonnie said.

"Then, would it be all right for me to pick some chippers from the bush in your yard?" Junior said, turning to me.

"It's not 'chippers', gooney bird. The word is *chispas* as in cheese-pas—'pas' with long ahh."

"*Chispas*" is what Mimy called the red peppers that virtually glowed like tiny Christmas lights on the scraggly bush in our backyard and burrowed into your tongue like sparks whose fire you couldn't extinguish no matter how much water you drank.

"It's okay then for me to take some of those 'cheese pas'?" Junior asked.

"Help yourself," I said.

Actually, I didn't think it was a good idea, but I was surprised at Junior's uncharacteristic bravado, and hated to discourage him.

"Instead of flipping for it, you can bet him something and let him win the apple," I suggested. I figured Milton Junior was just fantasizing about getting some payback for all the times he hadn't reacted to D.D.'s bullying. But soon enough Milton Junior would prove me wrong.

That Saturday morning I could see my mother wasn't herself. The previous night's scenario lined her face:

He is not gambling, Edward

You think not, Linda!

No

Then you tell me where he gets the money

I don't know where

He doesn't work—can't hold a job. If I ever catch him—

Those were whispers in the night that Mimy couldn't hear.

I myself wondered where Eddie had gotten the money to buy the motorbike he was always tinkering with. He'd done so much repairing and replacing, it wasn't the same bike he'd started out with.

On Saturday mornings, the poultry houses across the street from the Magazine Street Meat Market bustled with the cries of housewives vying for attention amid the squawking of chickens—white and gray and brindled birds clucking, scratching, and pecking in their cages one minute, yanked out by their heels the next—decapitated, doused in boiling water, plucked, packaged, and delivered to the waiting customers before the brainless creatures could realize what had happened.

My mother and I were up and out of the house by eight, hoping to beat the crowd that was already milling about by the time we got there. We had three stops to make. We began from the farthest point and worked our way back.

First we stopped at Carlos Christina's Poultry House for my mother to select a luckless hen. Then we stopped at the Magazine Street Meat Market across the street for the kidney chops my father loved and the lagniappe scraps that most times didn't make it to Queenie's bowl. Lastly, we went to H. G. Hill's supermarket to buy the things my mother and Mimy found "too dear" to buy at Matthews' Corner Grocery. It was a ritual that took up half the day and always made me sorry to wake up knowing that it was Saturday.

It was past noon when we got back from market. I was helping Mama hoist the bulging shopping cart up the front steps when Lonnie came running out of the alley.

"You won't believe what's happened to D.D.!" she cried.

At the time, Becky was home crying her eyes out because D.D. had been rushed to emergency at the Sara Mayo clinic, his head swollen to twice its normal size, and his face all lopsided. "Acute allergic reactions to a yet undetermined substance" had been the attending physician's diagnosis.

Lonnie paused, puffing her lip out with her tongue to demonstrate how bad she thought D.D. might have looked.

Becky told her that D.D. had started choking and turning blue; that he'd started acting funny after he'd eaten the candied apple Junior Moneypenny had given him.

My head rang with the word *chispas*! I ran to the Dillenkoffers' so that I could hear for myself exactly what had happened.

Becky started from the beginning, from when she heard Milton Junior's screams and ran downstairs in a tank top and panties and barefooted to find her brother on the ground thrashing and drooling, the apple cob still in his hand. She talked nonstop for twenty minutes straight, more than I'd ever heard Becky speak at any one time and in a high-pitched voice so unlike her own croaky voice that always sounded to me as if it had rusted in her throat from lack of use.

When the doctors at Sara Mayo gave D.D. the shots to reduce the swelling, she said they told her mother that he was swollen as much on the inside as he was on the outside, that that internal swelling was the real danger because that's what made it so difficult for him to breathe.

"You think he's gonna die, Vicky?" Becky asked me, her big brown eyes, so like D.D.'s, holding onto mine.

"Sounds like he had a pretty bad reaction, but once those shots begin to do their work, he'll be okay Becky," I said, seeing in my mind's eye the stripped clean pepper bush in our backyard.

Of course, D.D. didn't die. He returned from Sara Mayo a little worse for wear the next day, and still a little groggy from the antihistamines and whatever other shots they'd stuck him with.

Swollen lips and all, D.D. did his best to keep the hounds at bay, so to speak. He defended Milton Junior, saying that Milton Junior hadn't meant him any harm, that it was just a joke that had gotten a little out of hand, hardly different, he said, than any of the other jokes we were always playing on one another.

I was proud of D.D. He did his best to cover for Milton Junior but neither Ruth Dillenkoffer nor Mr. Moneypenny would buy it—not when they learned that Milton Junior had stripped the pepper bush clean and had marinated the candied apple in the juice from all those boiled *chispas*, the proof of the pudding being the hundreds of little husks lying at the bottom of the Moneypenny kitchen sink and the pungent odor that filled the funeral home, upstairs and down. The spicy smell might well have made the dead sit up had they not been sealed off in the basement that served as Mr. Moneypenny's embalming room.

When Lonnie and I walked into D.D.'s room and saw him sitting on the bed propped against a mountain of pillows, we were struck speechless. His face was lopsided, all puffed to the left with one eye swollen shut, and his nose was pulled askew by his upper lip, which had swelled to the size of an egg on a weak-walled bike inner tube.

"Y'all think thish ish bad. Thissh is nothin'. You shoulda *sheen* me *yesh*tiddy!" he bragged, looking at himself in the hand mirror Becky held up for him.

D.D. told us he'd taken the candied apple Milton Junior had offered him, not suspecting a thing. Well, who would've expected such deviance at the hands of wimpy little Milton Junior? he asked.

D.D. had licked the apple bottom to top, bit into it, got his teeth stuck in the crust, the juicy juice running down his chin, when he felt as if his whole mouth lit up, then his nostrils, and his ears! His tongue turned to burning wood. His eyes watered. He started whooping and wheezing and grabbing his throat.

"It closhed up tighter'n a crab's assh," he said, casting the hand mirror aside. Milton Junior must have gotten scared out of his wits on seeing D.D. having a seizure, as did Becky, who ran downstairs to see who on Laurel Street was getting murdered.

When D.D. fell to his knees and started making funny noises, his face turning from red to purple, Becky ran back into the house screaming for her mother, saying that D.D. was changing to a werewolf. By the time Becky and Mrs. Dillenkoffer came downstairs, D.D. was writhing on the ground and foaming at the mouth, and Milton Junior had vanished.

"Poor little whee-shul. He got sho shcared he dishappeared. Becky *sh*ed they've been lookin' all over the neighborhood and can't find him anywhere*shh*," D.D. slurred through his balloon-size lips.

"If it would've been you givin' me the apple, Vicky, I'd have thought twi*ssh* and it wouldn't've happened 'cuz you'd have had to tashte it fir-sht. But, I never would have believed it of Junior. Ju*ssh* wait 'til I get my han*shs* on the little ur-rat."

Wordy as he was with Lonnie and me, D.D. had offered no clues to the staff at Sara Mayo as to what might have caused so acute an allergic reaction. But the poisoned apple itself and all the husks of lethal little peppers in the Moneypennys' trash can were testament enough.

It got later and later and still there was no sign of Milton Junior. Mr. Moneypenny must have called D.D.'s house a half dozen times while I was there, sometimes angry, other times anxious about what terrible fate might have befallen his son.

"I did-dent wanta shay anything in front of anybody, but d'ya think Milton Junior coulda done shome-thing shtu-pid?" D.D. whispered to me.

"Don't even think about that," I snapped.

By the time I left D.D.'s, it was after five, and Milton Junior had been missing for seven hours. I decided to go out and look for Milton Junior myself, although I couldn't think of where else to look since all the places we usually went to had been investigated by Mr. Moneypenny ten times over. He'd gone to the farthest four points on our compass—Kingsley House, St. Charles Avenue, the Jackson Avenue ferry landing and wharf where the fireboat *Deluge* docked, and Clay Square.

"I've got to try to find Milton Junior," I said to Lonnie.

"Want me to come with you?" she asked.

"Maybe it's better if you stay by the phone in case he calls," I said. "I think he'll call one of us."

Lonnie nodded, curled her finger, and tucked it in her mouth.

I assumed Milton Junior's mindset, thought of where he'd think was the least likely of places anybody would look for him—least likely, yet not too far away, if I knew Junior. I headed for the carriage house behind the funeral home courtyard that Mr. Moneypenny used as the showroom to display his model caskets. I let myself into the side door he'd had cut into the carriage house wall to give him easy access without having to fuss with the cumbersome wide double doors of the main entrance.

"Junior, are you in here?" I called, muffling my voice with both hands. I didn't flip on the light switch, didn't have to. The caskets, outfitted with lighted nameplates to "enhance the personality" of each—Bronze Remembrance, Admiralty, Eternal Spring, Rose of Sharon, and so on—glowed softly from their open, come-hither lids.

"Milton Junior?" I whispered hoarsely, dropping to my knees to see if I could spot him through the skirted legs of the biers that supported the coffins. I pushed my glasses higher on my nose. "Junior?" I rasped.

"Vicky? Is that you?" Junior squeaked.

"It's me." I said, and breathed an inaudible sigh of relief.

I wouldn't have put anything past Milton Junior, him being the hypersensitive kid who'd have done anything to avoid facing his father's wrath. Not that he had a physical fear of the man; he just couldn't bear being out of his father's good graces. Then, too, there was the possibility in Junior's mind of D.D. having died as a result of what he'd done, the catastrophe having caused his father to fall off the wagon, the possibility of which might have caused poor Junior to do the unthinkable. Even then, I got chills thinking about it again.

Milton Junior was hunched under the farthest casket in a corner of the showroom, so scared that even in the stingy light that came from all the oblong boxes and the high, tiny windows on either side of the showroom, his face was deathly white.

I scrooched under the coffin and sat beside him.

"Is he—? Is D.D.—?" He faltered, and then he bawled, "Is D.D. dead?" His voice shivered, and his whole body did too, a shivering that passed like a current from him to me when I accommodated myself to sit alongside him, our heads now and again bumping the lacquered underside of the coffin.

"D.D.'s okay," I said, doing my best to control the quiver in my own voice. "He's been asking for you, Junior. He's been worried about you. We all have."

"He is? H-he really is okay? You're not kidding me are you Vicky?" Junior asked, unhooking the wire-rim glasses from behind his ears and rubbing his eyes with the knuckles of both hands.

"I promise you, he's okay," I said, crossing my heart.

"Oh, Jesus! Thank God! I thought for sure I'd killed him. I thought he was dead when the spit . . . when he began foaming at the mouth and fell to the ground and went into convulsions. It was awful. Thank God. Thank God," Milton Junior kept saying, crossing himself over and over. He was bending his fingers so far back I had to take hold of his hands to stop the self-mutilation.

"Stop blaming yourself, Junior. You had no idea the peppers were going to affect him the way they did. Who could have? Not me; not anybody. Come on. Let's go. Everybody's been worried , all of 'em asking for you."

"I can't go back. I can't," Junior said. He started bawling all over and steaming his eyeglasses again.

"Your dad's worried sick, Junior. He's probably got the police looking for you by now."

"My—father—is—never—going—to—forgive—me—for—this," he hiccupped.

"Yes, he will, Junior. It wasn't your fault. Like I told you, nobody, not even your father with all of his credentials could have known how allergic D.D. was to those chili peppers. And besides, it's usually the other way around, isn't it? If D.D. would've thought of it first, it would have been you or me running around with our mouths on fire and our lips swollen to goiter-size proportions, wouldn't it?" I said, laughing feebly.

I kept babbling on, saying anything to fill the silence that rose like a mist from between the coffins with their satiny interiors, little lights, and nameplates tilted just enough to look like invitations for you to try them out. All the while, I was hoping for Milton Junior's sake that his father wouldn't make the punishment fit the so-called crime, like sending him off to Timbuktu Academy in the farthest reaches of the Mississippi Delta, as he'd been threatening to do for the past several months.

By the time I coaxed Milton Junior out of the showroom and into the house, it was nearly seven o'clock. It was past dinnertime and I should have headed for home, but I was too keyed up. I needed to keep moving. I walked and walked, feeling that if I didn't walk fast enough it would all catch up with me.

I walked to Washington Avenue, turned back, found myself at the Jackson Avenue ferry landing at one point, then at Clay Square, and when I finally stopped I was standing in front of the apartment house where Valentina Dreyfus lived, staring at the sunken wicker rockers that were pitching back and forth all on their own on the wide-planked gallery.

"I pretty much downplayed D.D.'s condition to Milton Junior so that he wouldn't feel so bad, because to tell you the truth, D.D. looked a lot worse than he said he felt. I got Junior to calm down, but I'm worried about what's going to happen. His father was pretty upset. As soon as Junior and I walked into Mr. Moneypenny's office, where we found him hunched at his desk still dialing telephone numbers, Mr. Moneypenny took Junior by the arm, and promised him he was going to take measures to insure that nothing like this would ever happen again, that he was going to set Junior on 'the straight and narrow.'

"If by that he means he's going to send Milton Junior away, that'll kill Junior," I said, pausing because I had run out of breath.

Valentina folded her hands and pressed them to her lips.

"Mr. Moneypenny would never send Junior away—not for this. Milton Junior didn't mean to do anything bad. It was a case of overkill."

"What is overkill?" Valentina asked.

"It means 'going overboard,' like, taking things too far."

"By a case of 'overkill' you are saying that if Milton Junior hadn't boiled so many of the peppers, the brew would not have been nearly so potent and—"

"And probably the worst that would've happened would've been that D.D. would've had a swollen lip," I said.

"Perhaps the lapse in judgment was not about Milton using too many peppers," Valentina suggested.

"I know," I said, disappointed that she was not in total agreement with me.

"What is it that you know, *Dziewczynka*?" Valentina asked.

"I know that I could've stopped him—and didn't . . ."

A frown fleeting as a shadow crossed Valentina's face.

I had the vague feeling that that wasn't exactly it either, and that she was leaving it up to me to figure out.

"Excuse me, Valentina, but I need to be going!" I cried and ran out, careful not to let the door bang when I closed it behind me.

12

IT WAS EIGHT O'CLOCK and dark and nobody would have known where to find me. I was prepared for the worst tongue-lashing ever. But it never happened.

What happened, rather, what *was* happening when I walked in the front door, was the worst fight that I can ever remember happening in my family.

They were standing toe-to-toe, my father and Eddie.

"Don't lie to me, boy. I know it was you!" my father was yelling in Eddie's face.

"He was shooting craps in front of the Daigles', playing for money with those other hoodlums. He tried to hide. Didn't think I saw him," he said to my mother and Mimy, who were standing on either side of Eddie.

Eddie stood his ground, fists clenched.

"It's why you were fired both from Matthews' and from Ellzey's," my father said, nearly poking Eddie's eye out with his finger. "It's why you can't hold a job. You either don't bother to show up, or you're late, always late! Gambling and gallivanting the streets, that's all you're good for!"

"That's a lie! Ellzey's let me go 'cuz there were too many stock boys," Eddie shouted in my father's face.

My father fumbled for his belt.

"Edward! Don't!" my mother screamed. Her hair was standing on end, electrified as if she'd taken hold of a live wire and couldn't let go.

"*Basta!*" Mimy said. "Enough!" She pulled my mother back and put herself between Eddie and my father. "Here, Edward! Strike me, not this child!" she cried, slapping the very cheek she offered to him.

"Get out of the way Mimy!" my father bellowed. The very force of his voice, which became not so much louder as it did bigger when he was angry, seemed to displace the very air.

Mimy stood her ground.

"Get out of the way, see-nyor-ah. This is none of your business!" His arm swung out like a gate, ushering both women aside with one sweep.

My brother, sixteen years old and big for his age, broke from behind the two women.

"No, son! No!" my mother shrieked, horrified at the sight of Eddie confronting his father, fists held in readiness.

I thought my father would push Eddie away, maybe slap him, but that he wouldn't use his belt. And I thought Eddie was only posturing. But I was scared, scared of the way they stood their ground, glaring at one another.

Even as I saw my father grab Eddie by the throat I knew that he loved Eddie, and that he hated him at the same time—just as Eddie hated my father with all the fury that was in him at that moment. I forced myself between them, and in the scuffle I slipped.

"Vicky! You hurt? You okay?" my father cried, the wildness seeping from his eyes. He reached to help me up but I pushed him away. I struggled to get to my feet, shaken but unhurt.

After the scene had played itself out, instead of falling victim to one of her attacks of vertigo as she usually did, Mimy shuffled off to her room as fast as her swollen feet could carry her, leaving in her wake a flurry of maledictions uttered in Spanish, all of them aimed at my father. In no time she was at the front door, her *chal* wrapped around her shoulders, her black leather purse, stiff as a mortarboard, looped on her arm.

"I will call you, Linda, when I am settled. *Que Dios los bendiga,*" she said, giving us her blessing with a multiplicity of signs of the crosses.

With Eddie and I flanking her on either side, Mimy walked uncertain as a toddler trying its new legs on the dark uneven sidewalks of the Channel streets. We took turns persuading her to come back home, but she was deaf to our pleas.

With increased confidence in her footing, she crossed the streets, block after block, repeating my father's words when he ordered her from the house, when he blamed her for spoiling Eddie rotten, and blamed her for always coming between him and his family and not letting him be the head of his own house.

It took us forty-five minutes to walk five blocks and find a pay phone for Mimy to call for a taxi, and another ten minutes until a Yellow Cab pulled up.

"Go back home, *mijos*," she said, flattening the button lock with the heel of her hand. "Tell my daughter I will call her in the morning."

I was scared for her. I worried about what would happen were she to suffer one of her *vértigos* and lose her balance with none of us there to help her.

"Mimy, please don't go," I begged. But Mimy shook her head and signaled for the taxi driver to drive on.

It was the first time ever that I remembered Mimy going off without one of us along. Even so, I thought of what Mama had said when I'd remarked about Mimy's reclusiveness. "That's never stopped Mimy from getting things done whenever she wants to or has to," she'd said.

Even so, seeing the cab speed off, my heart sat heavy in my chest, reluctant to beat, reluctant, as well, to admit that what had happened at the house would never let us be as we once were—the five of us together.

"She wouldn't say where she was going?" Mama asked.

"She just told us not to worry, to tell you that she'd call you in the morning."

"Well—Mimy can take care of herself. It isn't as if she can't, you know," my mother said, with tear-filled eyes.

"We know," Eddie and I chorused.

I knew that when push came to shove Mimy could fend for herself. She'd already done it *solita*, propelled by the death of her husband; working her way with an infant girl from the Mexican town of Zacatecas to the Texas border and beyond; washing hotel bed linens in Juárez; picking pecans in a contract shop in San Antonio, working shoulder to shoulder with as many as a hundred other Mexican women who sat at long tables in a twenty-by-forty-foot room, picking, shelling, and sorting; breathing pecan dust so fine it hung in the air like a sepia mist.

In their rejection of the workers' appeal for better wages, the owners and managers of the shelling companies said that free pecans well supplemented the going wage of two dollars and fifty cents for the fifty-hour workweek. *They don't want much money; they're grateful to have a warm place in the winter for themselves and their kids while they shell. Whenever they're hungry they have permission to eat all the pecans they want. What more can they ask?* they said of the immigrant workers.

Mimy said that not since 1938 has she eaten another pecan.

I'd seen for myself that when it came to getting things done, Mimy was dauntless. She never bothered with telephone numbers; she simply dialed 0 for operator, and talked to the Southern Bell operators as if she were marshalling her troops. They, in turn, recognized Mimy's *Opeh-ray-tohr, will-jew-be-kind* requests for what they were: assignments for Bell Tel & Tel telephone operators to contact the parties of her choice. And it was nothing for Mimy to owe a balance at Matthews' Corner Grocery carried from the previous month. Mimy would send Eddie or me to pay the balance of one bill, and then promptly start another. Mr. Matthews would stab Mimy's charge book with his stubby pencil with every new item he listed. He'd vent his anger for those perpetual balances at me when I inherited the chore of running Mimy's errands from Eddie.

It was much the same at either of the two holy stores where Mimy did business—she'd pay for one dozen vigil candles, and right off charge a new dozen. But never once did I know of Mr. Matthews or the Umbach sisters griping at Mimy directly. Perhaps they saw her as Lonnie and I did—someone on whose good side you wanted to stay.

Thinking of Mimy the way she was, reclusive and disinclined to being unnecessarily sociable, it appeared that she'd fended so much for herself as a young woman that when she reached New Orleans she simply dropped where she stopped.

Much to our relief, Mimy returned early the next day. She announced that she was moving out of our house come September. She told us she'd already talked with the project manager, Mr. Micelli, at his office and had signed a lease for a one-bedroom apartment.

"I requested a two-bedroom *habitación* closer to the opposite end of the project, but there were none available. I had to take what I could get—the *habitación* that belonged to Norma and her mother," she said to Mama and me.

We begged Mimy to reconsider, but not all of our pleading, my mother's tears, or my father's reluctant apologies could get Mimy to change her mind.

True to her word, Mimy moved out the last week of August. For what would seem the longest time her room remained empty, then my mother began to occupy it little by little. She moved her sewing machine in, and a little settee she bought at Kirschman's Furniture downtown, a wood "cutting table" she bought secondhand, and she hung some pictures on the wall. But to me the room felt as empty as when Mimy had left it, taking everything she owned except the old El Popo Cigars calendar that remained tacked on the living room wall.

No matter how many excuses D.D. and I came up with to keep parading to the funeral home, Mr. Moneypenny always ended up by saying it was in Milton Junior's best interest for us to leave Milton Junior alone and to stop giving Junior false hopes, because he was in the process of making certain arrangements for his son.

"When my father says he wants to keep me away from the bad influence of a de-deteriorating n-neighborhood, he d-doesn't mean you all," Milton Junior assured us, his eyes big as marbles behind his bottle-butt eyeglasses. "He's referring to the neighborhood in general. He says there's an element coming in that he won't contend with, that could-might probably cause him to get out of the mortuary business altogether."

"When your dad said 'an element,' was he referring to the old colored lady, the one whose niece you said came down from Chicago to make arrangements for her funeral?" I asked.

"Miz Birdie—," Junior mumbled.

"Miz Birdie. The same Miz Birdwell that used to stop and give us mints on her way to church?" I asked as if I didn't already know.

"Uh-huh," Milton Junior said, his eyes trading thoughts with mine, asking the same question of how it could have finished this way for Miz

Birdie, who we remembered in her old-lady bonnet and her widow's weeds, a model from another age separated from us by decades that were eons to our youthful selves. From the looks on our faces, we were all having the same thoughts, all seeing ourselves accepting the cellophane-wrapped mints she took from her purse and gave to us one each, mints that had never been high on our list of goodies, although she could never have known that by the appreciative snaggletoothed smiles we gave her in return.

"It isn't my father didn't like Miz Birdie, it was the niece from Chicago whose attitude he didn't like," Junior mumbled. "But even that isn't the real reason my father was upset. He expected the niece, being from Chicago, wouldn't have known that her people went to the Connors Undertakers on Dryades, or to the Roseland Mortuary. Mostly it's a bunch of other things.

"It's 'the old familiar faces leaving and a whole different breed coming in to take their places,' is what my father says. Like, do you all know that the Matthews are leaving? That they're selling the grocery store to some rough-looking people from St. Bernard?"

"Well, I don't know who the heck your dad's talking about when he sez the neighborhood's goin' to pot, 'cuz, me, Vicky, Lonnie, all of us, we're still in the neighborhood," D.D. said petulantly.

"What my father means by the neighborhood deteriorating is that things are changing so fast, and as a businessman, he's got to stay in the loop . . ."

"What's that supposed to mean?" I asked.

"It means other than the changes in his clientele, which he can't do anything about, he's going to have to modernize; he needs to have brand new equipment, like for cremation and such." Milton Junior was clearly on his high horse.

We blanched. Everyone knew that cremation spelled excommunication in the Catholic Church's dictionary.

"It's what the *other* morticians propose, not my father," Junior was quick to add.

"They're talking about forming an association, a place where they could consolidate, have everything together, kind of an all-faiths place.

Not just for funerals, but for the whole works. The services, the funeral, the crematoria, the niches, the burial plots. It's all in the talking stages," Junior said.

"Sounds like a supermarket mortuary t'me," D.D. sniggered.

"Not funny, D.D.," Milton Junior said.

13

"THEY'RE GONNA MAKE mincemeat of poor Milton Junior," Lonnie lamented.

"Yeah. They're gonna chew him up like ground hamburger meat and spit him out," D.D. said.

"The other boys, or the Brothers, or all of them together," I said, putting in my two cents' worth.

What troubled us most about Milton Junior's leaving was that he was being sent to St. Stanislaus, the all-boys school in Waveland, Mississippi, across the lake.

The Christian Brothers at St. Stanislaus were strict disciplinarians known for their less-than-gentle methods of correcting wayward boys entrusted to their care. They were known for their liberal use of "the paddle"—a sawed-off canoe paddle—on any kid who needed disciplining. Not that Milton Junior would ever be such a problem, but those annoying habits of his could drive a saint to swearing. We'd heard of one kid who'd been paddled so hard one of his testicles was injured, and for a while it was touch and go as to whether or not he'd lose it. We just couldn't see Milton Junior lasting long enough to complete the school year.

The beginning of the '60–'61 school year brought other changes as well. Going into ninth grade meant more homework, more studying, more extracurricular projects, and less leisure time to be with my friends. Moreover, Lonnie was enrolled at McMain High in Mid-City, which meant she had to take two buses to and fro, and I was enrolled at the parish high school, a block removed from the elementary school building, so, except for weekends and holidays, we didn't much get to see one another.

According to the *New Orleans Times-Picayune*, that November was the coldest in forty years. It was Friday, the day after Thanksgiving, and Lonnie and I had spent half the night running from bed to window to door hoping the TV weatherman's forecast for snow proved accurate, each of us hoping to be the one to spot the first errant snowflake falling from the dark fluorescent sky—a miracle that until then existed for us only in the movies.

We raced from my house to Lonnie's, our running feet barely touching the ground in the bone-rattling cold. We were headed for the bowl of walnuts and Sunkist oranges Lonnie said was sitting on the kitchen table. Even though Lonnie's father had been gone for hours, out of habit we whispered and walked on tiptoe going through the first three rooms.

"Shh," Lonnie cautioned needlessly as she turned the doorknob that would take us through her brother's room to the kitchen beyond.

A palpable silence replete with the odor of sweat and urine met us as the door creaked open.

Despite the dingy light, our eyes were immediately drawn to the figure kneeling against the bedside.

We gasped, seeing that it was Rudy. His arms were clenched under his chest, and the muscles of his face strained from the effort to hold his head above the rumpled piss-stained sheets. His trousers were bunched at his knees and Miss Ada was standing over him, a leather belt looped around her hand.

In the half-light, Rudy's face was dark, his blue eyes as colorless as peeled onions. He struggled to free a hand from under his torso.

Lonnie and I stood mute as statues, willing ourselves to be outside, to be anywhere else but where we were. Both Miss Ada and Mister Rudy ignored us, or most likely, they hadn't noticed us standing there, dumbfounded by fear.

"Put your hand down, son," Miss Ada said in a voice obscene for its wheedling softness.

At Miss Ada's command, Rudy drew back his uplifted hand, and meekly tucked both his hands under his bowed chin as if he were praying.

Whoop! the sound of leather on flesh stung the air.

Lonnie turned and looked at me with eyes as colorless as her brother's. It was not fear, nor rage that I saw in them; as with his, it was humiliation.

"Keep your hands down like I told you, son."

"Ma, please don't!"

"You promised me you wouldn't wet the sheets again."

"Mama, I couldn't help it. Don't!" Rudy pleaded.

Whoop! was the hideous answer.

I turned to escape to the rooms from whence we'd come, but Lonnie clutched my arm with pincerlike fingers. She tugged for me to follow her. We veered to one side of the room as if we were skirting the scene of an accident. Lonnie bumped the kitchen door with her shoulder and turned the knob simultaneously.

"Lonnie—what are we—what can we do?" I rasped as if there was anything we could have done.

"Please, just don't say anything!" she muttered and closed the door behind us. Her face was so close to mine I could smell the nutty odor of the peanut butter toast we'd had at my house less than ten minutes ago. She let go of my arm, went to the table, and took a navel orange from the big ceramic bowl. "Catch," she said, pitching it at me.

I caught the orange and began to peel it like a zombie as Lonnie herself was doing. Like her, I was going through the motions of acting as if we hadn't seen what we'd seen, as if we still weren't hearing the whooping sounds of the strap coming through the door.

"I *hate* her," Lonnie hissed. She hurled the torn fruit at the door and covered her ears with both hands.

The hair rose at the back of my neck. I picked up the mangled orange and shoved it in the pocket of my sweater.

Just that quickly the whooping sounds stopped.

I cocked an ear, prepared to see Miss Ada explode through the door to come after us, leather belt in hand.

We held our breath, but all we heard coming through the door were the muffled sounds of Rudy's moaning and Miss Ada's wheedling voice telling him to stop it.

Lonnie plucked a second orange from the bowl and dug into it with her nubby thumbs, tore it open until the juice squirted from the broken skin.

I peeled back the skin of my orange with my thumbnails. "Your brother must not have washed the sheets," I said stupidly.

When I would spend the night at Lonnie's house sometimes I'd awaken to see Lonnie scurrying from the bed to Rudy's room to help him strip the sheets from his bed. And more than once, I peeked out of my kitchen window to the yard to see the two of them swabbing the red rubber sheet that protected the mattress and saw the mattress ticking with its traces of old and its new piss stains, sagging on the clothesline, but I had never mentioned any of it to Lonnie. The alley between us was so narrow we could both have hung from our bedroom windows and touched hands. Yet I'd been oblivious to the many times Lonnie must have lain awake praying that Rudy's bladder would not work overtime.

Lonnie gave me a cross-eyed look. It was as if her eyes had tried and had failed to focus. "Let's go back," she said.

"Back to where?" I asked, sucking the juice that was spilling from my lips.

"Back to your house."

I didn't believe that Lonnie hated her mother. I thought she hated what her mother was doing to Rudy. I thought she was confused in her feelings because her mother was a confusing person—hot one minute, cold the next.

It was after Mr. and Mrs. Cavanaugh signed the papers giving consent for their seventeen-year-old son Rudy to join the navy that I noticed a change in Lonnie; and it wasn't until Valentina mentioned it, on the occasion of the party she gave celebrating Gloria Callahan's admission to Rosaryville, that I came to realize that Lonnie had stopped sucking her finger.

Gloria always had one foot in the nunnery, the other on the stepladder to heaven. You'd have thought the Pope was visiting whenever her aunt, Sister Caroline—young, pretty, the classic model of nunhood—visited.

None of us were surprised, then, when Gloria told us that it was all set, that she was going to become a nun. Being only twelve, her parents had had to give their signed consent for Gloria to live at Rosaryville for the year preceding the four-year high school program and the two-year novitiate that followed.

We were all sitting at Valentina's dining table, besotted with punch and homemade pineapple turnover cake, and benumbed by Gloria's babble about the Benedictine Rule, her postulancy, her proposed vows, her this and her that.

We did a lot of talking and laughing and teasing, but we never dared bring up the subject of Father Butterworth's molestation of her, nor of Norma's rescue of Gloria by her bare-assed mooning of him. The mere mention of Ol' Butterfingers's name would have triggered bad memories for Gloria that would have wiped out the gaiety of the occasion.

After the party I stayed to help Valentina square things away. "Wonders never cease, do they?" I mumbled as I was putting one of the clean glasses on the topmost shelf of the cupboard.

I turned to see Valentina looking at me quizzically.

"Oops. Sorry. I was thinking out loud. I got a letter from Milton Junior last week. Not only is he adjusting to boarding at St. Stanislaus, but it sounds to me as if he actually likes the place. He still says he wants to come home, but says his father keeps telling him that boarding school will give him 'a greater sense of independence and instill a sense of leadership that is lacking in him.' I'm quoting Milton Junior quoting his father," I explained.

"My neighbor, Mrs. Carmody, has told me that her nephew has done very well at St. Stanislaus," Valentina said.

Mrs. Carmody's nephew was the kid who'd nearly been emasculated by one of the Christian Brothers' infamous paddlings, but I mentioned nothing of that to Valentina.

"That's good," I mumbled, while pulling gobs of packing material from the large cardboard box that Valentina's new shelving unit had come in. It was a four-shelf wooden unit she'd ordered from the Sears Roebuck catalogue, which we were going to assemble and fit into the small pantry.

"When you said 'wonders never cease,' I thought it was Lonnie you had in mind," she said.

It was my turn to give her a quizzical look.

"I note she has broken the habit of sucking her finger," Valentina said.

"And it's about time," I laughed. But it bothered me that I hadn't noticed before Valentina mentioned it that Lonnie had broken that lifelong habit of sucking her index finger. That wet question mark of a finger with its fleshy nodule peaking at the middle joint from having had to sustain so much drawing power had been as much a part of Lonnie as was the star-shaped scar on her forehead. Whatever the reason, I felt as if I'd been excluded from an important event in Lonnie's life.

"*Tak*, it *is* about time," Valentina said. She shook out the damp dish-towel, folded and hung it on the towel rack above the sink.

I went through the motions of sweeping, of taking the garbage bag downstairs and dropping it into one of the big canisters at the curbside, and of helping Valentina with the pantry shelves. But all the while I was thinking of Lonnie, of how in between all the laughter and talk she seemed to have drifted to some other place; of how distracted she had been at Gloria's party, studying the configuration of pineapple turnover cake crumbs on the tablecloth as if they contained some cryptic message.

"And Norma, no word from her yet?" Valentina asked, quite unexpectedly.

"Nobody's heard from her," I said, grateful for the change of subject. "I've written her a bunch of times. Norma has to be receiving her mail because none of us has gotten any of our letters returned to us."

"What about the *matka*—has anyone heard from Missus Costanza?"

"All we know is that her mother is living across the lake with a cousin so that she could be close to the facility where Norma's staying. But nobody's heard a thing from either of them, which comes as no surprise. Norma and her mother pretty much kept to themselves. Not that you could blame them, the way people treated them," I said, hoping that recollection of Mimy and my mother's contemptuous remarks about Norma wasn't written all over my face.

"Perhaps you might write to the office of the hospital where Norma is," Valentina suggested.

"I thought about that. I even thought of asking my parents if I could take a ride out to see her. They won't be any too keen on the idea. They never had any use for Norma—especially since the Father Murphy incident."

"I will be glad to go with you if that would make it more acceptable to them, *Dziewczynka*," Valentina offered.

"You would? That would certainly make it easier for my parents to say yes."

"But you must first contact the administrator's office to see if visiting is permissible and then get your parents' permission."

"It's as good as done. You'll love the north shore, Valentina. Last time I was over there was on an Easter Saturday about three years ago, when Lonnie's parents invited me to go with them on a picnic at Fontainebleau State Park. That's not far from where Norma is."

"I remember like yesterday the first time Zofia and I went on a holiday just the two of us for the first time," Valentina said. "We were about your age, twelve or so, and we took the train. We traveled over a hundred miles to spend a two-week holiday with our aunt in Rothenburg ob der Tauber."

"What was it like? The town, I mean, and the trip?" I asked, entwining my legs about the spindle legs of the chair, preparing myself for one of Valentina's recollections of a time when she and Zofia were girls in happier days before the war.

"Rothenburg is a medieval town, very much as one would imagine seeing in a fairy-tale picture book. There was a beautiful *Glockenspiel.* Zofia and I would gather with the other tourists every hour on the hour in the town square to see the life-size figures of the clock reenact an occasion in the town's history when the mayor saved the town from being razed by wagering with the leader of the conquerors that he could consume all of the beer in a giant tankard in one swallow.

"I remember I met a boy during the war. Siggy was his name. He was born in Rothenburg, that very same town, but not in the old walled section, is what he told me. He had a, how do you say it, a cowlick that made his hair flop always like a fan above his forehead . . .

"He was the son of a barber, very ready with his hands. Siggy learned, from cutting of the hair and working in the storeroom at Auschwitz where the victims' property was kept, that the Jews were bringing food with them because they were thinking they needed sustenance until they would arrive at the place, a Jewish colony in Madagascar, where they thought they were to be resettled . . ."

The air in the room felt suddenly cold, as if I'd been shifted from a patch of sunlight to the blue chill of mountain shadows.

"Siggy, he decided that he would risk getting some of the food that was being cast aside by the Germans. He tied up his trouser legs with his shoestrings and went over and managed to get close enough to stuff some crusts of bread and some sausages into his trousers.

"I was watching from the other side of the barbed wires when I heard a woman kapo shouting from behind me. '*Stoppen! Stoppen!*' I heard. I looked up and saw the kapo woman calling the attention of a German policeman with a rifle, who was standing perhaps a hundred feet away on the men's side of the fence," Valentina said, pointing to a place beyond my shoulder, as if by turning to look, I'd have seen what she was seeing.

"The policeman turned and looked at Siggy, and Siggy froze. The policeman commanded him to untie the strings at his ankles. Siggy obeyed at once, as if it was the natural and right thing to do. He nodded, bent down, and untied the strings, and the crusts of bread and the sausage tumbled out of his trouser legs.

"'Walk to the wire,' the policeman commanded to him. He meant for Siggy to walk to the fence. And Siggy did so. He walked straight up to where he stopped, inches from where I was standing frozen like a statue on the other side. His face was so close to mine I could see the irises of his eyes like the spokes of a wheel radiating from the hubs of the pupils.

"The German soldier lifted his rifle and aimed it at Siggy. I thought that he would shoot the boy in his back, and I was prepared to die along with him because I was frozen where I stood on the other side of the wire fence, in line to be shot with Siggy.

"Siggy's eyes locked on mine and, without turning or taking his eyes from mine, he said, 'Herr Kommandant, if you have children to go home to, you don't want it on your conscience that today you have killed a boy of fifteen.'

"I could not believe my ears what I had heard; that this young man, hardly more than a boy, spoke so courageously, so recklessly by appealing to the humanity of a German soldier. I had seen others bludgeoned to death for nothing more than silent obeisance.

"Siggy's eyes had never left mine, or mine his, but I did not have to look beyond him, nor did Siggy have to turn, to know that the German had lowered his rifle. Siggy had seen our salvation in the reflection in my eyes." Valentina paused, shaking her head as if to clear the images from her vision.

"There was at that moment an exchange between us, a mergence of Siggy and me. I cannot explain—there was no *other* . . . But I never again saw Siggy in the camp in the following months, nor among those who were released when the Americans came—those who wandered into the towns and villages, lost, or searching for their families . . . I think perhaps that he escaped."

There were times in the telling of her story when I wanted to stop Valentina, to make a comment, or to ask a question, but I had come to appreciate that she was not to be interrupted, that at some time the empty space at the center of the puzzle of what had caused the long years of estrangement between her and Zofia, would be filled.

14

My brother's life—hardly out of the ordinary for a teenage boy growing up in New Orleans's Irish Channel in the sixties—intrigued me simply because it was his and not mine. His freedom was his by birthright; mine had to be taken on the sly.

Some nights, waiting for him to come home, I'd leave my bed half-asleep, my bare feet glancing the cold linoleum as I made my way through the darkness, Queenie following me, her nails tip-tapping too close for comfort on the linoleum floor.

I'd bounce onto the living room sofa and drowse, the swirls of velvet brocade imprinting my face as I hunkered against the back of the sofa, listening for Eddie's three-note whistles that began with a mouthful of air forced through his thumbs and blown into the hollow of his cupped hands, the top fingers flapping to produce the ooo-*eee*-ooo that reverberated through the night, something that, try as I had, I could never master.

Weary from listening, I slumped down onto the sofa and fell asleep. What seemed not a minute later, I was startled by the sound of voices.

"Didn't I tell you to keep it down?"

"Aw, shit," one of them grumbled.

"You want to fuckin' wake up my ol' man?"

In the snug darkness behind the window screen I recognized my brother's voice, and I chuckled, thinking that Tutankhamen would sooner have been coaxed from his tomb than my father would have stirred from the blankets under which he and my mother were buried.

I rubbed the itchy imprint left by the dusty window screen on my forehead and squinted to sharpen my fuzzy vision. At the same time, I felt around for the eyeglasses that I'd tossed somewhere on the sofa.

The boys crowded the curbside—Eddie in the street on his motorbike, "Lima Beans" Greiner from the next block, Johnny Daigle from the projects, Charlie Simoneaux from next door, sitting on the sidewalk's edge, and a boy I didn't recognize straddling a black motorcycle so shiny-new it looked as if it were wet.

The gusting wind rustled the oaks across the street, jostled the streetlight that hung from a metal arm attached to the utility pole, making it bob like a paper lantern. I flipped on my cat-eyes and right off spotted Louis Champagne standing at the center of the semicircle of boys. In my surprise I shifted my weight from one knee to the other, pinning Queenie's poor little paw beneath it. Instantly, I wrapped my hand around Queenie's muzzle to keep her from yelping.

Louis's bumpy nose looked at odds with the rimless eyeglasses that glinted whenever he turned his head. He had a look of feigned indifference, a look that left me with a vague feeling of annoyance. By then the gatherings in Louis's upstairs apartment when we were kids playing games were a thing of the past, and except for brief encounters in our comings and goings, I'd seen little of Louis in the past months. He was, of course, the same Louis, but strangely enough, he looked different, posturing as if he were on display, preening in the occasional glare of the headlights that idled by.

One of the boys reached out and pinched Louis, tugging the front of his shirt so that it poked out like a twisted nipple.

Louis slapped at the boy with a motion that was as deliberate as it was unconvincing.

"Lima Bean*ths*, you *th*top doing that," Charlie Simoneaux lisped, flipping a loose-wristed hand at Lymon (hence, "Lima Beans") Greiner. Lima Beans laughed and took another turn at the twisted nipple of Louis's shirt.

Louis shied away, laughing.

"Don't you see how ticklish he is, boys?" the stranger on the black motorbike snickered. The boys howled.

"I told y'all to shut the fuck up. You're gonna wake up the ol 'man!" Eddie hissed.

Queenie emitted a low growl, and once more I wrapped my hand around her muzzle, all the while keeping my eyes on my brother and the strange boy who by then had dismounted his motorcycle and was joining in on the harassment of Louis.

"Let him alone!" Eddie snarled.

"What's it to you?" the stranger asked.

I could hear from the way he spoke that he was from the other side of town, from the Lower Ninth Ward, I speculated. I couldn't make out his face, but he was a stocky kid and his nubby hair in the dim light was the gray-brown color of clay.

He reached around Eddie, attempting to twist Louis's shirtfront as Lima Beans had done, but Eddie blocked him with an upward swing of his arm.

My heart tightened like a hand inside a too-small glove.

"Listen, goddammit. The fag owes me money. I want it now—the ten bucks he owes me," the boy spat, taking another stab at Louis. Not taking his eyes from Eddie, the stranger positioned his foot against Eddie's bike, and shoved.

The bike hesitated, then hit the ground with the sickening scrape of metal on cement. Eddie swiveled as effortlessly as a kickboxer, hit the kickstand of the boy's motorcycle with the brunt of his heel, and sent the machine crashing to the pavement.

"Son-of-a-bitch!" the boy screamed. He hoisted the motorcycle upright, and ran his hands over the liquid black fenders, the gas tank, everywhere, feeling for kinks and scratches. Then he turned and dove at Eddie.

The other boys backed away, lifting and straddling their bikes to give them ground.

"Chrissake! You gonna have everybody runnin' out t'see what's happenin' out here!" Charlie Simoneaux rasped. In the blink of an eye, they were all in the fracas, trying to pull Eddie and the stranger apart before the confrontation ballooned to an all-out fistfight.

I pulled Queenie, quivering with excitement, closer to me. "Be quiet," I whispered, pressing her spiky muzzle to my cheek.

The boys managed to pull Eddie and the stranger apart.

"Good thing for you there's a couple of scrapes and such, but ain't no dents," the stranger said.

"Asshole," Eddie muttered.

"I'll collect the ten bucks you owe me tomorrow," the stranger spat at Louis. He mounted his cycle, stomped the pedal, gunned the engine, and sped off with a roar that cut through the night like a buzz saw.

A little later, Daigle left, followed by Lima Beans, leaving Louie, my brother, and Charlie standing at the curbside. Louis touched my brother's shoulder and then the three of them moved out of my field of vision toward the alley between my house and Lonnie's, going to Louis's apartment upstairs.

I lay sleepless in the dark. I heard the church bells chime every half hour, and for the first time that I can remember, the thousand fiery stars that would crowd the hellish universe of nonsleep for months to come were crowding my vision.

When the panel door of the confessional slid open, I proceeded:

"Bless me Father for I have sinned It's been four weeks since my last confession I was disrespectful to my parents I was late for Mass I was lazy in school I lied to my parents about where I was going—I mean about where I had been, and I had some bad thoughts . . ."

The last words conjured the image of bumpy-nosed Louis Champagne preening in the circle of light and of my brother and Charlie disappearing from the limits of my vision through the window screen to the darkness of who knows what happened then?

"What kind of thoughts did you say, my child?" I dared look up then to see the priest through the latticed screen cupping his fleshy ear with his hand.

I drew in a deep breath, resigned to endure the consequences of my stupidity in not having taken into account that Butterfingers might be the confessor lurking behind the faded green drapery on which hung the nameless blank placard!

"What kind of thoughts, my child?" he persisted, his ear practically pasted to the lattice.

"Different kinds of thoughts," I said, deepening my voice in a desperate attempt to effect a disguise.

"Are those thoughts of yours impure thoughts?" he asked, his voice curling like ivy through the latticework pane.

"No, father," I croaked.

My throat constricted with the thickness of the lie, a lie that rendered the sacrament of penance null and void and added yet another sin to the pile of sins that were steadily accumulating and which I figured I would surely have to account for come purgatory time. But I reasoned that I hadn't lied, that I didn't really know if my brother had committed a sin of impurity. I hadn't allowed my mind's eye to follow my brother, Louis, and Charlie beyond the limits of the screened window to the alleyway and up to Louis's apartment. Nonetheless, thoughts of Louis, the stranger's demand for money, and the questionable source of Eddie's money buzzed in my head—thoughts obliterated by the brilliant red pinpoints that prickled my insomnia.

"If they are thoughts displeasing to God, then they are sinful thoughts that must be confessed to be forgiven. How would you describe them?" the priest urged.

"I guess they're what you could call doubtful thoughts," I said, making that all-important distinction.

"Well, then, my child, tell me about these so-called doubtful thoughts of yours . . ."

"These aren't my thoughts, they're a friend's thoughts," I said, my voice resonating in basso profundo tones.

"You needn't concern yourself with the wrongful acts of others! So long as you shun questionable acts, avoid temptation, and do not entertain bad thoughts generated by sinful acts of friends or companions, there is no sin."

I prayed he wouldn't become suspicious of the Tallulah Bankhead–like voice and decide to look through the grid before saying the magic words that would spring me out of the confessional into the boundlessness of the nave, past the niches where Saint Anthony stood on his pedestal with his doves and squirrels and Saint Lucy pleading to heaven with her plateful of eyeballs, out through the heavy stained glass doors, and into the street.

The priest finally traced a sign of the cross in the air, absolved me of my sins, assigned a penance of five Our Fathers and five Hail Marys, and told me to make a good Act of Contrition.

"Go in peace," he wheezed before I'd finished my recitation.

What had I expected? I couldn't have told any priest that since the night of the boys on their bikes, the diamond-point "reds" appeared whenever I tried to sleep, how the reds materialized even when my eyes were wide open, a slew of them tucked against the ceiling in a corner of my room, or strewn across the footboard of my bed. I couldn't have told any priest that I suspected the hellish stars were something I'd conjured to take the place of thoughts about my brother I had disallowed. I wanted to be forgiven, but I didn't know for what.

I couldn't confide in Lonnie, who had always protected her brother's bedwetting secret with her silence. I couldn't tell anyone what I'd seen, or thought I'd seen, least of all Mimy, who worried enough about my brother; and telling Valentina, to whom I'd always sung my brother's praises, was tantamount to a betrayal of him.

At school, things went downhill. At times Sister Clarisse was solicitous; at other times she called me down for being indifferent and inattentive, and for staring out the window. I might have told her that staring out the window was a way of blanking my mind, but I couldn't get past the black-and-white habit that made her subject to the black-and-white rules of Mother Church, which allowed no room for doubt, or skepticism, or for staring out the window.

"Is there something you want to talk about?" she asked, having kept me after school to clap erasers.

Sister Clarisse was the only nun who didn't wear glasses. She was young and pretty and had a lilt in her voice like that of Doris Day singing. She'd tried a number of times to get to the bottom of why staring out of the window had replaced Literature as my favorite subject. I'd never been at the top of my class, but I could ace it when I had to, and in Literature and anything having to do with the social sciences, good grades were effortless.

I was clapping erasers, creating a haze of chalk dust with every clap of felt on felt when Sister Clarisse came outside. She picked out a pair of erasers from the jumble in the box and clapped them together as demurely as if she were applauding a pas de deux.

"I've tried every which way to get you to talk to me and you will not, Vicky, you simply will not. So, I'll say no more on the subject," she said, her eyes on the little puffs of chalk dust that issued from her erasers. "Except for one thing—"

As I was clapping the erasers, I sneezed and sneezed from the cloud of chalk dust.

"—which is to say that when God favors you with gifts, you are obligated," she said, setting the erasers back into the box. She stood for a moment dusting the chalk powder from her habit. "When you've finished, you may put the eraser box in the cloakroom and go home."

In the second semester, when Cs and Ds became the grades of choice on my report card, Sister Clarisse sent me to the principal's office.

"Sister is concerned about your falling grades. She believes that you have—how did she phrase it?—'an originality of expression.' That you have talent, and she doesn't want that to be compromised. Sister's concern is that these poor grades might indicate a trend. What say you, Victoria Lumière?" The principal sat erect in her tufted swivel chair, her chin tucked in so that her cheeks overflowed the stiff-starched wimple.

Not knowing what she expected for an answer, I shrugged.

Sister Julian's steel-blue eyes jumped to the top of her metal-frame eyeglasses. "You have nothing to say for yourself, Victoria?" she asked, cocking her head.

I shrugged again, my thoughts snagging on the name "Victoria."

"Is Sister Clarisse's concern for you worth our while?"

I shrugged again.

"Do you think you're making good use of God's gifts?" she asked, taking another tack.

"I don't know, Sister," I said.

The starched panels under her black veil rustled against the bib that armored her chest like a breastplate. She bounced forward in the swivel chair and walked to the front of the desk, where she stood looking at me as if I were a specimen under glass.

"I told Sister that this conference would be a waste of time, that you would not be receptive to any advice, to any effort on our part to help change the course you appear to be taking, a course that has been clearly demonstrated throughout the years."

"I don't know what course it is you're talking about, Sister," I said, thinking of the course of years that went back to when she taught me in fourth grade.

"You're being disrespectful—and bold!"

"I don't mean to be disrespectful or bold, Sister Julian, but I honestly can't see that I'm headed in any particular direction." That came out not exactly as I'd meant it to.

"I'm told you've always had a clever way with words, that you've always exhibited antisocial behavior."

"If you mean by that that I don't have friends, I do. Lots of them here at school—" I thought of Becky Dillenkoffer and Gloria Callahan and was scratching my brain for other names to add.

"You run around with public school riffraff."

"If you mean my best friend, who goes to McMain—"

"—And with boys that are up to no good. Perhaps that's where your mind is instead of on your studies," she sniffed, adjusting her veil.

I pictured the coterie of nuns sitting in the dark of the screened-in veranda that served as the vantage point from where they watched the bunch of us cutting up.

The principal's face darkened to challenge the circles under her eyes that gave her the look of an unhealthy panda.

"Tell me who you go with, Victoria, and I'll tell you who you are."

"Sister Julian, I have to tell you, my name isn't Victoria, it's Vicenta."

"You're being insolent—"

"I'm not being insolent. I'm just telling you that my name is Vicenta, not Victoria. You can look it up in the file," I said, nodding toward the manila file on her desk.

"Ds are respectable enough grades for a girl like you," she said, flittering at my indignation with a wave of the hand. "And with some effort you can upgrade those to Cs. I see no need to confer with your parents, but if they wish to, I—"

"For a girl like me?" I said shakily.

Her hands disappeared inside the yawning cuffs of her black serge habit.

"—of your background," she hedged.

"Of my background?" I asked.

"Of your heritage."

I didn't have to ask her *what* heritage she was referring to because my French heritage had never come under scrutiny.

I wondered how she could have forgotten my name, since she was the principal of the school, privy to student records, and I'd always been listed as Vicenta Maria de los Angeles Lumière. Moreover, I'd been a pupil of hers in fourth grade, which was when the "What I Did on My Summer Vacation" incident happened.

It was our first assignment of the new school year and I'd decided to forgo the reality of the ordinary summer vacation I'd spent in the neighborhood to write about the wonderful, albeit imaginary, trip my grandmother and I took motoring across the Valley of Mexico, coming upon the snow-clad volcanoes at sundown, one asleep, the other awake, its smoke plumes rising to meet the navel orange of a moon that hung in an azure sky.

I could hardly wait for my turn to read in front of the class.

When Beverly Whittington, red-faced and timorous, returned to her desk directly in front of mine, I practically sprang from my seat to get to the front of the classroom.

Standing beside Sister Julian's desk I read from my spiral notebook, the written words fairly dancing on the page, eager for me to read their wondrous tale. I finished and curtsied to the applause of my classmates and turned to see Sister Julian stepping down from the dais on which her desk sat, as imperious as that of a queen's throne. She took me by the arm and led me to the back of the room.

"Stand here until after school," she muttered between clenched teeth.

"What did I do?" I asked, fairly quavering in my shoes.

"You could *not* have written that composition!" she hissed, her veiled back to the class. "No! You could not have!"

My parents hadn't yet arrived from work, and when I told Mimy what had happened she called the information operator requesting the telephone number of the Notre Dame Convent on Clementine Street. When she peeked through the window curtains and saw that my parents had not yet returned, she unwound the *chal* from her shoulders, donned her prickly woolen sweater, took me by the hand, and said, "*Vámonos.*"

We descended the steps slow as molasses in winter, crossed the street to the convent, and paid Sister Julian a visit.

"Sister Juliana—" (*Who-lee-ahna* is the way Mimy pronounced the name).

"Julian. It's 'Sister Julian,'" the principal protested.

"*Bueno*, as you say—," Mimy conceded. "Considering that my granddaughter's imagination is a God-given gift, it could hardly have been challenged by so simple and unimaginative a task as that of writing *un papel* on what she did during the summer vacation. And while it would seem to most that Vicenta's expressions—that being her way of writing—is so *sofisticada* for one so young, I am here to tell you that my granddaughter comes by it naturally. It is a talent inherited from *los poetas* who predated the arrival of *los conquistadores*. Do you understand what I am telling you Sister *Who-lee-ahna*? The greatest of these was the philosopher king of Texcoco, a city referred to in the books on civilization and culture as—How do you say '*el Atenas del mundo oeste*'?" Mimy asked, turning to me and promptly tweaking my ear.

"The Athens of the Western World," I said, feeling as if I had a whistle stuck in my throat.

"'The Athens of the Western World,'" my grandmother echoed. "Texcoco, sometimes called 'the navel of the moon' because it is said to be the origin of the word 'Mexico,' and indeed the very umbilicus of our culture, you understand . . ."

I'd been standing there wondering who the heck this philosopher king Mimy was talking about was, because in all her stories of Mexico, she'd never once mentioned him to me before!

"And I should be pleased to add that Texcoco *es el lugar de mi nacimiento*."

"Texcoco is her birthplace," I hastened to translate before Mimy could pinch my ear again.

Mimy was having a language meltdown toward the end of her diatribe, but that didn't prevent her from telling Sister Who-lee-ahna all she'd come to say. It was the most I'd heard Mimy speak in English at any given time. I could hear my mother saying that Mimy could rise to the occasion whenever she had to!

All the while—it couldn't have been more than ten minutes—Mimy had not let go of my hand, nor had she accepted Sister Julian's invitation to be seated on the brown velvet sofa that, together with the Mary Queen of Heaven statue standing on a pedestal, dominated the convent parlor.

She bade Sister Julian a good night and we left without Mimy's having acknowledged the miniature marble pietà on the pedestal in the nuns' foyer, twin to the framed icon in her bedroom.

Sister Julian phoned my grandmother the next day to explain that while my composition was indeed imaginative and well written, it was not what the assignment had called for, which was to write about what I did on my summer vacation. Regretfully, said she, she could not in good conscience allow my teacher to award me a gold star for having a good imagination.

"*Idiota*," Mimy mumbled, adjusting her pillows in preparation for her afternoon nap.

It would've appeared that Mimy had conceded she'd lost that one, but there was a timbre in her voice, and the trace of a smile on her lips that said otherwise when she laid her head on the pillow and bade me to be quiet.

I headed straight for the Encyclopaedia Britannica and learned that Nezahualcóyotl, which means "Hungry Coyote" in Aztec, was the philosopher king of Texcoco, from 1403 to 1473, and was considered to be one of the greatest poets America had ever produced, just as Mimy had said in her instruction of Sister Who-lee-ahna.

Further on I read that "Mexico" is a term of uncertain origin, and while some anthropologists believed the term came from the old Nahuatl word for the sun, others suggested that it is the name of a type of water plant that grows in Lake Texcoco, whose mystical name was "Moon Lake." But anthropologists and historians alike think that the term "Mexica" means "navel of the moon" from the Nahuatl *metztli* for moon, and *xictli* for navel. What the term had come to mean to me was totally different, known only to me.

To remedy my inattentiveness, Sister Clarisse moved me from the row of desks beside the gridded windows that overlooked the school yard to the row of desks closest to the chalkboard on the opposite side of the room.

It was just as well. The chalkboard with its eraser-made clouds stranded on a dull green sky proved to be a decent enough substitute for the view of the school yard with its boundary lines and goal posts, and its five-hundred-sixty iron picket fence—unchanged in number whenever I re-counted them.

15

THE ARGUMENT BETWEEN Lonnie and me began quite innocently. Certainly, neither of us could have foreseen that those points of contention, silly as they then were, would, down the line, lead to the breakup of our friendship.

"There's Francis. He's sitting on his bike in front of the grocery," Lonnie said.

"Francis the fruit?" snorted D.D.

"Take off your glasses. He's looking this way!" Lonnie said, reaching for my tortoiseshell cat-eyes.

When it came to boys, Lonnie had always been downright ridiculous.

"Kiddy, he's waving at you!" she giggled. She ducked low so that I was left in the open, staring in the direction of a mirage of blended colors—blond and suntan beige and blue and silver that comprised the blurred image of Francis Kettering sitting on his bike.

Lonnie took hold of my wrist, raised my arm, and started waving my hand as if I were a puppet unable to maneuver my own limbs.

"Stop being so ridiculous!" I said loud enough for everyone within a quarter-mile to hear me.

Francis Kettering was new in the neighborhood. We'd seen him hanging around the St. Andrew Street project courtyard where he lived, and riding his blue-and-silver bike in the driveway that ran the length of the project from Clementine to Felicity Street.

I thought the bike looked like Francis in the way some people's pets looked like them. He had flaxen hair and blue eyes, and he was slender and graceful. If I were to have described him in a single word, it would have been "bluesilvery."

"Why is it when it comes to boys you can be so imbecilic, Lonnie?"

"I'm not being imbecilic," she said, not taking her eyes off him. "Uh-oh. He's leaving, riding off the banquette, getting ready to cross the street . . ."

I let my eyes drift in that direction just as the blond and blue and silver blur disappeared in the complex of project buildings and courtyards.

"He waved back at you!" Lonnie said ecstatically.

"Y'all make me wanna puke," D.D. said, sticking out his fuzz-coated tongue.

"You are so disgusting," I moaned.

"Y'all are the ones who're disgustin'. That guy wouldn't be caught dead spookin' either of yas. Besides, he looks like a big fruit with all that floppy blond-looking straw he calls hair," D.D. said.

"You're just jealous 'cause he's so cute and you aren't," Lonnie said.

"He's more than cute," I interjected. "He's the cutest boy in the Channel."

"I wouldn't go that far," Lonnie remarked.

"He's The Ideal." I knew I'd gone too far the instant I said it.

"The ideal fairy you mean?" D.D. cackled.

"For your information, ignoramus, 'The Ideal' isn't a description, it's a concept. It's from medieval times when people loved purely and from afar."

"Jeez! That doesn't sound like it was any kind of fun! Do you ever sit down and listen to yourself?" he said stretching his arm while clutching at his chest. "You know what your trouble is, don'tcha? First of all, you read too much, and second of all, you believe everything you read. Yak! Yak! Yak!"

"S'true. You do read too much," Lonnie said, poking me in the ribs to make me think she was only kidding. "Francis Kettering may be cute, but he isn't *my* ideal, no matter which way you use the word. Everybody doesn't feel the same as you do y'know."

"Everybody doesn't have to," I smirked.

"You can call it 'ideal' or whatever you want to, but the way I see it, what you've got is a simple case of the hotsies," she said.

I was fit to be tied. "You mean like the hotsies you have for Vincent what's-his-name?"

"Who're you talking about?" Lonnie said, turning red from the throat upwards. At that moment her face would have been the perfect illustration for "discombobulate" in the OED.

"Oh, come on, Lonnie. Don't act so innocent. You know darn good and well who it is I'm talking about. Vincent, whose last name sounds like a drink of water—Vincent Glub-glubbidy-glub."

I'd seen the look in Lonnie's eyes whenever Vincent came riding up on that black motorcycle. I'd seen her face redden—just as it did then—her eyes dancing as if they were ready to jump from their sockets whenever she saw him. I'd seen how flustered she got when he winked at her, taking it as a flirtation rather than as a condescending gesture made to a goo-goo-eyed girl.

Lonnie's mouth flew open, but nothing came out.

"You're plain jealous, that's what's wrong with you!" she said at last.

"Of you and Vincent Glubbidy-glubbidy-glub?"

"Stop calling him that! His name's Gugliamo. Goo-gli-ah-mo!"

"Y'all give me the drizzles," D.D. said, "arguin' over those guys when neither of them would give either of you the benefit of a good fart."

In his own crude way D.D. was probably right, but after opening my big mouth about Francis being "The Ideal," I wasn't about to retract anything, however preposterous it might have sounded. Nor would I have admitted that I was out of line in having brought up the subject of Lonnie's crush on an older boy from the other side of town whom none of us knew anything about. Incensed though I was, I kept quiet about having once seen her roaring off with him on the back of his motorcycle, clinging to him as if he were master of the universe.

Lonnie jumped off my steps and ran into her house without even looking back. She was mad, but so was I. Mostly for how she'd sided with D.D. whenever it suited her. But on the whole I was more hurt than angry for the way she kept her motorcycle rides with Vincent Gugliamo a secret, even from me.

Lonnie didn't call me for a couple of days. I sat by the phone, picked up the receiver to call her, and set it back a dozen or more times.

When Lonnie did call neither of us mentioned the argument. I more or less pushed it all out of my mind until the day I came home from school and found my house key missing from its nail inside the screen door. I tried the doorknob, and when the door opened, I saw Lonnie and Vincent sitting knee-to-knee, staring into one another's eyes on the sofa.

"I can't believe you did that," I said to her after Vincent had left.

"Don't be mad, kiddy. It was a spur-of-the-moment thing. What happened was that when I came out of my house, I saw him sitting on your steps. He said he was waiting for Eddie, and I told him I thought it would be all right to go inside and wait because I was waiting for you to come home, too. I never would have done it if I thought you'd have minded."

Right then I should have let her have it! She knew the rules, and they didn't include her taking the liberty of unlocking our door and bringing a virtual stranger into the house. I should have asked her right off what was going on. I should have said I'd seen her riding off with him on his cycle not once but four times, but I knew she'd get mad and that was the last thing I wanted.

"The last thing in the world I'd want is to make trouble for you, kiddy. You know that . . . I knew that your parents wouldn't be coming home for a while—"

"That's not the point," I told her.

"What *is* the point?" she asked.

"The point is that he's too old for you. He's seventeen, maybe even eighteen, whatever he is, you're not even thirteen yet."

"I'm just about thirteen! And besides, what's his age got to do with it? He's not my boyfriend. He came looking for Eddie and I was just trying to be nice, that's all."

I put it all out of my mind until the day she told me what happened at the foot of Monkey Hill.

16

"I've got to talk with you."

"Soon's I can get this door open," I said, startled by Lonnie's sudden appearance. My parents weren't home from work yet, Mimy was in her apartment across the street, and Eddie was off, gallivanting.

I unloaded my book pack onto the sofa and let Queenie out into the yard to do her business. When I returned I found Lonnie lying across my bed crying softly.

"What's wrong?" I asked. I figured it had to have something to do with Miss Ada.

Lonnie sat up, tried a couple of times to tell me, but the words kept catching in her throat.

"Calm down while I get you a glass of ice water," I said, already headed for the kitchen.

Her eyes, when I returned, were the same reddish color as her face. I handed her the glass of water, drew a string of tissues from the box of Kleenex on the night table, and gave them to her in a clump.

"I couldn't help it," she shuddered. "I couldn't stop him." Lonnie started to cry in earnest then. I thought she'd cry until her heart would break.

"Come on, Lonnie. Stop it now. Just tell me—," I urged, patting her hand.

"I don't know how it happened," she sobbed. "We went riding along the River Road, doubled back to the park, and stopped where we always used to picnic. Remember? By the big oak with the leaning branch we used to climb that's right by Monkey Hill?

"Well—the moon was so bright the shadows on the grass were as clear and sharp as in daylight. I felt shaky from riding on the motorcycle seat, like the roar of that motor had taken over my heartbeat, and had sapped all my strength. I was scared to talk because I knew my voice would be shaking and I didn't want him to think I was acting like a wimp still wet behind the ears.

"He turned around without saying anything and he kissed me on the lips. Then he . . ." She lapsed into a long heaving sigh. "He took out some sort of blanket from out of the motorcycle satchel, then he took me by the hand and we went and sat on the blanket under that giant oak and he started kissing me and kissing me and he was sucking my breath away and I wanted it to stop but I felt myself slipping away. I couldn't help it, Vicky. I just couldn't help it!"

She was sitting in the middle of my bed, cross-legged, rocking and rocking, as if she'd ease away the pain.

"Get a hold of yourself, Lonnie. Besides, who'll know about it? You and him—and me; and that's it."

She threw her arms around me and we sat together locked in a clinch. The dampness of her teary face resting on my shoulder soaked through my uniform blouse. I felt that if I didn't do something, didn't say the right thing, she'd dissolve right then and there, leaving nothing but a puddle of regret and briny tears.

"Don't tell anybody, not even Mimy," she said.

"I promise."

". . . or Miz Dreyfus," she added.

"I swear . . ."

Since the day Lonnie told me about what happened at the foot of Monkey Hill, there'd been little I could say or do to lift her spirits. The only time I saw a flicker of enthusiasm was when she'd be at the house and Vincent called, looking for Eddie, or when she'd see Vincent's motorcycle parked out front.

"Did you get a letter from Rudy?" I asked, hoping to steer her out of the near-catatonic state she'd been in.

In the six months since he'd left, Rudy kept assuring Lonnie in his letters that although he missed being home, things had worked out for the best. He never failed to write how much he liked being in the navy and how much he wanted her to see California:

> *How are you sweetie? You coming along okay? I miss you. I miss the old neighborhood. I want you to see San Diego. You'd love the view of the bay, and the bridge and the old Coronado Hotel. I want to take you down to Baja. There's a great little Mexican village about ninety miles down called Ensenada where the ocean crashes against the rocks and the water is forced into these little cracks called fissures from which it shoots high up in the air like water spouting from the blow hole of a whale. Tell Vicky and Eddie hello and don't forget to write . . .*

But in time, the tenor of Rudy's letters changed. They were still warm and upbeat, but I detected an undertone in them when Lonnie read them out loud, that hinted he was happier in California than he'd ever been at home.

"Do you think he'll ever come back? I mean, do you think he'll come back home to live?" Lonnie asked, smoothing Rudy's folded letter on her lap.

"Why not?" I said.

"What if he meets somebody out there—a girl, and he gets married? He'll forget all about me."

"Rudy would never forget you, Lonnie. Even if he got married out there, it doesn't mean he'd stay. He'd bring his wife back home to live, or maybe he'd ask you to go to California to live with them."

"I guess so," Lonnie said, no more convinced of that than I was.

It was distressing to even think that Lonnie could leave for San Diego. We were together so much, had shared everything. She'd even named Queenie.

We were sitting on the kitchen floor playing jacks the day this little black-and-white mutt with amber-colored eyes wandered through the open backyard gate. She had bandit patches over both eyes, a white rivulet running down her snout, a big black spot riding sidesaddle on her back, and feathering on her rump as luxurious as a fox fur boa.

"Look at her. She prances around as if she were the Queen of Sheba. Her royal behind-ness!" Lonnie laughed. "That would be a good name for her, 'Queenie.' Don't you think?"

Lonnie cried as hard as I did when Fugly, the Greiner's mutt, wandered over from the next block and humped Queenie. We couldn't pull them apart. And when Queenie had her six puppies, it was Lonnie who found a home for two of them with her cousins who lived across town.

Knowing how much Lonnie had suffered over the incident with Vincent Gugliamo, I'd vowed to wipe it from my mind and never mention it again. So, when she asked me, flicking the point of her ballpoint pen in and out, "Do you think I should mention in my letter to Rudy about Vincent being my boyfriend?" I was flabbergasted.

"Why would you tell Rudy a thing like that?" I blurted. I should have added then that doing it once with a boy does not a boyfriend make.

"I just thought I ought to, that's all," she murmured.

"It's a bad idea, Lonnie, and it makes no sense. Rudy would worry and he'd start wondering who this guy is his little sister is calling her boyfriend. He'll start asking questions about where you met him, where he goes to school, and how old he is—," I stopped short. "I can't understand how he did what he did. Do you think your brother will?"

"You act as if it was all Vincent's fault," she said.

"Well it was! He's practically an adult."

Lonnie's eyes brimmed.

The last thing I wanted was to see her shed another tear over that jerk.

"Lonnie," I said calmly, "your mother could find out what happened by reading one of Rudy's letters answering yours."

"The old bitch's been all over my room rooting around," Lonnie snapped. "I can tell." Lonnie's hostility toward Miss Ada was blatant. It surfaced when Rudy left for the navy, but it had been festering a long time—probably since the first time Miss Ada woke Rudy in the middle of the night and beat him for wetting the bed while Lonnie stood helplessly by and while I, not thirty feet away, lay sleeping in my bed, or blissfully reading under the covers by the fading beam of a penlight.

"It's a real bad idea," I said again.

What I didn't realize was that Vincent Gugliamo was indeed Lonnie's boyfriend in the biblical sense and that Lonnie had been seeing him on the sly every chance she got.

It wasn't long before half the neighborhood found out about Lonnie and Vincent. Having had to forfeit their Saturday night bourrée card game because Lonnie's Aunt Esther had come down with an acute case of food poisoning, Mr. and Mrs. Cavanaugh came home earlier than expected to find Lonnie and Vincent making out on their wide double bed.

Lonnie said later that she and Vincent didn't even know her parents were in the house until Miss Ada was on top of them, punching and cursing and pulling them apart.

"Sounds like they're killing each other over there," my dad said, when he heard all the commotion.

"It's none of our business," my mother said.

"But, Mama—," I protested.

"It's no worse than any of the fights our family has had under this roof. We never saw any of them running over here and interfering," she said softly, without looking at my father. But her words stopped him dead in his tracks.

I didn't see Lonnie all next day and whenever I called, her mother wouldn't let her come to the telephone. I went from one window to the next, trying to catch sight of Lonnie, but the window shutters of her house were always closed.

When I got home from school the following day, I found Lonnie sitting on her doorstep. She looked terrible. She had dark circles under her eyes and from the way she was dressed, barefooted, wearing jeans and one of Rudy's old Warren Easton football jerseys, I knew she hadn't been to school.

"I wanted to come over a bunch of times, but my parents wouldn't let me," I said. "I made up my mind that if I didn't see or hear from you today, I was coming over to see you no matter what."

"Mama swears if ever Vincent shows his face around here again she'll have him picked up for contributing to the delinquency of a minor," Lonnie said. "I think she's blowing a lot of hot air, trying to scare me. She doesn't even know Vincent's last name . . ." She hesitated. "What if she asks your brother? Do you think she'd do that, question Eddie, and that he'd maybe tell her something?"

"What big secret can my brother tell your mother about Vincent?" I said angrily.

"Vicky, don't get mad at me," she said, tugging my arm. "Listen, if I tell you something, you swear to God you won't tell anybody no matter what?"

"You know I wouldn't betray a secret," I said.

"I'm running away," Lonnie said in a harsh whisper.

"Good God, Lonnie. You scared me. I thought for a minute that—"

"That what?

"That you were—"

"Jesus, Vicky!" she said, her eyes flaring.

"It can happen, you know."

"Not to me," she said.

"It only takes one time—"

"Did you even hear what I said?" she urged.

"You said you're running away."

"You don't believe me, but I'm dead serious."

"You're crazy is what you are," I murmured, the hair at the back of my neck standing up. "Where'll you go? What'll you do? Live in the streets?"

"You're beginning to sound more like my mother than my friend."

"Whose idea is this—his?" I demanded. "It is Vincent you're planning to run away with, isn't it?"

"To tell you the truth—," she said, hesitantly, "I haven't told him yet."

"I don't get it! Did he ask you to run away with him, or didn't he?"

"He hasn't asked me to run away with him exactly. And it's not going to happen tomorrow. There's no exact date. But we've talked about going away together . . ."

"You mean, getting married? Are you crazy? You're not even fifteen yet!" I sounded like a broken record even to myself.

"I told you it wasn't going to happen right away! But I've got to get out of this stinking house, and the sooner the better."

Lonnie's eyes were searching mine, wanting me to say something positive, something other than what she was reading in them.

"When are you planning to run away? Where'll you stay?" I felt that in asking questions I was giving credence to her plan.

"I don't know when exactly. What I'll do first is stay with friends of mine and Vincent's that live across the river."

It still sounded like make-believe to me. "Lonnie, you've got to promise me one thing; you've got to give me your word of honor that when you're ready to do this—meaning *before* you do it—you'll tell me."

"I promise," Lonnie said without hesitation.

I wrestled with the idea of talking to Valentina about Lonnie's intention to run away. I needed to tell someone nonjudgmental, someone older that I could trust. I told myself that confiding in Valentina wouldn't be a betrayal of Lonnie's confidence. Her secret would go no further, and if Valentina came up with a solution that would help me to change Lonnie's mind, it was a good enough reason to break my word just that once. But I put off talking with Valentina for a day, and then another, and before I knew it, the days became weeks, and the scenario I had in my mind of Lonnie using a fake ID and marrying Vincent at a thirty-dollar ceremony in some justice of the peace's parlor in Biloxi, Mississippi, with the justice of the peace in slippers and his bored wife and a paid yokel acting as witness faded from my mind altogether.

17

"The supervisor approached Daddy about a promotion to foreman of his floor," my mother said, obviously delighted by the prospect of what this would mean to our family.

"I'm thinking that with Daddy's raise, I'll be able to quit work. But you know Daddy; he's not one to count his chickens. He won't say anything on the subject until it's ready to happen. So, both of you don't say a word until he does," she said, looking from Eddie to me.

My mother had a number of reasons for wanting to quit Whitney Bag. She said my father needed more of her time, that he was always skulking about with a folded newspaper under his arm, restless, uncomfortable in whatever chair or sofa he fell into; that I was growing up faster than she could keep up; that Mimy needed more of her time; and that Eddie, who was hardly ever home except to eat and sleep, had become little more than a stranger under their roof.

After Mimy moved out, my mother depended on me as never before. I'd get dinner started before she and my father returned from work. I'd make salads, chop onions, turn a low flame under the perennial pot of red beans my mother left soaking on the stove, and follow whatever instructions she left to get dinner started.

It was lucky for me that Mimy lived across the street, what with all the traipsing back and forth I had to do. There were hot meals to bring over to Mimy every day and since I had become solely responsible for running all of her errands and doing the things that needed doing around her apartment, I was over there two or three times a day.

Eddie had outgrown the errand-running stage some time back, even reneging on the chore of going to Matthews' for the gallon cans of kerosene that fueled Mimy's small heater, which Mimy, despite the heating system in her project apartment, insisted on keeping in her bedroom and lighting on cold winter nights, just as she had done at home.

I had awakened on many a winter night to find Mimy's cylindrical little heater glowing where she'd moved it to the center of my room. The lit patterns of its lid casting floral designs on the ceiling reminded me of the pictures I saw of the Rose Window of the Cathedral of Notre Dame de Paris—more warm and alive, and just as lovely, though not nearly so intricate.

With the removal in the spring of 1961 of the giant kerosene drum wedged between door and show window at the entrance of Ruffino's Grocery, Mimy's little heater was relegated to a hook under our backyard shed and Mimy was forced to resort to the floor heaters in her project apartment—contraptions she disliked and mistrusted and disparaged every chance she got.

Around that time, D.D. and Becky were waiting to hear about the fate of Miss Ruth's job at Earl's Restaurant.

"Mr. Earl told my mama that he might sell the business," Becky croaked in her froggy voice.

"I heard, but I can't believe Mr. Earl would give up the restaurant," I said. "Anytime you pass there on weekends, Fridays especially, you can see the people crowded at the bar and hanging out front, waiting for tables."

"Yeah—well—Peacock's been after Mr. Earl to buy out his lease after the elder Mr. Young died. He says he wants to expand the business, says his customers have always complained about the seafood and crab boil smells that don't go too good with his antiques. Old Mr. Young wouldn't hear of it because Earl's had been a paying tenant for so long.

"The Youngs own the two buildings, y'know," D.D. added with an authoritative air. "Peacock told Mr. Earl that the antique business has picked up steadily, that antiques and collectibles are the comin' thing and that he could use the extra space.

"Mr. Earl told Peacock he wouldn't make a decision 'til after it comes time to renew the lease 'round the first of the year. He's got an option to lease for another five years. Ironclad, Mr. Earl told my mother."

"What does your mother think will happen?" I asked.

"That Mr. Earl won't sell," D.D. said.

A couple of weeks later, my father got formal word of his promotion and Mr. Earl told D.D.'s mother that Peacock had offered him a deal he couldn't resist.

It took some getting used to having Mama at home every day—something I'd longed for throughout my grade school years. Even so, and despite Mimy's supervision, I was mindful that it was my mother's absence—the work at Whitney Bag that took her away from home five days a week—that had allowed me my freedom, such as it was.

At first it felt as if her daily presence in the house was tentative, that it would pass as soon as the family felt the pinch of that missing paycheck that had for so long supplemented my father's salary. The flip side of it was that my mother and I got to spend more time together, going downtown to Kress's when there was a fabric sale, and putting our heads together to modify the patterns to fit the designs I sketched on paper.

Those times I'd catch a glimpse of the girl I saw in our family photograph album—the black-and-white not-to-be-believed photos of an impossibly young Linda Arroyo wearing a plaid tube skirt that touched the top of her socks, and with her arms wrapped around a slender young man with a shock of hair peaked high as an ice cream vendor's cap: my father, Edward Justin Lumière, fresh in from Cloutierville.

I bumped into D.D. at Ruffino's, formerly Matthews' Grocery.

"What's been happenin'? I haven't seen nobody around since forever," he said. "I mean nobody."

It was easy to figure D.D. was alluding to Lonnie because everybody else's whys and wherefores were known to us both: Milton Junior wouldn't be home from St. Stanislaus until Easter break; we received weekly reports from Gloria Callahan at Rosaryville; Ollie DeSales was coming less and less from Gretna to visit his great aunt. And as for Stanley Cunningham, he and D.D. were practically joined at the hip.

"If you want to know what's happening, why don't you pick up that newfangled contraption called the telephone and call?" I said, hoping to swing his attention in another direction.

"'Cuz last few times that I called, you either weren't home, or when you did answer the phone you hardly said anything."

"Bull," I scoffed, but it was true.

"And Lonnie . . ."

"Lonnie's been busy," I snapped.

"Yeah ya right! She's been busy, if 'busy' is the word you wanna use for what she's been doing."

"What do you mean by that?" I asked, pulling a loaf of Merita from the bread rack.

"It's just somethin' I heard," he said.

"What did you hear?" I asked, pummeling him with the loaf of Merita.

"Better look out, if you know what's good for you," D.D. taunted, jabbing at the loaf of bread.

"Say, you two! That ain't no punchin' bag ya got there. Smash it to a pulp if you wanna, but pay for it first and go outside with your shenanigans," Mr. Ruffino growled from behind his cash register.

"I'm paying for it," I said, waving the dollar bill my mother had given me.

"Good! And when's your grandma supposed to pay her bill? She's got a three-week runnin' balance here," he said, reaching for his ledger of accounts receivable.

I fluffed the bread slices inside the plastic wrapper, went and put the dollar bill in Mr. Ruffino's outstretched hand, a hand as beefy as the luncheon meats and baloney sausages he sliced by the carload, gauging his slicing machine with the precision of a mathematician.

"You'll have to call my grandmother and ask her yourself, Mr. Ruffino," I said, thinking *and good luck* because he knew as well as I that Mimy would pay the bill in her own good time.

"I'll do just that, little miss," he muttered.

"So? What've you heard about Lonnie?" I asked, turning back to D.D.

"I knew I'd get a rise outta ya!" he said, pressing the Red Devil jawbreaker he'd gotten from the gumball machine against the inside of his cheek.

"Godssake, D.D., get that damn thing out of your mouth and tell me what you heard."

"This ain't no teenagers' hangout. You're blocking the doorway!" Mr. Ruffino yelled, stretching over the counter.

D.D. drew the jawbreaker from his mouth, and held the glistening ball with pincer fingers. He drew in a long breath to have me understand that he was being pressured by me. "If you wanna know, I heard Lonnie's gotten herself really involved."

"Jeezuzgod, that's your big news?"

"Lonnie's gotten in*volved* with that older friend of your brother's."

"What older friend?"

"You know damn good and well what older friend. They're pretty tight, Lonnie and him . . . pret-tee tight, if you know what I mean."

"Quit trying to sound like you know so much and tell me who's been saying these things," I demanded.

"I never said anybody was saying these things," he said. "I said, it's what I heard."

"You're so stupid, D.D.!"

"Keep your voice down!" he hissed. "One of my mother's customers told her she sees Lonnie comin' back home at all hours of the night—*every* night, that some guy on a motorcycle drops her off at the far end of the block and she runs by like a ghost—that's how this lady put it—and disappears into the alley. No doubt she's been sneakin' back in through the window without her parents ever knowing she'd left."

"That couldn't have come from anyone other than that big snoop, Miz Simoneaux, poking her head out the door all hours of the day and night," I sneered. "It's her you're shielding, isn't it? Miz Simoneaux ought to be watching what her own kid is doing!"

"Whaddaya mean? You heard somethin' about Charlie?" he asked, beside himself with curiosity.

"No, I haven't heard something about Charlie!"

D.D. shrugged his shoulders and jimmied something from out of his pants pocket.

"Wanna hear somethin' cool? I sent away for it. Got it through an L.L.Bean mail-order catalogue," he said, yanking out a small transistor radio.

"What exactly did Miz Simoneaux say about Lonnie?" I asked him, giving the boxy little radio a glance. It was inside a perforated red leather case and was hardly bigger than the palm of his hand.

"She told my mom, she didn't tell me 'cuz I'd have told her off real good."

"I know you wouldn't let anybody talk bad about Lonnie," I conceded.

"And you know somethin' you ain't tellin' me," he said. "I c'n tell."

"You can tell!" I mocked. "Let me go, I'm holding up supper."

In spite of past differences, D.D. was a good friend and didn't deserve being left with the impression he couldn't be trusted.

He spit the jawbreaker out into the street, wiped his sticky fingers on his cutoffs, and stood there waiting.

"What?" I said, somewhat distracted by the new sculpted haircut that banished his cowlicks front and back, and by how tanned and fit he looked in the sleeveless tee shirt and faded cutoffs, his arms and legs smoothly muscular and glinting with little gold-brown hairs. A deep-down fluttering quivered inside me.

"Why're you lookin' at me that way?" he asked.

"What way?" I said, nonplussed.

"The way you were lookin' at me, starin' like you were turned on or somethin'."

"You wish."

"What do you mean, I wish? I saw you. You were starin' at me."

"You wish," I repeated ineffectually.

"What were you thinkin'?" he asked, coming up and taking hold of my wrist.

"Are you going bats? Let go of me!" I said, jerking away from him.

"Come on, Vicky—tell me what you were thinkin'," he pleaded.

"I *told* you it was nothing!"

"I think I know, because it was the same thing I was thinkin'."

"I was thinking that I heard you and your family were moving," I said, plucking that out of thin air. "That true?"

"Let's not change the subject," he said.

"Get serious."

"I'm being serious," he said. He paused then, his aura of self-possession dimming momentarily.

"To answer your question, if Mr. Earl closes the restaurant, which Mama now sez she thinks he might, bein' that Peacock offered Mr. Earl a bunch of money to break his lease, Mama's friend Miz Hazel told Mama she can get a job at Swanson's out at West End. She told Mama that on weekends, Friday nights especially, she can make a killin'. But let's get back to what we were talkin' about," he said.

"What is with you?" I said, hoping to conceal the sense of embarrassment, or foolishness, or nervousness, or whatever it was creeping inside me by degrees.

"What's with you, you mean!" He was imperturbable, aware of the spell of the moment, aware that we were on an even plane, that for once he might even have the upper hand.

"The older you get, the goofier you get, y'know that?" I turned to conceal my agitation. I hurried across the street, swinging the loaf of Merita with as much nonchalance as I could muster.

When I glanced back, D.D. was still standing on the corner in front of Ruffino's with a look on his face as if he were wondering what *that* was all about, something I couldn't have answered because it was easier for me and much safer to keep D.D. in the familiar pain-in-the-ass place he'd always occupied in my mind.

When I reached my doorstep, I turned to wave at him, as much to say "see ya later" as to shut away that disturbingly unfamiliar image I had of D.D. that hinted of fear and excitement—something akin to what I felt when I first entered the underground tunnel following those boys in the close confines of the passageway under the Robert E. Lee monument.

When I turned, D.D. was practically on top of me—his face against mine. Then his lips were on mine, parting, moist, salty, and tasting of the cinnamon Red Devil jawbreaker. My nostrils filled with breath that was both his and mine. His hand slid under my middy top, went to my solar plexus, and hesitated at the hard-soft place between my breasts, and then he began to wiggle his fingers under the band of my bra.

I jerked his hand away and slapped it hard.

"Let me," he said. "Please. C'mon."

"You have lost your mind!" I hollered in his face. I grabbed his now hesitant hand and twisted it, nearly toppling us both off the step.

"Ouch! C'mon Vicky. You don't wanna do that," he said, practically whispering.

I slapped his face, barely glancing his cheek because, knowing me, he'd anticipated my next move. I took the steps by twos and went into the house, slamming the door so hard I thought the glass pane would shatter.

"Jerk!" I muttered loud enough for him to hear.

"Don't be that way," I heard him say, laughingly I thought.

I was shaken by him in a way I never thought possible, and long afterward something inside me kept shuddering, or tingling, or both.

At six o'clock sharp I brought Mimy the dish my mother had prepared for her supper.

She was sitting at the little dining table snuggled against the wall of her snug efficiency kitchen. It still surprised me to see how well Mimy had adjusted, to see how much she liked being by herself in the project apartment she called her *casita*.

She removed the big cloth napkin with which Mama had wrapped the dish, draped it across her lap, peeled away the foil, and inspected the steamy dish as if it were an assortment of foods of questionable origin that she might or might not deign to sample.

I sat there sipping a glass of iced tea and dutifully listening to Mimy grumble about all the things she wasn't supposed to eat. I noticed that she kept pressing the fleshy underside of her armpit with her thumb, now and again smoothing the slope of her breast with the palm of her hand, quite unconsciously I thought, because all the while she never stopped chattering.

"Got an itch, Mimy?" I asked her.

"No, *niña*, I don't have an eetch," she said, dabbing her mouth with the napkin.

"I keep seeing you touching there. You've been doing it the whole time I've been here. I thought something might have bitten you under your arm."

"*Nada me picó*," she said, shaking her head. But her answer sounded like an open-ended statement, something I might or might not choose to explore.

"What is it, then, if nothing bit you?" I asked.

"It is nothing but a little bump," she said, rubbing the flesh under her arm.

"Like a boil?"

"A *qué*?"

"A boil. You know, a big pimple, kind of."

"*Un furúnculo?*" Mimy said. "*No. No es un furúnculo.*"

"A fu-*roon*-colo?" I chortled. Spanish always made things sound better or worse than they really were. "That sounds awful, like it was going to reach out and bite you—fu-*roon*-colo!" I teased, reaching for Mimy with clawed fingers.

Mimy turned away from me.

"I remember when Miz DeSales said that the big boil on Lonnie's forehead was called a *furoncle* in French. *Furoncle* doesn't sound at all the way it's spelled. It doesn't compare to 'fu-roon-colo.' You can dig your heels into fu-*roon*-colo."

"I don't understand you when you talk such nonsense," Mimy said soberly. "No, it is no boil. I think it's a gland, a swollen gland." She felt the place again with questioning fingertips, as if the swelling might have diminished in the minutes we'd been talking.

"Let me see, Mimy," I said, not waiting for a response.

What I felt under the fabric of Mimy's dress was a smooth solid lump the size and shape of a half-submerged pecan.

"Does it hurt?" I asked, worried, but trying not to look it. "How long's it been there?"

Mimy shrugged.

"When did you first notice it?" I persisted, afraid of what she might tell me.

"A while ago, *niña*," she said, her voice hinting at irritation.

I pulled my hand away, the words *that's no gland!* frozen on my lips.

I didn't know what swollen glands felt like other than the sore nodules that appeared at either side of my throat whenever I had an earache, or a sore throat, but I knew that *this* lump was something else. My mind shrieked to a halt, refusing to go farther than that. Even so, my legs would swing out from under the table, my feet would take me across the street, and I'd tell my mother I thought something was very wrong with Mimy.

Mimy's brow furrowed. "What do you think that is, Bee-Kee?" she asked.

"It's probably a swollen gland, like you said Mimy, but I think it'd be best for Mama to come over and have a look," I asserted, a marvel of self-control for what I felt at that moment was suffocating fear.

My mother returned from seeing Mimy, got on the phone, and said she was making an appointment for Mimy to see a specialist at Mercy Hospital first thing in the morning.

That suffocating feeling I had for not having let myself think of what that pecan-size lump was under Mimy's arm would last through the weeks after Mimy's mastectomy, and the months of chemotherapy that followed.

"Please don't take this wrong, Vicky," Lonnie said. "I think Mimy looks real good, but she shrank kind of. Don't you think so? I don't mean she just lost weight, her whole frame looks as if it's gotten smaller."

The picture of Mimy that Lonnie had in mind was surely the same as mine—that of my grandmother standing in the doorway, a graying wire-haired angel defying the forces of nature with her sparking Palm Sunday palm, and shielding us from harm with the wide berth of her behind and wind-whipped skirts.

"Mimy was never a big woman. She was always on the plump side, but she wasn't a big person like your Aunt Lizzie was," I said defensively. I never bothered to mention Mimy's wig, and Lonnie had the good sense not to say anything to me about Mimy's new curly hairdo. It was an expensive wig, bought at Holmes', downtown, but the way Mimy wore it, a little askew, even the most casual observer had no doubt as to what it was.

I found it hard to admit, even to myself, how much the cancer had dissipated my grandmother. It was as if, like a set of Russian matryoshka dolls, month after month a smaller and smaller Mimy emerged from inside the stalwart encasement of the original Mimy.

When it seemed that all of the vomiting and treatments and medications threatened to diminish Mimy to less than the half-sized person she had become, she started to make a turnaround. One day she complained about the tasteless "chalk malts" Mama made and the cups of Jell-O puddings that turned to rubber on the plate.

Mimy never regained her original weight and size, nor did she resume the spit-and-vinegar persona of her former self, but when my mother and I walked in one day and found her sitting on the side of her bed on the telephone scolding Mr. Ruffino as she had Mr. Matthews before him for overcharging her for six bottles of Barq's Root Beer and a small-size box of Lorna Doones and threatening to take her business elsewhere, we knew that she was getting better.

In the years to come, the disease would recur, taking her, and leaving us stunned and as perplexed by the void of her absence, which was as palpable for us as the reality of Mimy's *bultos* had been for her.

18

I WAS SITTING AT THE kitchen table doing my homework when Lonnie rattled the screen door.

"All right already!" I said, scrambling from the table. "Quit banging on the door. I'm coming."

Lonnie stood there waiting, her head lowered, her hands shoved deep inside her pockets.

"What's the matter, Lonnie?" I asked, unlatching the door.

"My friggin' mother, that's what's the matter," she said, practically growling. She was wearing her brother's gold varsity sweater with the big purple *E* for Easton High.

"The old bitch has been snooping around. She's been going through my dresser drawers, lifting the linings, digging in pockets, pulling my shoes out of the closet, and finding excuses every chance she gets to look in my book bag! She knows something," Lonnie grumbled. She plucked a glass from the drain board and poured herself some cold water from the fridge. "Where's your mom?" she asked, craning her neck to see if we were alone.

"She took Mimy for her checkup. She said they were going to stop at St. Patrick's to light some candles, and grab something to eat and wouldn't be back until five. Why?"

"Because I've got to ask you something. I need to ask a favor, kiddy. I'd like for you to keep something for me, just for a little while. I wouldn't ask you to, but I can't take the chance of hiding it at my house with *her* snooping around."

I didn't want Lonnie to see how uneasy I felt and started flipping through the pages of my math book. "What's this about, Lonnie?" I asked.

Lonnie was already slipping her hand into one of the drooping varsity sweater pockets. She drew out something and held it out for me to inspect.

"It's about this," she said. It was a plastic bag with, from what I could see, an assortment of different-colored pills and capsules.

"What are they?" I asked, already knowing. I looked up to see Lonnie looking at me, her eyes gone pale, the pupils larger, sharper, and deeper than I'd ever seen them.

"They aren't mine, kiddy. They're Vincent's. He asked me, he *begged* me to do him a favor and hold them for him a couple of days, that's all."

"Lonnie, for God's sake!"

"Well, what would you have done if it had been your friend, your brother, even, who'd asked you to do this for him?"

"I'd have told him 'no' that's what! Besides, my brother wouldn't have asked me to do such a thing for him, and neither would yours."

"It isn't as if they are hard drugs or anything like that. They're just uppers and downers."

"For God's sake—how do you know they aren't hard drugs? How do you know *what* they are?"

"Because—because he told me," she said, looking away as if somebody else had come into the room.

"Whatever he told you, these are drugs, they're narcotics, don't you understand?—You can get arrested."

"I'm a *ju*venile—"

"So what? So, you can get picked up and sent to juvenile hall for something like this. Jeez, Lonnie, you'd have a record. Do you know that? A record!"

"Yeah, if I'm stupid enough to get caught. That's why I'm asking you to keep them in a safe place just until tomorrow night. You have a good imagination, and besides, there's no chance anybody'd ever think of looking here. I know you'd find the best of all hiding places once you put your mind to it.

"Would you, Vicky? Please do this one little thing and I promise I'll never ask you for another favor as long as I live."

"I can't believe that slime bag asked you to keep these friggin' pills knowing what could happen if you got caught," I croaked.

"How many times are you going to keep saying the same ol' thing?" she demanded, stomping her foot. "And he's not a slime bag."

"He's using you."

"Look! He didn't ask me. *I'm* the one that offered."

"What?"

"That's right. He can't afford to take any chances. He's been picked up before. One more time, and he'll be sent to Parchman. That's one step from Angola, y'know."

"I don't give a flyin' fuck what happens to him!"

Lonnie blinked, speechless at my anger.

"I care about what happens to you," I said. "Don't you think your mother suspects something like this the way she's been snooping around your room? And she's got to know about your sneaking out nights. Frankly, I don't know how she hasn't found you out on either count."

"I told you, she doesn't have the frigginest idea what she's looking for, but I can't take any chances. She's nuts. One minute she wants to keep me in the house like a prisoner, next she wants to kick me out. One minute she wants me there with her, the next she wishes I'd never been born. Doesn't matter, I'm leaving, no matter what."

"But you said you were seeing Vincent tomorrow—"

"I *am* seeing him tomorrow. I'll wait 'til I hear the old farts snoring—she snores worse than my dad does, then I'll tippy-toe out."

"You sneak around at night," I said, as if it were a declaration.

"How else do you think I'd ever get to see him?"

"You aren't afraid they'll catch you?"

"You're really something, Vicky, you know that? You, of all people, talking to me about being afraid. You, who's always breaking the rules."

"This is a whole lot different, and you know it."

"Will you do this for me?—Just until tomorrow night?"

I looked at the algebraic symbols I'd been writing in my loose-leaf binder when Lonnie appeared at the door: neat letters that represented numbers and operations I'd been racking my brains over that I knew I'd never put to practical use, and which, in the grand scheme of things, were as meaningless as chicken scratches.

"I'm begging you—please, Vicky. I can't take a chance that Mama'll find them."

"All right," I said and slammed the textbook closed. "But just until tomorrow night. Call and let me know right before you leave to meet Vincent. I don't want to take any chances either."

From the minute I accepted the bag of pills, I had a bad feeling. Lonnie must have sensed it because she knew well enough to keep her mouth shut. She was virtually shivering with satisfaction and hugged me especially tight before she left.

I hid the bag of pills at the bottom of the chiffonier in my room, deep inside the big plastic storage box under all the heavy winter garments that had remained folded in mothballs throughout the season because the winter had been so mild.

I tossed and turned all that night, dreaming I was roaming back and forth through a house that, at the same time, was and wasn't mine, unable to find a hiding place, and dreaming that Miss Ada was following one step behind me, ready to pounce. I awoke with a start only to find that it was still night, that I was lying in my bed wrestling with my musty pillow, that a swirling storm of fiery stars was taking possession of my room as I sat in the dark, eyes wide open.

I awoke the next morning with the perfect hiding place in mind: the little crosspiece wedged in the inverted V-support above the door just inside Queenie's doghouse set against the fence under the landing of the broken stairway. It was the unlikeliest place that anybody would ever look, the easiest place for Lonnie to retrieve the bag without having to come inside the house, and it would require no further involvement on my part.

No sooner had I jumped out of bed to dig for the stash at the bottom of the storage box inside the chiffonier than my mother called from the kitchen.

"Vicky, I ordered a stewing hen from Sciortino's and I need for you to pick it up right after breakfast, and a couple of things from the market, too. Okay?"

"Okay," I called and stashed the bag of drugs back under all the blankets and folded winter garments at the bottom of the chiffonier.

My mother had the grocery cart waiting at the door. This was standard procedure since she'd quit work. She did most of the grocery shopping during the week, leaving the things she wanted "bought fresh" for me to pick up at the Magazine Street markets on Saturdays. I didn't mind because I could do in forty-five minutes what used to take half a day.

When I got back home not an hour later, I found that all hell had broken loose.

I walked in to find my room in total disarray: the mirrored doors of the chiffonier wide open, the clothes, some still on their hangers, strewn about my bed, the twin bottom drawers of the chiffonier gaping, and the plastic storage box of blankets gutted.

I heard the grocery cart I'd hastily propped against a chair in the living room crash to the floor. I couldn't think fast enough to make up something to tell my parents, who were standing about the table watching as I walked through the shotgun rooms to the kitchen to find the plastic bag open and the pills and capsules strewn all over the table.

"Whose are these?" my father demanded.

"Whose are what?" I asked, dumb-faced.

"Don't smart-mouth me, Vicky," he said.

"I was going to air out the clothes in the chiffonier when—," my mother interjected.

"They're not mine!" I blurted.

"I'm not accusing you. But I want you to tell me whose they are, if you know where they came from," my father said, standing and pushing the chair back with his foot. "Tell us if you know anything."

Just then the back door opened and in walked Eddie. He looked at me, at my parents, at the table with the scattered pills.

"What's going on?" he asked. His forehead was furrowed, his eyebrows knitted with all the questions he wanted to ask me but couldn't.

"You tell me!" my father said.

He was in Eddie's face even before Eddie could unzip his jacket.

"What're you talkin' about?" Eddie said.

"*That's* what I'm talking about!" my father said, pointing at the table.

The crease above Eddie's nose deepened. His eyes, dark blue like my father's, looked like purple nail heads. "You think these are mine? Is that what you're sayin', that you think they're mine?" he asked, and for the first time in a long time his voice cracked, sounding as if it had split in half.

"I want to know who the hell that dope belongs to! Are those yours?" my father demanded.

"No! This dope, as you call it, ain't mine. Why do you think right away they're mine?" Eddie yelled, backing off as if to push himself away from us.

"Who the hell else could they belong to? Your mother? Your sister?" my father shrieked.

"You mean, who else *but* me would bring drugs into the house! That's what you mean!" The cords in Eddie's neck were ready to burst.

"I *asked* you if they were your drugs!"

"You didn't ask me anything. You just as good as accused me!"

"Who do you think you're talking to!" my father said, his clenched fist crashing on the table. The pills popped up like Mexican jumping beans and the capsules rolled willy-nilly to the edge of the table.

"Please, Edward! Let's not have another fight!" my mother cried. "We can sit down and talk this out calmly."

For as long as I could remember my father and brother had rubbed each other wrong, but things had worsened since they'd begun to argue over the mysterious source of Eddie's money. Every time my father saw Eddie tinkering with his motorbike, gunning it, or whenever he heard the motorbike puttering to a stop in front of the house, he all but popped a blood vessel.

"It all makes sense to me now. There we were wondering where you got money and now we know how you got the money to buy that motorbike, and all of the stuff to fix it up with, and the money to gamble besides."

Louis Champagne's bespectacled face flashed before my eyes. The last time I met him on the street I wouldn't even look at him.

"Goddammit, sonuvabitch!" my brother screamed. The spit bubbled at the corners of his mouth and he was wiping away the traitor tears fast as they appeared.

My father went purple with rage. "What's that you said? What's that you called me?"

It happened so fast I couldn't think, let alone come up with something that would have exonerated Eddie without implicating Lonnie. All I could do to keep my father from flying at my brother with clenched fists was to jump between them as I'd done once before.

"Stop it, Dad! Stop it! The pills aren't Eddie's! They're mine!"

My father looked at me with eyes that didn't focus.

"They belong to me!" I said.

"Vicky, honey, they can't be yours," my mother gasped.

My father grabbed me by both arms. "I don't believe you!" he said, shaking me like a ragdoll. "You're shielding him, that's what you're doing." He was shaking me so hard I bit my tongue.

"You're hurting her!" my mother cried.

I swallowed the blood taste and told them that I was the one who'd brought the drugs into the house, that I was keeping them for someone whose name I couldn't divulge. It was a favor I was doing; a favor that was to have been for just a few hours; that I should never have agreed to do it because it was an endangerment to everyone in the house; that Eddie was innocent of all wrongdoing.

"I don't believe that for a minute," my father said. He scooped the scattered pills still on the table into the plastic bag, gathered the capsules that had fallen to the floor, went to the bathroom, emptied everything in the toilet, and flushed. Then he shut himself off in the living room to puff on one of his asthma cigarettes.

My mother took to her bed.

My brother stormed from the house.

I expected there'd be more to it than that. And there was.

The time it took for me to get from my house to Lonnie's was a blur. I was knocking and then banging on her door with my fists.

"That you, kiddy?" she said through a crack in the door. Her voice was sluggish, drugged-out perhaps. The door parted a couple of inches more and I barged my way in, pushing with both hands.

"Jeez! What's happened?" she said, instantly alert.

"My parents found the bag of pills."

"Oh God, no!" she gasped.

"Oh God, yes!" I said.

"Who'd you say the pills belonged to?" she asked with admirable control.

"I didn't tell them they belonged to your precious Vincent, if that's what you're worried about!"

"Oh, kiddy, I'm so sorry—"

"The only thing you're sorry about is that you're going to have to tell Vincent his pills are gone—kaput, flushed down the toilet."

"Vicky, I can't tell you how sorry I am. Whatever you want me to do, I'll do."

"Then go over and tell them the stash was Vincent's. They think it was my brother's."

"I can't do that."

"You'd let Eddie take the blame? You'd betray me, your friend? There's nothing you wouldn't do to protect that slug, Lonnie. That's exactly what he is, a stinking slug!

"It doesn't matter one bit to you that my father and Eddie practically came to blows over this, that my mom's crying her heart out, or that my brother left the house and hasn't come back. None of this matters so long as you come out okay with Vincent!"

The tears welled in Lonnie's eyes. "That's not true, kiddy, and you know it."

"What I know is that you don't care about anyone but yourself!"

"I wouldn't hurt you or your family for anything in the world . . ." She wiped her nose against the crook of her arm. "I got so nervous trying to think of where to hide the stuff, and I knew you always came up with such cool ideas. I didn't mean to get you involved. I didn't want to ask you but—"

"But you did."

"I asked you because you're my friend."

"Oh, please. Don't do me any favors," I sneered.

"Can't you at least try and understand . . . ?" she said, stamping her foot. Her indignation only served to fuel my anger.

"I understand, all right. I understand that you're the most selfish little bitch I know."

"Me? You're the bitch who always thinks she's right no matter what," she spat back.

Her retaliation took me by surprise, but I was nothing if not fast on the comeback.

"Let me restate my opinion of you, Lonnie," I said, cocking an eyebrow. "You're conniving and self-serving and I don't care if I ever see you again!" I grabbed hold of the wobbly doorknob and yanked the door so hard behind me, I was sure I'd broken something.

19

Eddie hadn't returned since he sped off on his motorbike. My parents had left shortly afterward, my father having coaxed my mother into going for a ride, no doubt to talk over what had happened by themselves. When my parents returned, they found me just as they'd left me hours before—lying on the sofa, staring at the ceiling.

We went to bed early that night, each of us awake and listening for whatever sound wrinkled the darkness. When St. Mary's tower bell chimed at midnight and there was no sound of Eddie's motorbike puttering to a stop outside, I heard my father get out of bed.

He padded to the front room and sank into the cut-velvet chair to smoke another of his musty smelling asthma cigarettes. Later, I heard his hushed wheeze when he climbed into bed to lie beside my mother, and then their twistings in the bed, each attempting to feign sleep for the sake of the other.

My eyes burned from staring at the winkless red stars, and when daylight appeared and the pieces of my room resumed their places—the bed frame gleaming dully at my feet, my clothes strewn over the back of the chair, the tall two-mirrored chiffonier sulking against the wall, the light fixture hanging from its twisted cord, the faded wallpaper with its smudge-print flowers—I drifted off to sleep.

The phone jangled and I was instantly awake.

Thank the good Lord I heard my mother whisper.

It was Mimy. She'd called to tell my mother she'd gotten up during the night to go to the bathroom and found Eddie asleep on her sofa.

I heard my mother tell Mimy she'd tell her what had happened when she went over with her breakfast. I could hear the forced casualness in my mother's voice as she answered Mimy's questions, and thought of Mimy at the other end of the line—wigless, touching the hairs that clung to her head like the sparse strands on a coconut husk—whispering so that Eddie couldn't hear her from the next room.

That afternoon Eddie waited until my parents were gone before he crossed the street to come over to the house. He breezed in the front door, headed straight for his room, and started packing some of his things into his gym bag.

I flopped onto the bed to watch him.

"Where'd they go?" he asked me.

"To eleven o'clock Mass, then they'll probably stop at Earl's for something to eat. Mama said she isn't cooking today. She isn't feeling so hot. You know how nervous she gets."

"They say anything else after I left?"

"Not really. Like I told you, I tried, but they wouldn't talk to me."

"They'll come around, punkin. And when they do, you're gonna have to tell them the truth about that stash." He stopped his packing, waiting for my response. "You know that, don't you?" he said.

I nodded, but I didn't answer for fear of blubbering. I picked up a ball of his rolled socks and stuffed it into his gym bag.

"Are you moving for good?" I asked over the lump in my throat.

"Yep," he said, checking over the contents of his gym bag.

"You mean you're never coming back home to live?"

"Isn't that what 'for good' means?"

My eyes stung from the sharpness of his response. "Eddie, I feel terrible. I wish with all my heart I never would have—"

"It isn't your fault, little sister."

"At the time I thought I was doing the right thing—"

"You did what you thought you had to." He reached over and tousled my hair the way he used to when I was a little girl. "I know who the stash belongs to and who you did it for, Vicky."

"It isn't what you're thinking," I said.

"Now, how do you know what I'm thinkin'? I know who the stash belongs to, and it isn't the person you're shielding. I'm not stupid," he said, zipping the bag. "I told that sonuvabitch I don't want him comin' around here anymore."

"You knew about all that, I mean about Lonnie and him?" I asked.

Eddie looked at me as if I were retarded.

"When it started I told Vincent to lay off. He laughed and said she was just a kid and he was just humorin' her." Eddie held up his hand to stop me from commenting. "If he ever shows his face around here again, I'll break his neck," he said between clenched teeth.

"I explained to Mom and Dad that you had nothing to do with the stuff. I know they believe me."

I could never have admitted it, but I understood my parents' suspicions about the pills. *How else could Eddie have gotten the money to shoot craps and buy a motorbike?* is what they'd thought.

"No need apologizing for them, punkin. It was natural for them to think I was the one the pills belonged to. How could they've thought otherwise?" He laughed then, attempting to make light of it. But I could hear the hurt in his voice, and see the traces of it in his bloodshot eyes.

"Hey, this has been comin' on for a long time between me and the ol' man. If it hadn't been for this, it would have been for somethin' else. I just figure I'd better split before somethin' worse happens."

"Are you moving in with Mimy?"

"I'm gonna wait there until my seventeenth birthday in September and see if I can talk them into signing the consent papers to let me join the Marines."

"They won't—"

"Oh, I think they will," he said.

My heart sank at the thought of my brother leaving.

"C'mon punkin. I'll be comin' back. It'll only be for a while, y'know. Besides, what really matters isn't gonna change."

"I know," I said cheerfully as I could, but I didn't believe it any more than he did.

"Gotta go," Eddie said, hoisting the gym bag from the bed.

Queenie nudged my hand.

Eddie reached down and tweaked her ears.

"Do me a favor before you go?" I asked him. "Queenie's got to do her business, but I have to go somewhere before Mama and Dad get back. If I'm still here when they get back, they won't let me go. Would you mind watching Queenie in the yard for five minutes so I can get away without her knowing? If she thinks I'm leaving, she'll start making a racket."

"Just put her in the yard and let her howl," Eddie said, obviously aggravated by the thought of being detained.

"She'll jump the gate, and I don't want her to follow me," I said.

Queenie could take the gate easily, but she was a small dog and it made me nervous to think of what could happen when she plunged from that six-foot height and hit the bricks on the other side. Eddie's condescending attitude toward Queenie had always griped me.

"Okay, I'll watch her, but I'm not gonna hang around for long. I don't wanna be here either when they get back. C'mon girl," he said, urging Queenie with his knee toward the back door.

Queenie faded back, ready to scoot.

"See? She knows," I said.

She wiggled and whined and nearly jumped from my arms when I picked her up and carried her to the back door, where I brushed the velvety dome of her head with a kiss before I nudged her out.

I watched my brother going down the steps, following Queenie into the backyard, and I was overcome with longing for those winter nights when Lonnie slept over and Queenie snuggled in the bed between us, and the low, blue-flamed ring of a wick burning in Mimy's kerosene heater lulled us to sleep; and Mimy, Mama, Dad, and Eddie slept in their beds; and the wind moaned outside, rattling window panes and tree branches, loosening eaves and clapboards, looking for unsecured things to take with it, while everyone and everything I loved and needed in the world to make me happy was safe under the roof of our house.

I knocked on Valentina's door, needing to talk with her, needing to siphon from the wealth of her experience so that I might sort things out, like a deck of cards that I could shuffle and set in order on a table before me.

I heard the door at the far end of the hall open.

"Is that you Vicky?" It was Miz Carmody.

"Yes, ma'am," I said tentatively. "Is Miz Dreyfus home do you know?"

"Ah, Miz Dreyfus—," she sighed, wringing her apron front. "I hate to be the bearer of bad news, but Miz Dreyfus took a bad fall. She tripped on the bottom step going downstairs for her mail yesterday. Lucky for her I was fixing myself something to eat and didn't have my soaps on yet so that I was able to hear her when she hollered. Lucky for her, too, I left my door propped open to let in the breeze from the hallway," she said, walking over to where I was standing.

"At first I didn't know what to make of it, where she was calling from, she sounded so far away. 'Help me,' I heard, 'Help me. Missus Carmody, somebody please help me.' And when I came out farther in the hallway and looked down—my God! I couldn't believe my eyes. There she was, lying at the bottom of the stairs.

"She was trying to push herself up, poor soul. I ran down to help fast as I could with my bad knees and all. I made her comfortable as I could and then I came back upstairs and called for an ambulance. Shame on shame—it took them a good twenty, twenty-five minutes to get here.

"They told me last night when I called the nurses' station that Missus Dreyfus had broken her arm in two places. But worse, she fractured her hip, the left side, I think they said. They had taken her to surgery. I know she'd have called you already if she could have."

"What hospital is she in, Miz Carmody?" I asked, already seeing myself rushing into some shiny-floored emergency unit.

"Hotel Dieu."

"Thank you," I called, halfway down the stairs.

"Vicky, wait a minute. If you're going to visit Miz Dreyfus, I think you'd better call first. She could be in intensive care 'cause they might have needed to put a pin in her hip and they might not let you in to see her . . . Well, you oughta check first and see if she's out of recovery."

I thanked Miz Carmody but I wasn't going to waste time on the phone trying to get connected with the right person on the right floor only to be told the patient couldn't receive visitors other than from a family member. I had to go there myself.

In the few minutes it took me to get home I was envisioning myself sitting in the passenger seat of my father's car, or on the back of Eddie's motorbike, speeding up Tulane Avenue to Hotel Dieu. When I got home, my father's Chevy Impala was nowhere in sight.

I figured I'd run in, jot a note to my parents, then run over to Mimy's and ask Eddie for a ride to the hospital. Not wanting to waste time unlocking the front door, I ran up the alley to let myself in the back door, which would have been unlocked.

Queenie hadn't barked. She wasn't making the racket she'd have made hearing me running like a nut through the alley. That's what I was thinking when at the end of the alley my eyes set on a sack-like thing slung over the gate.

I ran without breaking stride, slid on the moldy bricks, thudded against the gate, and gathered the still-warm bulk in my arms. I held it high as I could to slacken the tautness of the rope and worked my fingers under the prickly cincture that was buried in the furry neck while I supported the precious weight, not wanting to believe. I cradled it against me like a baby, lifted it with both hands, meaning to thrust it upward, to lift it high as I could and cuddle it so that the dead-weight blue-tongued thing would become Queenie again.

Queenie! Oh, Queenie! I begged for someone to answer, to tell me how mistaken I was in thinking that the still-warm furry mass I held in my arms could be my Queenie, who even then was inside the house, waiting for me, and whining with indignation for having been left behind.

My brother kept saying he was sorry. He explained over and over how he'd left Queenie tied securely to one of the posts that supported the shed, that he'd left her with enough rope to run about the yard to do her business. He begged me to understand that he'd left because he couldn't chance being there when my parents came home. He wasn't ready to face them. He couldn't have known that Queenie would jump the gate.

My mother and Mimy took turns at placating me in Eddie's behalf: "Your brother feels terrible . . . It was an accident . . . Talk to him, Vicky."

Even my father, who still wasn't right with Eddie, made excuses for him. But I was inconsolable. I blamed Eddie and swore never to forgive him for the obscene way in which Queenie had died.

"You there?"

It was D.D.'s voice, which I hadn't recognized at first.

"Jeez, I'm sorry about Queenie. Can you believe it—ol' Queenie? I'm comin' over, if it's okay," he said.

"It's not okay," I croaked.

"Are you still mad at me for—for when I last saw you?" he asked.

Same ol' D.D.! I couldn't believe that he could be so self-absorbed as to assume I could still be thinking of him at such a time.

"I would've called sooner, Vicky, had I known, but Becky just told me what happened. God, that's awful. I can't tell you—I can't picture—I mean, we're all so used to havin' her around. Did y'all—did you get the chance to bury her yet?"

"Yes."

"I'da helped . . . Where'd y'all put her?"

"In the backyard, next to the fence, under the landing where she and I used to . . . Aw, Jesuschrist, D.D.!"

"My mom says there's a city ordinance against buryin' pets in backyards. But what nobody knows won't hurt 'em, huh? Vicky? You still there?"

"I'm hanging up," I said and dropped the receiver in its cradle and let myself fall back onto the bed.

I could hear how bad D.D. felt about Queenie, but I needed to be left alone, to do nothing but lie in bed without moving, as if not moving could freeze time and with it the painful reality of Queenie's death.

When I found the will to drag myself from the house and make it to Hotel Dieu to visit Valentina, I had my father drive me.

Eddie offered. He did everything but pick me up and set me on his motorbike. But I couldn't stand to be near him, to have to listen to him telling me yet again how sorry he was.

My father took his newspaper and sat in the lobby to read while I took the elevator to the semiprivate room on the third floor, where the reception desk personnel said Valentina had been moved. Hotel Dieu, with its black oak grandfather clock that looked as if it had come from the heart of Bavaria, its oak-paneled lobby cluttered with Victorian pieces and worn carpets that looked more like it all belonged in an old-timey hotel lobby than it did a hospital.

The light behind the opaque curtain that divided the room cast indistinct shadows that intensified the feelings of uncertainty I had about how I'd find Valentina and what I could possibly say to cheer her up, as heartbroken as I was over the loss of my darling Queenie.

She lay with her eyes closed. Her hair, grayer and longer than I remembered (actually, I had never before seen it loosened from the plaited chignon she always wore) was spread on the pillow. Her left arm, encased in a plaster-of-Paris V-form cast, was propped on a metal rod that stood on the blanket. Her free hand was half clenched, as if she'd meant to grip the covers and push them back. The narrow plastic tubes that snaked from her nostrils onto her chest and across her shoulder were clipped to the tucked sheet and slid into the squeezed space between the bed and the machine whose dials and innards clicked and buzzed.

The rounded bulk of the hip cast covered by the pale blue blanket reminded me of the whitewashed cement encasements of above-ground crypts I'd seen in an Italian cemetery in Independence, Louisiana.

I leaned in close as I could manage without touching the bed and let my hand hover just above hers, hesitant to touch the translucent flesh. I drew my eyes from the all too fragile tracery of veins and bones and thought of the Auschwitz tattoo concealed by the plaster cast, slipping, as it were, into oblivion.

I don't know whether or not I whispered her name when her eyelids, dewy in the lightning that flashed silently through the Venetian blinds, fluttered.

"*Dziewczynka?*" she whispered.

"I'm here Valentina," I managed to say just above a whisper. I reached for her hand, hardly daring to touch the parchment-like flesh. "Don't talk. You don't need to . . ."

She smiled a smile of light playing on water.

Outside, the thunder rumbled, the lightning crashed, the raindrops that pelted the windowpane fell in rivulets down the glass.

"It is a storm," she said groggily.

"*Tak*," I said and felt the movement of her fingers in my hand, slight as the stirrings of a newborn chick.

"I am tired," she said. I cupped my ear to catch what she was saying.

"You're tired, Valentina?" I whispered tentatively.

"I am very tired, *Dziewczynka*, yes," she said.

I eased back into the nearby chair without letting go of her hand and buried my face in the blanket bereft of any semblance of downiness, and I wept soundlessly and without tears.

My father and I were barely inside the house, still brushing off the droplets of rain from our clothes, when Miss Ada appeared at the door.

"Ada, come in out of the rain for goodness' sake," my mother said. "Let me get you a towel."

"Don't bother, Linda," she said to my mother. "All I need is for Vicky to tell me where my daughter is." And without so much as a nod when I walked into the room she demanded that I tell her where she could find Lonnie.

"How am I supposed to know where Lonnie is?" I asked brazenly. I stopped just short of saying I didn't give a good goddam where Lonnie was.

"Vicky!" my parents cried simultaneously.

"Well, how *am* I supposed to know where she is?" I asked them, chastened by their anger.

"We'll deal with you later," my father promised. "Vicky and I just returned from Hotel Dieu," he said, turning to Miss Ada. "Missus Dreyfus took a bad fall. Vicky sat with her a few hours. I went back and only now picked her up from the hospital."

"Lonnie's been gone since yesterday," Miss Ada said, more distressed, less angry than she was before.

"Have you called the police?" my mother asked.

"Her bed wasn't slept in. She sneaked out. It isn't the first time, as you all must well know by now," Miss Ada said, her eyes boring into mine.

"Vicky, do you know anything about this?" my father asked.

"No, I don't," I said with as much control as I could muster.

Actually, I had an idea of where they might find Lonnie, but if I'd known *exactly* where, I wouldn't have told them. Nevertheless, I was as surprised and angered by Lonnie's abrupt disappearance as was her Jekyll-and-Hyde mother.

20

EDDIE GOT WHAT HE WANTED. My parents signed the consent form allowing him to join the Marines. At the end of October, a month to the day after his seventeenth birthday, he left for basic training at Camp Lejeune in North Carolina.

Since my father's promotion, my mother had talked of moving from the old six-room shotgun on Clementine. She dreamed of renting a house farther uptown, away from the Channel. And, after Mimy had sworn that she'd never again be caught dead living under the same roof with Edward Lumière, my mother had gotten her to move back in with us.

I think it was because of her declining health rather than because of my mother's powers of persuasion that Mimy decided to come back home to live. The radical mastectomy she had to submit to after yet another mass, small and malignant, left her in a state of imbalance.

Mimy underwent a second mastectomy. Yet, although my grandmother insisted she loved her *casita* in the projects and cherished her independence, she relented to my mother's pleas. It all happened about the time Valentina was transferred from the hospital to a convalescent home in the neighborhood.

The Good Shepherd Convalescent Home sat on the corner of Jackson and Camp, not far from where Valentina had lived. It was a Spanish-Creole-style mansion with added wings and ramps and walkways and an enclosed courtyard protected from the busy street by a low picket fence that was buried inside a thicket of sky-reaching ligustrum through which you could see the occasional wink and flash of passing cars.

I found Valentina sitting in the courtyard, tall and erect and looking all too fragile in the stoutness of her wheelchair.

"*Dziewczynka!*" she called when she spotted me. She gripped the wheel rings of the chair, preparing to maneuver her way over the herringbone brickwork.

I usually walked the seven blocks from my house to the convalescent home, but I'd gotten a late start. "Sorry. I'm running late," I said, rushing over to take hold of the handles at the back of the chair. "I had to wait what seemed like forever at the bus stop."

I sped Valentina's wheelchair up the ramp of the passageway leading to the rec room.

"Valentina, guess what?" I said, braking the wheelchair once we got to the rec room.

"*Nie, nie,*" Valentina said shaking her head. "First you must tell me about your grandmother, how she is. Then you can tell me to guess what."

"Mimy? She's doing okay. Same ol' Mimy, sassy as ever," I added, disingenuously.

Valentina cocked her head, waiting for a more detailed response.

"She's finished with the chemo, and her appetite's improved; it's not quite a hundred percent, but getting there. She's even gained a little weight."

That much was true, but the whole truth was that Mimy would never again be a hundred percent—as much from having had cancer as from Eddie having left the way he did, deaf to their pleadings—hers and my mother's.

"*To jest bardzo dobry,*" Valentina nodded, smiling.

"It *is* very good—Mimy having gained a few pounds!" I said, unabashedly proud of my increased, albeit very limited, knowledge of the Polish tongue.

"Now, *Dziewczynka*, what is it you wish to tell me? And don't make me to guess what," she laughed.

"I finally got an answer from them."

"What answer from whom?" she asked, her eyes searching mine.

"From the administration office at Mandeville. Remember you suggested that I write them to try and determine what happened to all the letters we wrote, if Norma was receiving them or not?"

"Yes, I do remember that," Valentina said.

"They said that Norma has been receiving our letters all along. I'm going to let Lonnie and the others know." I took care to drop Lonnie's name in the course of normal conversations whenever I could. If Valentina suspected that Lonnie and I were estranged, she never said so.

"They said Norma's in good health, that Miz Costanza goes to see her every day, and that they'll mention to her mother that I got in touch. It's the most they can do, since Norma doesn't want to answer our letters."

"Perhaps Norma does not know how to—"

"Oh! I know for certain Norma can write. I think her reluctance to write is her way of keeping her pride. She may be a little ashamed, or even embarrassed, for what happened."

Valentina nodded and shrugged her shoulders at the same time, a gesture that had me shrugging my shoulders as well.

She had reserved the use of the rec room television a week in advance so that we could watch the first-ever live performance at Carnegie Hall of Ruggiero Ricci, a virtuoso violinist whom I'd never heard of before Valentina introduced me to him via her old RCA Victor 33⅓ records. She so looked forward to the occasion that I'd have taken a bus from Timbuktu at the peak of rush hour not to have disappointed her.

"This promises to be a doubly auspicious occasion," Valentina said, "because not only is Maestro Ricci the undisputed master of the Paganini caprices, but he will be performing them using the master's violin. The instrument is one hundred and seventy-five years old," she added, fairly chirping.

I knew little of classical music, and nothing of virtuoso violinists, but Valentina's enthusiasm was positively contagious.

"Ruggi*ero Ric*ci, the Italian virtuoso," I said practically kissing the words in my best pseudo-Italian accent.

"Nicely said, *Dziewczynka*, but Ricci isn't Italian, he's a one-hundred-percent American."

"I guess that makes it even better—that the, what did you call him, 'the undisputed master of the Paganini caprices' is an American? How did he come by Paganini's violin?" I wondered aloud.

"The violin was lent to him especially for the televised concert. According to Paganini's will, the instrument was never to leave Genoa, the place of his birth. The instrument has been kept in the city chambers since his death and it hasn't left Italy but once prior to this performance. It was in homage to Ricci's artistry and prominence that the instrument was lent to him."

"What do you think, Valentina? Do you think Paganini's violin will make a difference in Maestro Ricci's performance?" I asked, rolling my *r*'s deliciously. "—In the way he plays, is what I mean."

Valentina straightened herself in the wheelchair. "Your question is not an easy one to answer. It's very similar to the question the maestro was asked in a recent interview. When asked if he anticipated an appreciable difference in his playing, he said that other than the joy he derived of playing the violin that once belonged to Paganini and the privilege that had been accorded to him, he didn't expect that the master's violin would enrich his performance. I think that response took the interviewer by surprise."

"It does sound as if he was bragging a bit, don't you think, Valentina?"

"Ricci's answer wasn't braggadocio. I think what he meant to say was that it would be his individuality, his own joie de vivre that will be heard via Paganini's violin."

"But don't *you* think that because it *is* Paganini's violin it'll make a difference?" I asked.

"Perhaps in playing that instrument Ricci's joy of expression will be heightened. I do not know," Valentina paused, shrugging her shoulders. "I think that to add more to that would be to go over Ricci's head, so to speak, to imply that Ricci's artistic brilliance will have resulted because the instrument has kept in itself Paganini's expression, his soul, as if such was—how should I say it?—transferable."

"Oh—now I understand what you're saying," I hedged. "At least I think I do."

"Ah, *Dziewczynka*, now *you* understand, and now I think *I* do not!" Valentina said, laughing so heartily her shoulders shook. She reached to squeeze my hand as the Westinghouse logo announcing the Carnegie Hall production appeared on the television screen.

"I do understand, Valentina," I insisted, but had she chosen to pursue the matter, I'd have been hard-pressed to put in words what it was I understood.

When I got home the telephone was ringing with nobody there to answer it.

"Where is everybody?" I called, picking up the receiver that was sounding off even as I put it to my ear.

It was Etheline Costanza.

"It's Norma Mae. She's done run away from that God-forsook place!"

"When?" I said, in place of a heartbeat.

"Two days ago. Right away the guards came and axed me where she was, as if I knew. Ha! As if I'da told them bastids anything at all! Lawd, Gawd, what's happened to my girl? Two whole days and nobody's seen her. Where c'n she be gone?"

I tried not to think of where, but thoughts, crazy thoughts about where she might be and who she might be with, buzzed through my head.

"Miz Costanza?" I ventured.

"Who else d'ya think it is, girlie? You seen Norma Mae? I'm callin' 'cuz I figured she woulda come straight to you."

"Why me?" I asked, flustered.

"Norma Mae's slow, but she ain't stupid, girlie. Norma Mae always put more stock in you than in all of them others put together."

"Miz Costanza, can you tell me what happened?" I asked.

"Didn't I jus' finish tellin' you what happened?" she scolded. "Norma Mae's done run away from that place! She's been gone since Thursday. They don't know what time she left. They only guessin' it was in the mornin' 'cuz her bed hadn'ta been slept in when they went to wake up the girls in her dorm.

"Two sheriffs come to my cousin's trailer where I'm stayin' lookin' for her, and I'm a-scared of what they'll do when they find her. They'll put them handcuffs on her. Put her in one of them straitjackets that'll for sure make her go crazy. Might even give her them electromagnetized shock treatments they give people to calm 'em down. I wouldn't put it past 'em." She paused long enough to catch her reedy breath.

"They treated her good enough, and truth be told, it wasn't such a bad place, but Norma Mae hated it there. I could see it in the way she was whenever I visited—not able to stay sittin' in one place, so restless she'd pitch back and forth whilst standin' on her feet with her arms wrapped tight around her, holdin' herself like she was holdin' a baby she was tryin' to make peaceful when all along what she was holdin' onto was her plan to ex-cape."

I thought that what Norma was holding onto was the doppelganger of her baggy. I stared at the punch-holed mouthpiece as if I were looking at the sunken-cheeked face of old lady Costanza herself. I couldn't picture Norma being cunning enough to fool anybody, let alone sly enough to plan an escape from the Mandeville institution.

"How did she . . . ?"

"She jus' up and walked away purdy as you please—that's how. Jus' walked off, big as you please, right from under their noses when the other patients was outside sunnin' theyselves. Or maybe she ex-caped in the night. I dunno. But they said a couple of the patients said they remembered Norma Mae being out on the lawn, jus' walkin' around is how they put it. There ain't but a low white fence surroundin' that area. It woulda been nothin' for Norma Mae to jump over that fence and disappear into the woods. It's all surrounded by woods around there, y'know."

Etheline Costanza's dentures were clackety-clacking like a mini typewriter trying to keep pace with her monologue.

"They mean to arrest her and bring her back there." She paused and for a while I thought she had set the receiver down and walked away, just like Norma might have done.

"She's on the childish side, but she's got a good heart, a real good heart . . . my poor girl . . ." Her voice wound down like a mosquito flittering off to another room while the picture in my mind changed from Norma climbing over a razor-wire protected fence to her walking away big as you please over sun-sprinkled lawns, into the woods, and into deeper, pine-thatched hollows, and then emerging from the cool shadows and coming to the grit of the open road—the placards and billboards looming at her, the busy highway running in contrary directions, a sudden panic clutching her heart, unable as she was to detach her feet from the gravelly shoulder of the road to tell them which way to go to get home.

"Norma Mae mighta gotten lost. I told her about my new place being not a mile from where she was, but she don't know shit from Shinola, pardon my French, about where I was stayin' 'cuz she ain't never been there before.

"She don't like wearing shoes, no, and she don't like wearing step-ins. She just pure don't like no constraints. But my girl ain't no criminal," Etheline Costanza was saying. "She just ain't no criminal."

I tried to calm the old lady, promising I'd call her if Norma came around.

"She'll be there, girlie. You can count on it. Take down this number. You call me collect the minute she shows up, which I know she will, if she ain't lost, or if somethin'—God help us—ain't already happened to her, the way—" Again the pregnant pause.

Norma's window on the world had been the bedroom window that overlooked Clementine Street. I had never seen Norma in any place of business other than the corner grocery, not even in any of the Magazine Street shops or restaurants where you'd bump into just about everyone else from the neighborhood, including Etheline Costanza.

"She'll be okay," I said not too convincingly.

"She's too trustin', too believin'. Always has been. Anybody could take advantage of her if they's kind enough to show her some attention. They jus' havta know how to treat her. I told Etheline Costanza not to worry, and gave her my word that I'd do everything I could to help Norma.

"Tell her the baggy's safe with me," she said.

"The what?"

"Her baggy! Tell her not to worry, that it's safe. I told her I was keepin' it safe, but she has to keep bein' reminded when she don't see it. By now she's forgotten and she's probably thinkin' she's lost it, or she left it with you—you bein' her friend. If you ask me I think that's what she's huntin' for."

"Tell her I don't have it, Miz Costanza."

"Didn't I jus' finish sayin' I got it, girlie? Scooped it up when them sonsabitches came to the house to pick her up."

"I'm glad you have it in safekeeping. She would never have given it to me. She wouldn't let anybody come within ten feet of it," I said, exaggerating because Norma was all right as long as you acted as if you hadn't noticed the damn thing. A couple of times I even thought she was going to let me hold it, or tell me to, the way she smiled and set it on the step as if it were a third person sitting between us.

"What does she carry in it, the Hope Diamond?" I asked, hoping to elicit a laugh.

"You mind your own business, girlie!" the old woman snapped.

"Okay, okay," I said. I hunched my shoulders, as if the old lady was standing there to see me shrug. I heard myself promising her again I'd do everything I could to help Norma, but I hadn't the vaguest idea of how I'd manage to do that.

Feeling the weight of my weightless thirteen years, I set the telephone receiver in its cradle.

I must have gone in and out of our front door a hundred times that day on lookout for Norma. On the hundred and first time, I peeked out and there she was, sitting on my front steps looking up and down Clementine, just as if it was an ordinary day and she hadn't a care in the world.

Her fringe-cut hair clung to her head as if it were wetted down. Her dress was zipped halfway up the back. She didn't turn around or budge an inch. She was looking across the street, at the apartment where she had lived, at the dark-screened window set in the brick wall the color of unripe tomatoes, at the dark pointy-leafed oleander bushes that bracketed the wall where we'd stood countless times calling for her to come out and play.

When she turned, throwing one leg over the other to get a good look at me, I saw that her feet were scratched and dirty, which made me wonder if she'd hitchhiked or walked across the bridge that spanned the lake.

"I couldn't get into my house," she said. "The door was locked."

"The locks are changed but I've got a key," I said, lowering my voice in the hope that she'd do the same. I looked up and down Clementine to make certain nobody had taken notice of Norma.

"That's good you got the key. But where's Mama?" she asked.

"She'll be coming."

"Where's my baggy," she asked, tucking a strand of hair behind her ear.

"Not to worry, Norma. Your mother has it," I said, taking her by the hand to lead her across the street.

Ever since Etheline Costanza called, I'd racked my brain trying to figure what I'd do with Norma if she showed up, and how I could keep my promise to the old lady to keep Norma safe.

When Norma and I walked into the apartment, I could see her mouth—thin-lipped and supple—working curiously, questioning her mother's absence and the few pieces of unfamiliar furniture she saw there, her nose twitching like a rabbit's, sniffing scents that weren't hers or her mother's. She wandered through the rooms, peeking into closets, pressing surfaces with rag-nailed fingertips, running her hand along the washbasin in the bathroom, across the countertops in the kitchen, and brushing herself against corners and doorjambs like a cat claiming its turf.

"It's your house, Norma, just a little changed. But you'll be okay. Your mama will be here tomorrow."

"Where *is* Mama?"

"I told you, she's coming from across the lake. She asked me to call her as soon as you got here . . ."

Norma spied the black telephone sitting on Mimy's small porcelain-topped table in the kitchen. She walked over, picked up the receiver, and held it out to me. "Call Mama," she said.

"I can't call her from here. That telephone has been disconnected."

Norma put the dead receiver to her ear, listened, then set it back in its cradle. "Then, how're we going to call Mama?" she asked petulantly.

"I'm going to call her from my house as soon as we get you freshened up. I borrowed a couple of dresses for you until your mama can get your own things together. I want you to be as quiet as a mouse 'til I get back. Okay?" I zipped my fingers across my lips and Norma did likewise.

"Where's my baggy?" she asked, rocking on her feet.

"I already told you, Norma, your mama's got it. She said for me to be sure to tell you that. Even so, I'll remind her to bring it with her, so don't worry."

Norma's small crowded teeth gleamed like golden kernels. She was smiling so hard, I thought she was going to laugh out loud.

I reached for the wraparound housedress belonging to my mother that I'd stashed on the uppermost shelf of the bedroom closet, just in case. "Here, Norma. You can wear this while I take your dress home and wash it. Okay?" I handed Norma the dress together with a pair of my mother's nylon drawers in case she might break down and wear them, and a pair of old terrycloth scuffs.

"Okay, Vicky," Norma said, inspecting the items. She hooked her hair behind her ears and silently mouthed the words *Okay, Vicky* again to herself.

"Soon as you shower and change, I'll run over to my house and call your mother."

In ten minutes flat, Norma was in and out of the shower and changed, her wet hair soaking the collar of the housedress when she stepped out of the steamy bathroom.

"Okay, you can go call Mama," she said.

I got Norma settled in front of the antiquated black-and-white television of Mimy's that had been left behind and ran over to Ruffino's for a carton of milk, a box of Lorna Doones, bread, a pound of sliced chicken loaf—items that wouldn't arouse Mr. Ruffino's curiosity when I charged them to Mimy's account. I brought the groceries to Norma, ran to my house, called Etheline Costanza on the sly, and then hurried back to the apartment.

"I can't stay, Norma. But you'll be all right. You have to remember to keep the windows drawn and the door locked. Locked, okay? Don't answer if anyone knocks until you hear my voice. Be as quiet as you can," I instructed before I left. "We don't want anybody surprising you, but we want to surprise your mama when she comes."

I left satisfied I had things pretty much under control.

I was looking at Mimy, who was looking back at me with a curious expression on her face. The pocket of her cotton housedress was drooping, weighted by her rosary beads, her change purse, and the ring of keys she carried with her as faithfully as a super in charge of a multidwelling apartment house.

It was a matter of pride for my grandmother that she'd kept up the rental payments on her project apartment, the same stubborn pride for which she went around flat-chested, refusing to be measured for "a sawdust *chiche*," as Mimy called the prosthesis the hospital's rehab center wanted to order for her, even though the hospital file showed she'd refused the first prosthesis they'd wanted to order for her.

"Let's go sit at the table, Mimy," I said, attempting to usher her toward the kitchen. "There's something I have to discuss with you."

"I can see that, *niña*," she said.

"Mimy, this is what I have saved," I said, getting directly to the point. I pointed to the $83.93 figure in the balance column of my Hibernia Bank savings account book.

"I need to pay you back for the things I charged at Ruffino's, and what's left ought to cover what Norma and her mother will need from the grocery until Miz Costanza can straighten things out."

Mimy looked at me as if I were the *bulto* come back. "You're talking between your teeth, *niña*. Explain to me what you said."

"I charged some milk and sliced chicken loaf and things on your account at Ruffino's and gave them to Norma," I explained.

"Are you telling me you took it upon yourself to buy these things at Roo-filla's without my permission to feed that crazy woman?" she asked, huffing with indignation.

I nodded reluctantly, trying to dispel the images that that epithet conjured.

"I thought they had her in *la casa de los locos*," Mimy said, not one to mince words.

"Norma wasn't in a crazy house, Mimy. She was in the mental hospital at Mandeville, but she left."

"What do you mean 'she left'? What is it, a mental hospital or a hotel with a revolving door where *la señorita* Costanza can come and go whenever she pleases?"

"Norma walked out without permission is what I'm saying. They're out looking for her now. I promised Miz Costanza that I'd help her and Norma—and I hope you don't mind, but both Norma and her mother have been staying in their old project apartment for the last two days.

"*Their* old project apartment?" my grandmother said, squaring her shoulders.

"*Wait, Mimy,* please. Before you say anything, before you start hollering at me, I'm asking you not to tell anybody. Not Mama, not anybody. If you do, I'll have to get Norma and her mama out of the apartment and help them find some other place to live until Miz Costanza can straighten matters out with the hospital administration, and the police, and stuff."

"I want you to know something, Bee-Kee. That when they cut this," Mimy said clutching her chest, "they did not cut out any of this," she said, tapping her forehead. "I don't need anyone, least of all a *mocosa* like you, making my decisions for me!"

"I'm not making your decisions for you—"

"What do you call it when you inform me that these two women are staying in the apartment that I am paying for, without my consent? What do you call it when you tell me, 'Mimy, I charged things on your Roo-filla's account,' without first having asked my permission? What do you call it when you tell me, 'Mimy, if you don't do such and such, I'm going to have to do such and such'? If that is not making my decisions for me, what is it?"

"I didn't say those things," I protested.

"You put things up in my face in such a way that I have no alternative but to say 'yes, yes, yes.' It's the same thing, Bee-Kee. Don't fiddle with fancy words or try to make me out to be the crazy one."

"Fancy words? I haven't used any fancy words," I sputtered.

"'Fancy words' is what I said, and 'fancy words' is what I meant. Don't argue with me, *muchacha*!"

"The last thing I want to do is to argue with you—"

"Put that away," Mimy said, sliding the slim savings account book back across the table.

"The rent for my apartment is paid until the end of the month. Norma and her mother can stay there for the next two weeks or until the mother has straightened things out with the authorities—whichever of these happens first."

"But, supposing Miz Costanza can't get matters settled by then? Supposing they find out where Norma is staying and come to get her? You can extend the lease if you need to, Mimy. I know Mr. Micelli will let you if you ask him."

"If Mrs. Costanza can't get things underway in two weeks, *niña*, you have no recourse but to let matters run their course."

"Run their course? Don't you understand what can happen? Norma might wind up being sent to Jackson!" I said, desperation mounting in my voice.

"What is Jackson?" Mimy asked, as if she'd never heard of it.

"You know, the state insane asylum at Jackson. Once she's declared insane, they won't send her back to Mandeville, they'll send her to Jackson and they'll keep her there forever. Do you want to be responsible for that? Jesus H. Christ, Mimy! Norma's not insane and she's certainly no threat to anyone. She never meant to hurt anybody, least of all Father Murphy. She's like a child almost."

"She was charged with assaulting a priest, and with indecent exposure, no? She exposed herself not to one, but to two priests, no? And what is the meaning of 'Jesus H. Christ'? Is it a joke? Is that it? That you make a joke of that most sacred name?"

I think Mimy would have smacked me then and there had she been able to reach across the table.

It was useless to argue with her. There were certain issues about which my grandmother was adamant. For Mimy, as for just about everyone of my parents' generation for that matter, priests could do no wrong; priests could not lie. Norma Costanza stood as much of a chance against them as a snowflake in a frying pan.

What Mimy had said was true—Father Murphy, believing he was saving the neighborhood from a fate worse than death, had filed charges against Norma, and Ol' Butterfingers had chimed in, saying he had not filed those selfsame charges against her for an earlier offense because he assumed that the act of indecency committed against him was an isolated incident. He'd been willing to forgive and forget until the morning Norma assaulted Father Murphy.

I couldn't shake the image I had of Norma being in that hellhole of a place called Jackson, where patients went around in sackcloth dresses, oblivious as zombies from mind-numbing electro-shock treatments, or flittering about tormenting one another like demons with pitchforks. I was confident that someone or something would intervene within the next two weeks—seventeen whole days, to be exact, until the time when Mimy would turn in her apartment keys.

"Put that savings book away, *muchacha*, and go to Matthews'—"

"It's Ruffino's now, Mimy."

"Roo-filla's!" she snapped.

"Ruffino's," I corrected.

"Bee-Kee, do not interrupt me again. You can work off the debt by doing the chores that need to be done, beginning with those front steps that haven't been scrubbed since—well, I can't remember when they were scrubbed last, and then, by going to Umbach's to buy some *vee-gee* lights. After that, we'll see."

Front steps scrubbings and vigil lights would just be the beginning. Mimy had assumed her staunch no-nonsense voice, but I could see from the tilt of her head and the heave of her chest how little it took to sap her reserve of energy.

"Thanks, Mimy," I said. I gave my grandmother a peck on the cheek and hurried off, concealing my own fragility and fear behind a phony smile.

"One thing more, my girl," Mimy called, catching me before I could bound out of the door. "There is something, call it luck or call it *el destino*—no matter your plans, things will happen as they are meant to happen."

I heaved a huge, deliberately loud sigh.

"*Basta!*" she said. "Promise me one thing—that you will *not* go any further with this if in the next two weeks your plans do not work out, and that you will *not* use the 'Jesus H. Christ' name ever again!"

"Those are two things, Mimy, but I promise. I promise!"

21

VALENTINA WOULD HAVE SAID that the rattle of pots and pans parrying with the kitchen voices, the piquant culinary aromas blending with the delicate scents of juniper, acacia, and sweet olive in the courtyard were a polyphony of sounds and scents.

I'd entered the grounds of The Good Shepherd Convalescent Home through the Chestnut Street gate in an effort to avoid the delay at the nurses' station—an island of push-button phones and gleaming surfaces that stood at the center of the spacious reception room.

I waited just inside the picket gate to catch my breath, to press the puffiness from my eyes that was threatening to become a permanent facial feature. Then I skipped over the low boxwood border that separated the flagstone walk from the shaded courtyard and I found Valentina as I'd expected, sitting in her wheelchair, reading in the dappled light that filtered through the foliage of sweet olive trees.

"Hi!" I said cheerily.

"*Dziewczynka!*" Valentina set the book she was reading in her lap. "What a pleasant surprise."

I smiled, letting the corners of my mouth lift like curtains parting to let in the sun.

"I wanted to surprise you. Hope it's not too close to supper time," I said.

"And if it is, we will love to have you. Calvin will be happy to make another place at the table," she said. Calvin was the jack-of-all-trades peripatetic handyman who unfailingly announced his proximity with one of the old R & B songs he was forever singing or whistling.

"I told Mama I'd be home in time for supper, but I can call and tell her I'm having supper with you," I said.

"Then it is settled," Valentina said and called for Calvin, who was close by singing in his best falsetto voice the jump blues number, "*Caledonia? Caledonia! What makes yo' big head so hard? . . .*"

"Are you okay, Vicky?" Valentina asked me.

"Sure. Why?" I said, plunking right down on the brick floor in front of her.

She slipped a bookmark into the small book in her lap. "What I'm reading is that you have something weighing on your mind."

"Uh-uh. It's nothing," I said, scrambling to my feet. I went and sat against the rim of the small dry fountain at the center of the courtyard, reached in it to stir the brown leaves that lay at the bottom of the reservoir. I turned and stretched my arms and legs in an effort to effect a languid pose, reminding myself that I hadn't come to burden Valentina with my problems, that I had come in the hope of finding a measure of ease and the sense of things turning out okay that being with Valentina always gave me.

Throughout the long months of her convalescence I'd been reluctant to bring any news I thought would impede her speedy recovery. I had not told Valentina about Norma's plight, and I still avoided, whenever possible, any mention of Lonnie's disappearance.

"Let's go to my room, shall we?" Valentina said, nodding toward the French doors nestled under the eaves of the veranda.

"Okay. It is cool out here," I said. "I didn't realize—"

"I'm fine. It's you, Vicky. You have the goose bumps," she said.

"I don't know why, because I'm not cold—really," I assured her, rubbing the crepey flesh of my arms. "Let's stay out a while—that is, if it's okay with you."

"Of course," Valentina said, inching her wheelchair closer to me.

I cracked my knuckles, a habit that Mimy kept warning would result in my knuckles getting bigger than my brother's. I cracked, squeezed, and pulled until I ran out of knuckles and joints to torment. I sat on my hands and drew in a breath so deep and involuntary that I shivered anew.

"Tell me, *Dziewczynka*," Valentina urged, slipping the book with its oversize bookmark into one of the side panels of the wheelchair.

No bus in sight, I had run the many blocks from my house to the convalescent home with Mimy's words still ringing in my ears. *Three days left, niña, and you have not yet told Norma and her mother that the apartment lease is finished. It has to be done. You must tell them no later than today. Give them the time they need to make other arrangements.*

"I'm okay, Valentina, really. I get like this sometimes. I sh-shiver when—," I couldn't finish the sentence. "—when I'm tired out."

Under Valentina's gaze, from which there was no escape, I broke down and told her the whole sad story—well, most of it.

"It's been two weeks now, and time's run out. I can't say that I blame Mimy. She's helped as much as she could. I just thought—I'd have bet my life that something would've happened before now . . ."

"What is it that you thought would happen?" Valentina asked.

"That Miz Costanza would've made some connection with her cousin in Hammond who would've helped. Or, that Father Murphy would've written a letter to the authorities, telling them it had all been a misunderstanding, like I'd asked him—*no*! like I'd *begged* him to do! Missus Costanza went to see him, too, explaining to him how Norma is. He was very sympathetic and very understanding, but he didn't budge.

"The police have already come around knocking on doors asking if anybody's seen Norma, saying that we should report it to the district police station if she's seen in the neighborhood.

"Nobody but Mimy and I know that Norma and her mother have been staying in the apartment Mimy leased after them. Had anybody guessed, they'd have turned Norma over to the police faster than you can blink."

"Isn't there some other place where Norma and her mother can find shelter for a few days until, as you say, Missus Costanza can make the necessary connections?" Valentina asked.

"The Y on Gravier Street, downtown—I thought of that. But Mimy thought that even if the Y agrees to take Norma and her mother in, they'd get in trouble for harboring a fugitive. I told Mimy they don't have to know the details, that all they'd be doing is taking in these two women for a few days . . ."

"I think your grandmother is right, because Norma is a fugitive from the law."

"Norma's no criminal!"

"Vicky, my dear . . . Norma is not a criminal, no, but—"

"I don't know what else to do," I said. "I went to the apartment today to tell Norma's mother that she and Norma had to leave the day after tomorrow. But I just couldn't do it. I wound up telling them we'd work something out for the long run. I don't know what else I could've said to give them any hope."

"You might suggest to Norma's mother that it would be in Norma's best interest if she would contact the authorities before Norma is found by them," Valentina said.

"That's what Mimy keeps telling me to do. But I can't see them taking Norma and treating her like a crazy person again. People don't understand that she does odd, you might even say, strange things, but she doesn't mean to harm anyone. There isn't a mean bone in her body. But let them try and put their hands on her again, and I think she might go nuts."

"Sometimes the only thing left for one to do is to persevere," Valentina said softly.

"Persevere?" I scoffed. "What does that have to do with anything?"

"Sometimes one must accept that there are problems for which there are no immediate or even satisfactory solutions."

"You mean as in, 'what can't be righted has to be borne'?" I said, thinking that it was what Mimy had said to me, only in different words.

I nodded respectfully, but to me that kind of thinking was for old people who, like trees, had to stand and tolerate the infirmities brought on by nature.

Later, sitting beside Valentina at one of the tables in the dining hall, I vowed with every forkful of squash and roast beef that I'd do whatever it took to help Norma even though it meant breaking my word to Mimy. I'd get Norma and her mother into the Y, or I'd use my $83.93 savings to help them find a place outside the Channel, maybe even in one of those fleabag motels along Airline Highway in Jefferson Parish, if only to have enough time until a better solution could be found.

For some reason that night, sitting in her room after supper, Valentina resumed the narrative of her "life stories," as she called them.

She would recall these episodes not all at once, nor in the chronological order in which I have recapitulated them, but randomly, as if she were standing under a tree, plucking the nearest fruits and passing them to me one at a time.

Her hands would fidget as she spoke, the long blunt-edged fingers weaving the narrative, as it were:

> Zofia and I were born in Krakow in 1903. As you know, my sister and I looked very much alike. We were twins, *tak*, but we were not identical twins.
>
> When we were yet very young children our family moved to Munkács, a Czech town renowned for its flourishing Jewish community. My father, Daniel Hirsch, was a cabinetmaker, very much in demand for his skills in repairing and duplicating rare antique pieces. Later, my father's business took us back to Krakow.
>
> I met David Dreyfus, my husband-to-be, there. We were both very young when we were married. Zofia, on the other hand, did not marry until she was into her late thirties, and, in 1941 when she gave birth to little Magda when she was nearly thirty-nine years of age, it was like a miracle.
>
> Magda was a gift from heaven, a breath of life in our stodgy family. And to us, to me and to my dear husband David, who died of consumption not long after Magda was born, for an all too brief time, Magda was like the baby daughter we never had.
>
> By the time of the war, our family was living in Wieluń. After the invasion, the Germans split Poland in two, and because our town of Wieluń originally belonged to Germany and was close to the German-Polish border, the Germans reclaimed it. They told us to take whatever we could carry and go to Krakow. There they registered all the population according to age groups.
>
> Our mother, father, brother, and Zofia's husband, Nathan Borack, disappeared. They never returned to the ghetto after being ordered to gather in the town square early one morning, supposedly to be sent to work at a labor camp.

Zofia and I stayed behind with Magda. We hid in a crawl space of our apartment that was concealed under a cabinet fitted by my father with a false bottom. We stayed hidden there for three days and were able to stay another week more in the apartment without being detected. Then the Germans made their forays and we were discovered and evacuated with the last of the Jews remaining in Krakow.

What I remember most about that day, *Dziewczynka*, what I will not forget, were the shoes. Yes, the shoes, the feet. Why is it, I have asked myself, that my mind shuts down, that I remember not the ravaged faces but the dull sheen and the dust of the shoes and the raggedness of the socks of those who wore them? That is what I remember most of our leave-taking from Krakow in 1943.

On the train that took us to Auschwitz, we took turns, Zofia and I, one holding the languishing little Magda while the other slept, unable to fall from being held up by the others packed like cordwood standing on end in the cattle car. We could then have only guessed at the bad things that were happening at Auschwitz, but never, *never* did we dream of the horrors.

Sucking the air from between the slats, even in the stench of human oppression in which we stood, when the train screeched to a stop at the depot, I could smell in the outside air, in the fumes and in the soot and the smoke of the train, something horrific, something unnamable. And I knew then . . .

I knew to linger, to hold back as the human cattle were herded from the boxcar, my sister among them. I clung like a tick to the wooden slats. I managed to stay back to the last, and then I set Magda down, left her to sleep her fevered sleep in a corner on that vile floor.

My sister was frantic to find us among the crowds of people. When I stepped out from the car, I could see her jumping above the heads of the crowd. It was a superhuman effort. Then I saw him, the man we came to know as Dr. Mengele.

He was impeccably tailored, even handsome, separating with the movement of a finger the chaff from the wheat—right left, left right. He signaled for me to go with the ones going left. All the while a guard was going along the lines yelling "*Zwillinge. Wir wollen zwillinge.*" What they said was, "Twins. We want twins."

To this day I am not sure why I volunteered that I was a twin, what difference I thought it could make. Once the doctor learned that I had a twin sister, he went looking for her and personally plucked Zofia, hysterical as to the whereabouts of Magda, out of the lines marching to the gas chambers.

Zofia and I, of course, were too old to be counted as "Mengele's children." But we were important in that we were twins. I was to be the control, while my poor sister Zofia underwent the injections. Hence, we were a cut above the genetic specimens that Mengele liked to collect for his experiments: the dwarfs, the giants, and the hunchbacks that caught his fancy.

The world came to equate the name of Auschwitz with the gas chambers, but it was at Birkenau, a couple of miles away, where Mengele worked in his laboratory, and from where the Nazis dispatched the inmates to the crematoria.

After the Russian front moved closer to Auschwitz in 1944, most of the camp was evacuated. When the American forces closed in from the other side, the Germans evacuated the remainder of us from Auschwitz and we were made to walk first to Loslau, then to Dachau. Many wore wooden shoes or rags on their feet, tramping over the hardened mud. We had shoes, my sister and I. We had shoes.

Along the way, we passed small towns, and the people came and looked at us. We were not allowed to slow down. If you fell, the guards killed you on the spot.

When we arrived at Dachau, there was another selection. If you were too sick, too weak, if your feet were frostbitten, they left you there; otherwise, you were made to march all the way to Austria.

My feet were cracked and swollen, Zofia's were not. My sister supported me despite the danger that by so doing my injuries would condemn us both to death.

When a young German officer saw Zofia holding me, he said, "Hold on a little longer, *Mutter*, the war will soon be over."

It was happenchance that it was that young soldier who saw us and not another soldier, less compassionate, indifferent to our suffering. We were in Dachau a few weeks, perhaps months, I do not know as there were no barometric instruments by which to measure hours, days, weeks, months—well, when the Americans found us it was the morning of April 29 in the year of 1945. This I know.

Zofia, who had risked her life to save me, fled from me once we were liberated.

After the war, I searched for her. I sought her forgiveness for my arrogance in having made a decision to hold back, to have that evil man call her out of the line headed for the gas chamber, as I myself would have been had I not identified myself and my sister as twins. Zofia wanted Magda with her to the very last, whatever the cost. But I had made the decision to leave Magda hidden in the train—a decision that was not mine to make.

I wanted to tell Zofia that I had acted without thinking—that the panic of the moment urged my decision to leave Magda to a fate where hope, however ephemeral and near nonexistent, was more than the certainty of what awaited her outside that car.

In all the years I searched for her—and there were times I suspected when I was very near to finding her—I did not expect that she would forgive me for having stolen from her those final precious moments with her child; I wanted only the chance of asking her forgiveness . . .

We survived Auschwitz and Mengele. We survived the death march to Dachau. What we did not survive was the loss of Magda.

Was I right in having left Magda? Was I wrong? Sometimes there are no rights or wrongs, there is only the decision, after which we are left to face the consequences of our actions.

I thought of the old WAR BONDS poster that had hung on the wall of Aunt Lizzie's and Grandpa Eli's laundry shop so many years before, and my own dark fascination with the look of fear on the child's face—the girl cowering with her doll in the shadow of that giant spider of a swastika.

I thought of the Cat Lady, her stooped shoulders, her ravaged face, her soul devastated by her great loss. I thought, too, of Puss and her kittens in the gas chamber on wheels, and the twenty years that had separated the two sisters, and I had to ask: *Where was he, the God who the Sisters said abided in our bodies that were temples of the Holy Ghost, who saw to the fall of a sparrow, to the drop of a leaf, but who had failed to look in the corner of that filthy boxcar for a little girl?*

One particular evening when I was visiting Valentina, it got dark so fast and rained so hard that I called home and asked my father to pick me up at the side entrance of The Good Shepherd.

"Valentina?" I said, already on my way out, for in no time my father would be at the Chestnut Street curbside waiting, car door open, ready for me to hop in out of the downpour.

"Yes?" she answered.

"You never stopped looking for Zofia, did you?"

She smiled wistfully. "Accepting what we can't change does not mean we give up hope."

"You okay?" my father asked, between the ump-umpping of the windshield wipers on our way home.

"I'm okay," I murmured, content to rest my head on his shoulder.

Etheline Costanza had barely walked into the apartment when Norma ran to her and started searching the bulging mesh shopping bag she was carrying. From out of the jumble, Norma drew out her baggy. She fairly ran with it to the bedroom, and flopped onto Mimy's bare mattress.

"Come on in, Vicky," she called after a while.

Norma was sitting on the side of the bed, the canvas bag propped in her lap, her toes *en pointe* to make a level surface for it. She patted a space where I was to sit, then she lifted the canvas bag, set it between us, and began to unknot the frayed straps. She worked the opening until it was loose, then she gently squashed the bag down on all sides so that the contents, a towel-wrapped bundle, sat unencumbered by the swaddling tote bag.

I sat there enthralled by the grace and precision of her movements, so unlike the freneticism that was characteristic of the Norma that I knew.

She lifted the bundle, unwound the striped towel, and let it fall to the floor. Then she held the object aloft with both hands, gazing at it with eyes that scintillated in their adoration.

"Look, Vicky," she urged, "look."

I was transfixed by the look of utter bliss on Norma's face, an engrossment so absolute that I had to tear my eyes from hers to focus on the object she held up for inspection.

It was a mason jar filled with a liquid as transparent as air, in which there was suspended a tiny human being, pearl-white, very fragile-looking, but perfect from head to rump. It might have measured seven or eight inches long, as far as I could tell. Before I could recover my breath sufficiently, Norma reached for the towel, rewrapped the mason jar, and put it back into the baggy.

"I have wanted to show you my baby for a long time," she said, smiling so sweetly, my heart practically melted.

22

For months I'd gone about in a daze.

I brooded over my brother, who seldom wrote. I fretted about what would happen to Norma should she be institutionalized in the state mental facility at Jackson. I worried over the fate of the embryonic baggy child Norma had left with me for safekeeping. I contemplated my attendance at the new school with trepidation. And as excited as I was by the imminent move, I was distressed by the thought of leaving the Channel. Perhaps it was the uncertainty wrought by all the changes that had taken place. And underneath it all and despite my anger and hurt and disappointment in Lonnie, I was concerned for her and wondered about her whereabouts, for it had been a long time since I'd last seen her.

It was not long before we moved from Clementine Street that I saw Lonnie "on the outside" for the very last time.

The grade school kids were scurrying by me, hurrying to get home early for supper so that they could return to school in time to line up for the May Procession.

The student bodies of St. Mary's and St. Alphonsus would walk through the streets of the Channel strewing flower petals from beribboned satin-lined shoe and cigar boxes they decorated and carried filled to the brim with flower petals in observance of the annual Queen of May celebration that honored the Virgin Mary, patron saint of the parish. The procession would culminate in the big school yard, where the life-size statue of Mary, borrowed from the Grotto for the occasion, would be crowned with a circlet of flowers.

From out of the muddle of so many thoughts on my way back home from helping with the decoration of the platform on which Mary's statue would be set, there emerged the image of a strange-looking woman sitting on my front steps, waving frantically for my attention.

I took my time getting there, trying, as I got closer, to figure who this person was. She had blue-black spun-glass hair, and she was wearing a scarlet-red halter top and white short-shorts. In place of her mouth there was a splotch of red and as best as I could see, she had on doorknocker earrings. For sure, she was nobody that I knew, I said to myself.

Watching my slow-drag approach, the woman drew on her cigarette with grim determination and then she flicked the lit butt and crushed it with the heal of her shoe in the little plot of dirt in front of my house. Closer up, she smiled at me and then she started laughing.

"You didn't recognize me, did you kiddy?" she chided.

I started to confess I hadn't, but instead I blurted, "Lonnie, it's you!"

"Of course it's me," she said, her red lips working inside the dark lipliner outlines. "Who'd you think it was, Elizabeth Taylor?" she asked, fluffing her rigid puff of blue-black hair.

"What do you expect, your hair being that color? I could have made a wild guess, y'know," I said, instantly regaining my composure. "It changes you, makes you look totally different."

"That's what it's supposed to do," she laughed. "And thanks. I hope that was a compliment!"

"What happened to you?" I asked, getting past the hair, the lip liner, the black winged eyebrows and puffy eyelids.

"Jeez! Aren't you even glad to see me?" Lonnie asked.

"I'm surprised, that's all. It's been a year, almost."

Eleven months, three weeks, and a day, to be exact."

"A lot has happened," I said. I dropped my book bag onto the step.

"I know. Ada's been keeping me up on things. But I want *you* to tell me all about what's been happening," she said. "Aren't you going to ask me in?" she added.

"Sure," I said. I watched her from the corner of my eye as I fumbled for the key hanging on its nail inside the screen door.

She'd gotten up from the step and was stretching. Her shorts had accordion-pleated wrinkles in them, and there was a pearlized pink leather cigarette pouch with a Zippo lighter poking from one of the gaping pockets.

For all the changes—the dyed black hair, the winged eyebrows, the lined lips, the attitude that had nothing to do with the Lonnie I knew—I noticed that her fingernails were again bitten to the quick; that she still had that fleshy peak on the knuckle of the forefinger she'd stopped sucking what seemed a lifetime ago.

"What've you been up to?" I asked as casually as I could.

"Can we talk?" she said in a whisper.

"To our hearts' content. Mama and Mimy won't be home for another hour, maybe more. But they'll be back before the May Procession begins. You remember the May Procession, with the flowers and the crowning of the statue of Mary and all that?"

"Sure do," she said, pausing to press her exaggerated lips together.

"Ada told me Mimy moved back with you all," she said.

"A while ago."

"So! You think I've changed that much, huh?" she said abruptly. "I know. You're thinking I look older than my age. But that's the point—I want to look older than I am." She slipped the pink leather pouch out of her shorts pocket.

"No ashtrays. Mama got rid of them all when Eddie left. You'll have to use a saucer maybe."

Lonnie headed for the kitchen cabinet in search of a substitute ashtray while I flopped into one of the kitchen chairs.

"You do know Eddie left, don't you?" I said in a voice replete with sarcasm.

"Uh-huh. Ada told me he joined the Marines, was it? Where's he stationed? How's he doing?"

I couldn't get used to hearing Lonnie calling her mother "Ada." It sounded as phony as her blue-black dye-job hair looked.

"He's in North Carolina. The Marines are right up his alley. He doesn't know for sure yet where they're sending him. He thinks maybe to the West Coast before he gets sent overseas." I talked as jauntily as if Eddie had been writing home nonstop.

"Rudy's going to stay in California when he's discharged," Lonnie said, plucking a cigarette from the packet. "So—then—you think this changes me that much, huh?" she asked, fluffing her hair again.

"For God's sake Lonnie, when I asked what happened to you, I wasn't referring to your hair. What I was asking you was why'd you disappear without a word? Why didn't you ever bother to get in touch?" I stopped short. I hadn't meant to be so blunt, but my curiosity and my temper had gotten the better of me.

"Let me explain," she said, soundlessly tapping the tabletop with her nubby fingertips. "What happened the night I left was that Vincent called my house and Ada picked up the phone before I could get to it. She blew a gasket when she heard it was Vincent. She cursed him out, told him she was going to sic the police on him. Called me the worst names ever, said that I was a liar and a sneak and a no-good whore. She accused me of everything under the sun.

"Right then and there I made up my mind I wasn't going to wait any longer to leave—not another day; I was going to run away that night. I just couldn't take it anymore. Y'know kiddy, it wasn't so much that she was being any different than before—it was, as the saying goes, the last straw."

"Why didn't—?"

"Please—let me finish," she said, smushing her cigarette stub in the dish, before lighting another.

"At first Vincent was okay. In fact, he was very sweet about it when I told him I'd had a bad fight with my mother and wasn't ever going back home.

"We couldn't go to his house because of his parents and my being so young and all that. So, he took me to stay with some friends of his that live in Gretna. I stayed with them a few weeks. He'd come over to see me whenever he got the chance. Then one day he tells me that he's tired of having to catch the ferry every time he turns around, and tired of me always getting on his back about him getting a job so that we could get our own place.

"After that, everything went downhill. Little by little he stopped calling. He made excuses for why he couldn't come, said I nagged at him, and then one day he just didn't show up, period! After a while his friends got tired of me hanging around. They never said anything but I could tell. I felt terrible, kiddy. Lower than a snake's belly.

"Then I hooked up with the guys that ran Buzzy's Bar, the juke joint in Gretna where we used to hang out, Vincent and all of us. They let me work—"

"They let you work there—you, a minor?"

"They couldn't let me work behind the bar, no, or put me on the payroll or anything like that, but they paid me under the table for running errands, sweeping up, busing tables, and letting them know when things were running low in the stockroom—things like that to earn my keep, y'know?"

"And where'd you live?"

"In a little room next to the storeroom. It was hardly bigger than a closet, but it accommodated a cot, a little table, and a box to store what things I had. It worked out good for everybody. Not that it made any difference to them, but that's when I decided to get my hair colored this "raven's wing" shade to make me look a little older. After a while I started working regular hours at Buzzy's. And, well, *ta-dah*, here I am," she said, doing a little shuffle. She set the saucer with the lit cigarette onto the table.

"You're wondering what my parents think about all this," she said. She took a long drag from her cigarette and blew out the smoke in a hard steady stream.

"To tell you the truth, they surprised me, the both of them. They seem to be pretty well satisfied with the way things worked out. We've even been talking regularly, Ada and me. Well, I guess she told you that."

"No, she hasn't. Your mother would never answer me whenever I asked how I could get in touch. All she'd say was that you were doing okay, that she'd tell you I asked about you—"

"And she did."

"Other times, when I'd pass her on the street she acted as if she didn't even see me."

"Same ol' Ada," Lonnie said, shaking her head. "Forget about her. Tell me what's been happening around here? How's D.D. doing?"

I thought of D.D. with his cracking high-low voice and the peach fuzz that coated the cleft above his upper lip curved as delicately as a girl's, and

I felt an emptiness in my chest that forced me to catch my breath, and a sadness, too, for how much things had changed between us.

"I don't see him all that much anymore. We talk now and then. I guess you can say that in some ways he's still the same, and in other ways, he's changed. Really, I haven't seen him or Becky but twice since they moved."

"They've moved?"

"Yeah, well, after all those months and months of talking, Mister Earl finally sold out. Miss Ruth went to work with one of her friends at Bruning's, a seafood place at West End."

"Is D.D. still the goofball he ever was?" Lonnie asked, as if what I'd said just flowed through her, so much air through a sieve.

"I told you, I don't get to see or talk to him much, but he did call yesterday to tell me they're tearing down the big library."

"The main library on St. Charles?"

"They're razing it to build an insurance company and a parking lot, of all things. D.D. said he saw it on the evening news. I saw it, too, in the morning paper. They're going to build a new main library at the site of the new civic center."

"I just can't believe they'd tear down that beautiful old building! Remember how we used to ride down there on our bikes?"

I nodded, but that wasn't the way I remembered it. I'd gotten Lonnie to go with me a couple of times, and I remembered how restless she'd gotten once we got there; how she was ready to leave not twenty minutes afterward.

"And what about Gloria?"

"We all went to see Gloria at Rosaryville when she got her novitiate veil—"

"Uh-huh. And Milton Junior?"

"He's coming home for summer vacation."

"Remember how much he ranted and raved, how much he hated being sent to Stanislaus?" Lonnie said.

"You'd never know it by the way he is now. Guess it was his getting away from all those coffins and cadavers that let him live, you could say. I heard that Mr. Moneypenny was selling the mortuary and going to work as a salesman in the insurance business."

"You're kidding."

"Nope."

"What about Ollie DeSales?"

"Never see Ollie anymore. But I was thinking about him earlier. His aunt told my mother that the long flight of stairs has gotten to be too much for her. Doesn't trust herself going up and down, and she's thinking of taking a ground floor apartment in the project."

"What's gonna happen to Louis when she moves?"

"How should I know?"

"Just asking," she said, abashed by my curtness.

She hadn't asked about Stanley Cunningham, but I offered, "Stanley looks real good since he got rid of that old wooden peg. He got fitted with a new prosthesis."

"A what did you say?"

"A prosthetic that has a shoe with a built-up sole and heel. Thick like. Reminds you of the platform shoes the tico-tico dancer with the mound of fruit on her head used to wear in those old-time musicals at the Happy Hour," I said, undulating my hips.

"Carmen Miranda!" Lonnie said, laughing. "Oh, kiddy, if you only knew how much I've missed you!"

She snapped off a doorknocker earring and tossed it onto the table. She rubbed her earlobes, wincing, and for an instant, under the spun-sugar black hair and all the garish makeup, the Lonnie I remembered appeared—petite and clean and fresh as the sparkle of sunlight on pine needles.

I was struck by a longing to tell her everything, to fill in the things she'd missed, to tell her of our oncoming move from the Channel, to lighten the burden on my shoulders of all that had happened. There was so much I wanted to tell her—to share the news that Norma and her mother had been found at the Y and taken by a policeman and two orderlies to the psych ward of Charity Hospital and held there until it would be determined where Norma would be placed, Mandeville or Jackson; to tell Lonnie that the shock of it had been too much for the old lady, that she'd suffered a stroke that left her paralyzed, and that she had died of a massive brain hemorrhage two weeks later, but not before she'd bequeathed the care of Norma to me; and that Norma had gone crazy with grief on learning of her mother's death and had to be restrained and taken to Jackson, just as we had all feared.

And I longed to tell Lonnie about the contents of Norma's baggy we'd all wondered about for so long, to show her the mason jar I'd secreted for Norma in an old writers box I'd bought at Young's Antiques, a maple box scored by ringed stains, with a patchy blue velvet interior and a lock you could open with a bent bobby pin. But it was a secret entrusted to me by Norma, and it was only hers to impart if that was what she wished.

I left so many things unsaid.

"You're not saying much. You're still mad at me, aren't you?" Lonnie said, lighting up again.

"Lots of things have happened," I said, "being mad with you is just one of them."

We went and sat on the back steps to keep from stinking up the house with cigarette smoke.

"You'll never know how much I thought of you and how many times I started to call. I was so scared and lonely.

"No matter what, though, everything's worked out okay. Don't you think so, kiddy?"

"I guess so," I answered, and got up to squash the lit butt she'd flipped out into the yard.

"Wait," she said, grabbing me by the wrist.

"What?" I said.

"I don't know if what I'm about to tell you will make any difference about what you think of me, but I'll feel better if I tell you—

"Remember the time I told you about Vincent and me at the foot of Monkey Hill? Jeez, I don't know why I'm telling you now, after all this time." She faltered, the color of her face waned.

"It didn't happen exactly like I told you. What I'm saying is I'm not just blaming him for what happened because sooner or later, the way things were going, it would've happened anyway. I was so mixed up . . ."

"You're talking in circles, Lonnie."

"That night I was so scared and mixed up and weak. I was trembling when we got off the motorcycle. All of a sudden he pushes me down and he's on top of me. It happened so fast. I was crying, screaming, and trying to get him off me. He told me to holler all I wanted, that nobody was going to hear me out there on the field side of Monkey Hill. He kept laughing, calling me a prick tease, telling me I wanted it as bad as he did. And I did, kiddy. Inside myself, I did! I cried hard, and I never ever told him how I felt."

"Regardless—it was rape, Lonnie! He should have been reported."

"What good would it have done?"

"It would've gotten that bastard what he deserved."

"I can't help but feel it was just as much my fault," Lonnie said.

"Why didn't you ever tell me?" I said angrily.

"What I'm telling you, kiddy, is that you wouldn't have understood. I'm telling you I let it happen. I wanted it to happen because I needed it. It was more than physical. I needed it in a way that I myself didn't understand enough to put into words. But I'm telling you now," she said.

The schoolkids were already trekking back to gather in the school yard for the May Procession when Lonnie and I stepped out of the front door, kids holding their satin covered cigar and shoe boxes brimming with flower petals they would scatter in the asphalt, shelled, cobblestone, and cement-paved streets of the Channel.

We waited at the curbside until the procession and attendant crowds moved onward to the school yard, where the Virgin Mary waited on her flower-bedecked pedestal, and the loudspeakers bled their speechless noises, and the clergy sat in their creaking folding chairs waiting to begin the Queen of May ceremony.

"Don't forget to let me know when you all get situated in the new place. Ada knows how to reach me," Lonnie said.

"I won't forget," I promised. "And take care of yourself, Lonnie—really."

"I will, kiddy. I promise," she said.

We hugged one another one last time and stood in awkward silence waiting for Lonnie's ride to pick her up.

I was picturing a black Harley to come roaring around the corner any minute when a green Studebaker with a Bondo-patched rear fender rounded the corner and pulled close to the curb.

Lonnie ran around the car, opened the door, and threw me one last kiss. "See ya, kiddy," she said. And with a splutter of exhaust fumes, she was gone.

"You wouldn't have recognized Lonnie she's changed so much," I said to Valentina.

"How so?" she asked.

"She didn't even bother to ask about how Mimy was doing, sick as Mimy was. She had to know about what happened to Queenie, but she didn't mention it! And not a word from her, not anything about—"

I caught myself just in time. I had never told Valentina about the bag of drugs episode, and all of the grief that had followed because of it.

"That may well be true that Lonnie has changed, as you say—but it is also true that what we see depends on what we're looking for," Valentina said, her eyes searching mine.

I nodded petulantly, letting her know that I understood and that she needn't bother to elaborate.

Valentina made a palsied gesture—as if she were nodding "yes" and shaking her head "no" at the same time.

"Lonnie loves you, *Dziewczynka*," she said at last, "she loves you."

At that the dyed-hair image of Lonnie with her outlined lips and the too-tight shorts, the cigarette-gruff voice and the fleeting goodbye kiss gave way to the sweetness of her face glistening with the purifying waters, the star scar marking her forehead glowing in the lambent light of the Grotto the day of her baptism—the image of Lonnie that I fixed in my mind, and that I would retain throughout all the times to come.

There are places in the heart that we could never hope to reach—and that is as it should be. This is what I understood that Valentina, in her inimitable way, was saying.

23

When it was balmy Valentina wore her piqué peignoir with the little yellow flowers and the oversized satin ribbon that looked like an artist's smock. When it was cooler, she wore the quilted blue robe my mother and I had bought at The Vanity Fair Shoppe on St. Charles Avenue the day of Valentina's discharge from Hotel Dieu. It was a rose-tinted shade of blue, like the color of the sky caught between daylight and dusk.

How did I know it was her favorite color? Valentina had asked me, stroking the crushed velvet robe just out of its china-paper wrappings.

I'd shrugged, utterly gratified by her delight in my choice of a get-well gift.

It was the end of August, a mild day, unlike the lion's-roar-heat-of-a-day that typified summer's end in New Orleans.

I headed for the courtyard, expecting to find Valentina, as usual, reading in the dappled shade of the sweet olive trees.

The days and weeks had flown since I'd last seen her. What with the impending move from the Irish Channel to the new house and the new school uptown, and all that the move entailed, I hadn't found the time to have a decent telephone conversation with her.

Not having found Valentina in the courtyard, I walked along the flagstone pathway to the covered veranda and on to where the small double-door entrance to her room was. Even before I tapped on one of the glass panes of the French doors, I could see through the fluted curtains that the room was in darkness.

From somewhere on the grounds, I heard Calvin singing—*Hunh, hunh, hunh-hunh-you gone and lef' me—hunh—baby*, but he was nowhere to be seen, and there was no one close by whom I might ask about Valentina's whereabouts.

"I thought dat was you!" Calvin said, appearing from nowhere.

I jumped, startled.

"Oops. Didn't mean to scare you, Miss Vicky," he said. "I been on lookout for you. Didn't want to miss you. Nurse Franklin said if I was to see you fo' she do, to be sho' not to let you get away and to tell you to stop at the main desk."

"I'll be sure and stop by and see her, Calvin. Thanks a lot. Can you tell me where I might find Miz Dreyfus?"

"You don't know 'bout her, do you?" he asked, hushed.

"What about her, Calvin?"

"Miz Dreyfus ain't here no mo'. She gone. Gone since Thursday two weeks ago."

"Gone? What are you saying, Calvin? Where'd she go?" I knew she'd given up her apartment a while back, and couldn't imagine where else she might have gone to. "Is she back at Hotel Dieu, or at Charity Hospital?" I asked faintheartedly.

Calvin rolled his eyes. "She wheeled herself outside like she always do, and dat's where she was. Dat right over dere is where I found her," he said, motioning with his chin in the direction of the courtyard.

I clutched my chest, hoping to calm the fluttering that had me wheeling. My legs felt as if they'd disengaged at the knees.

"You okay, Miss Vicky?" Calvin asked, cupping my elbow. "Me wid my big mouth! I shoulda waited fo' Miz Franklin t'tell you. I'll let her tell you da rest but I wants you to know Miz Dreyfus didn't suffer none. I could tell from da look on her face, peaceful like. She passed easy, doin' what she lak; listenin' to dem birds singin', and wid a book of poems in her hands and wearin' dat pretty robe she lak so much you give to her." He cocked his ear in the direction of the sweet olive trees as if to recall the twitter of the birds. Calvin stooped to level his eyes with mine. "You sho' you okay?" he asked again.

"Oh, Calvin! I should have been to see her . . . I would have, but the family's been packing, boxing up everything, getting ready to move, and between times I had to go and be fitted for new uniforms at Villere's on Dryades, and I had to make a list of all the things I need for the new school, and everything else. I wanted to wait until I had enough time to sit down and visit with Miz Dreyfus like before. I wanted to talk with her in person, not over the telephone, so I didn't—"

"Hold on now, Miss Vicky," Calvin said. He pulled a rumpled red workman's handkerchief from the bib of his overalls and handed it to me.

"You think Miz Dreyfus don't know all dat? You think she don't know you thinkin' 'bout her and carin' 'bout her all dat while she didn't see you?" he said, watching me blot the tears from my eyes. "Now, you stop worryin' and be sho' to stop by and see Nurse Franklin. She holdin' somethin' for you."

"Her heart gave out, Vicky," Miss Franklin said, reengaging the bobby pins that secured her butterfly cap atop her head. "Our medical director, Dr. Lucas, says it was congestive heart failure. That's what happens with a lot of elderly people. It's a condition that creeps up before anybody realizes—but I think Mrs. Dreyfus knew," she said, interrupting herself. "She certainly knew more than the doctors, that's for sure, 'cause there was no mention of any heart problems in her medical chart when she came to Good Shepherd from Hotel Dieu. But she came—how shall I put it?—she came prepared.

"I was looking at her chart this morning. Her birthday was Tuesday a week ago. She wasn't that old. But with the accident, and the surgery, and the good Lord only knows what the poor ol' soul went through during the war . . ."

The pain of it was so hard to bear, Vicky could only nod.

"It all took its toll," the nurse said.

"Miss Franklin, I didn't realize—I didn't know Miz Dreyfus was sick. I thought she was convalescing. I forgot about her birthday being last week. I just kept putting things off. Y'know how you do? I had so many things on my mind, so many things I had to do, time just flew by, and—God! If I'd only called her; if I'd only remembered her birthday. I should be horse-whipped. I should have remembered," I blubbered, my eyes welling with tears.

The nurse put a flattened box of Kleenex in my hands.

"We wouldn't have known about her birthday either, sweetie, if it wasn't our business to know such things," she said. "We always like to have a little something for our residents on their birthdays, particularly for residents like Mrs. Dreyfus that have no kin.

"She was an odd bird, though. She thanked us when we added her name to the list on the bulletin board of birthdays to be celebrated this month, but she forbid us to make any fuss, or even to make further mention of her birthday to any of the other residents.

"And the reason I say that she was aware she had this heart condition is, like I told Dr. Lucas, by the time she was admitted here she had already made arrangements to see to the disposal of the contents of her apartment. And she wrote out exactly what she wanted done with the things she brought with her. We sent everything to St. Vincent's Poor just as she instructed, except for the package we found on the shelf of her night table with your name on it, which is why I asked Calvin to send you in to see me. Just a minute, sweetie . . ." she said taking the Kleenex box from me.

"Jackie, where'd you put that package with Vicky Lumière's name on it?" she crowed above my head.

"It's there on the shelf right under your nose, Franklin," the other nurse called from across the room. "If it was a snake, it would have bitten you."

Miss Franklin reached under the counter-top and drew out a book-size brown paper package with "For Vicky Lumière" neatly inked in Valentina's handwriting in one of the squares made by the double-crisscross cord with which it was tied.

"C'mon now, sweetie," Miss Franklin urged, "Mrs. Dreyfus—bless her heart—wouldn't have wanted you to be all nervous or crying over a forgotten birthday, now would she?" She kept nodding her head as if she meant to coax the package into my hands and the tears from my eyes.

"She thought the world of you, and you of her, and that's all that really matters, isn't it?"

I took the package from Miss Franklin and waited until I was outside to open it, but even before I'd gotten down the front steps and stumbled over the hedge of lavender phlox that bordered the flagstone pathway leading to the rear of the courtyard, I was untying the cord and opening the brown paper wrapping.

It was an old-fashioned stationery box with the cameo of a feminine profile embossed at its center. I opened the lid and found Valentina's note under the overlapping leaves of the vellum lining.

> Mój ukochany Vicky,
>
> I found this photograph among my sister's possessions in the house on Clementine Street, the same as when it was taken in front of our house when we were girls in Krakow in the month of October of 1916.
>
> She kept it with her throughout all of the years I searched for her, throughout all of the years of our estrangement.
>
> We have spoken our hearts, you and I—but I was not ready to share this with you until now.
>
> Na zawsze,
> Valentina

Under the note there was a sepia-toned photograph of two young girls, twelve or thirteen—spindrift hair, wind-riffled skirts.

I held the photograph to the clearer light. It was labeled:

Zofia i Valentina, Zawsze ragem.

Październik, 1916.

I left the Good Shepherd home and walked the few blocks on Jackson Avenue toward St. Charles.

I walked for many blocks after that, conscious of nothing but the rectangularity of the box tucked under my arm that held Valentina's gift—an old photograph that for all of its simplicity seemed to me grand and enigmatic and mysterious.

In a state of timelessness, I found myself standing before the familiar Bedford stone building, its gray facade streaked and rosied by time and the elements, its Corinthian columns standing in welcome. I clutched Valentina's gift against my breast, took the steps by twos, and entered the recessed portico. I nudged one of the bronze doors of the soon-to-bedemolished library, and when it swung open, the late-day sun, refracted by the beveled edges of the leaded glass insets, shone iridescent as a prism shining in morning light.

I sat at an isolated reading table and opened the box whose crumpled brown paper wrapping crackled in my nervous hands.

Sitting at one of the oblong tables, I studied the picture of the girls—the two sisters, hugging one another, the slanted light lifting their laughing faces from the shadowy background. They seemed to shiver in the clear cold long-ago air as I myself was shivering in the hushed vastness of the library.

In my other hand I held Valentina's note. I took off my glasses to rub my eyes, and holding the note inches from my nose I read the inscription again. *Mój ukochany* Vicky I was certain meant "My beloved Vicky." *Na zawsze*, I already knew, meant "forever."

EPILOGUE

Whenever my heart hungers and loneliness swells to a crescendo displacing all else in its hurtful habitation, it is Mimy I long for, and Queenie, and Norma, and, of course, Valentina—those whom I have loved and lost throughout the years. And Lonnie, who became lost behind the gridded gates of the Orleans Parish Detention Center for Girls, and the Orleans Parish Prison when she was picked up by the vice squad, and lastly the women's prison at St. Gabriel—I hear a voice, and it is Valentina's, and once again I see the sacramental water-splashed sweetness of Lonnie's face with its star scar glowing softly in the lambent light of the Grotto.

Author's Notes

The king of Texcoco, Nezahualcóyotl, which in the Aztec, or Nahuatl, languages means "Hungry Coyote," is described by Luis Valdez, professor of Chicano studies at the University of California at Berkeley, as "a philosopher king and one of the greatest poets America has ever produced." Unlike other high-profile figures from the century preceding the Conquest, Nezahualcóyotl (1403–1473) was not an Aztec. His people were the Acolhuas, part of the third migratory wave of northern tribes into the Valley of Mexico.

Mexica, source of the word "Mexico," is a term of uncertain origin. Some say it was the old Nahuatl word for the sun; others contend that it was derived from the name of their leader, Mexitli. Still others say it is a type of water plant that grows in Lake Texcoco, whose mystical name was "Moon Lake." Mexican historian Miguel León-Portilla, a leading authority on Aztec history, literature, and philosophy, suggests that the term *Mexica* means "navel of the moon," from the Nahuatl *metztli* for "moon," and *xictli* for "navel."

Acknowledgments

This book was started after the publication of *The Fifth Sun* and the onset of my husband's illness, after which I could not write anything of worth for some time. I am profoundly and deeply grateful to my husband, Will Lagasse. What beauty there is in this book, it is because of his attention and his caring.

I am profoundly grateful to my loving sons—Donald and Gary—who've supported me throughout, going back to my first published works—the freelance stories that gave me the confidence, the experience, and the assurance that "I could do it!"

I thank my family of friends, related to me by our mutual interests, love, and respect.

My thanks and profound gratitude to Sigmund Borack, friend, neighbor, and survivor, for sharing memories of his experiences as a young prisoner at Dachau and Auschwitz.

My thanks to my agent Pamela G. Malpas, at Harold Ober Associates, for her friendship and continued belief in my work, and to Gianna F. Mosser, acqusitions editor at Northwestern University Press, and the staff whose expertise contributed to the publication of this book.

Last of all, I thank the furry four-legged member of this family, Maggie, whose warm presence dozing peacefully beside my desk during the writing of this book is deeply, lovingly appreciated.

"One of the gracious ladies of the time" is Mrs. J. J. Collins as quoted by Isabelle Dubroca in *Good Neighbor Eleanor McMain of Kingsley House* (New Orleans: Pelican, 1955).